THE DELVE

THE TIME BEFORE #1

DAN FITZGERALD

DRAGONHEART PRESS

CONTENT WARNINGS

This book contains adult material and should not be read by anyone under the age of 18.

Specifically:

Graphic violence;

Coarse language;

Explicit, consensual sex scenes, including some bondage.

AUTHOR'S NOTE: The events in the Time Before Trio take place several millennia before the Maer Cycle and the Weirdwater Confluence. Each of the three series is independent, and they can be read in any order. The Time Before is a set of linked standalones, with different main characters in each book but numerous throughlines and recurring characters as well.

1

Ardo adjusted his circlet, hoping for better reception, but the Stream had been intermittent since they'd rounded Titan's Elbow and had dropped out entirely by the time they stopped for lunch. The last he'd checked, three other mines had gone dark on the same day as the Deepfold, but there were unconfirmed reports of more. It was grim news for the Maer, whose supply of brightstone was already strained by the buildup for the looming war with the humans, though the High Council did its best to downplay the troubles.

The Orator's official view had been all over the Stream, spouting the usual denial and propaganda. "A temporary setback in the supply chain," the Orator had said, standing on a cliffside veranda, the hair covering his face glowing golden in the sunlight. "Our reserves are more than sufficient to continue at full strength until we have achieved our goals."

Ardo pocketed his circlet and shucked the heavy pack, leaning it against a twisted cedar shrub next to the large flat rock he'd selected for their picnic. He took a long swig from his waterskin, scanning the sparse branches of the tall pines overhead and the carpet of rusty needles and vivid green moss all around. They'd diverged from the path to approach the entrance to the Deepfold from the hill to the east in case there was trouble outside. The forest was eerily quiet, devoid of all sounds of life. Yglind stood gazing down into the crevice, the wind molding his maroon cloak to his square frame. He swiveled his head around and grimaced at Ardo.

"The door is closed, and there's not a guard in sight." He turned to look back down, then shook his head. "That door is solid stone, probably a couple feet thick. There's no way we're getting in if the Timon don't answer our knock."

"More like ten feet, and it's technically not a door," said Aene, who materialized beside Ardo. "It's a cube of granite, held in place by mechanisms hidden deep within the rock. We're not breaking our way through that."

"How do you know all this Timon shit anyway?" Yglind turned all the way around, looming over Aene, who stood her ground. Ardo understood Yglind's disdain for the Timon, given his family's history during the wars, but they'd been at peace for eighty years.

"I studied their work in school. Their ingenuity easily equals our own, though it may take different forms." Aene had shared little tidbits of Timon culture with Ardo along the way, and he found it fascinating. He wished he'd had the chance to study foreign cultures at his leisure, but he'd been lucky even to be accepted into squire training, given his background.

"Well, I hope with all this schooling you know how to get us in if there's no one at the door."

"Leave the problem solving to me, and I'll leave the posturing and bravado to you."

Yglind sneered, and Ardo stifled a grin. Aene was the only Maer he'd ever seen go toe to toe with Yglind in verbal sparring.

"Right. You get us in, and I kill whatever we find inside. A classic Delve."

"Egg, we're not here to kill anyone. We're here to—"

"Speak for yourself. I just received my Forever Blade, and I intend to give it a proper breaking-in. And if you call me that again, I'll break it in on your fucking head."

"And how would you get through ten feet of solid rock without my help, *Yglind?*"

Yglind waved her off with his gauntleted hand, annoyance stamped onto his face. Ardo wanted to kiss a smile back onto it, run his fingers up Yglind's neck and hear his cocksure voice melt into a velvety groan.

Yglind never let his soft side show in public, but Ardo knew the Maer behind the mask, knew the kind of tenderness Yglind was capable of. He sighed wistfully, realizing it might be days or even weeks before they could be together again, depending on what they found inside the mine. Something told him it wouldn't be a feather bed and a tray of scented oils.

"Ardo, hand me my whetstone."

"My lord..." Ardo shook his head. He tried not to call Yglind that, except in bedroom play, but he'd burned it into his brain during training, and it was hard to root out. "You haven't used it since you sharpened it last, and that blade will keep its edge through a dozen cuts or more."

"It's part of my process, love." Yglind held out his hand, still staring at his sword.

Ardo rustled around in his pack and pulled out the leather case, which was embossed with the same patterns as the stone itself and the ones that were on the Forever Blade. He undid the brass clasp and handed the stone up to Yglind, who spit on it several times, then sat on a rock and lay the sword across his lap.

"Preparing for battle is not just about the sharpness of your sword," he said, running the stone across the blade's edge with slow, practiced strokes. "You have to make yourself ready, mentally as well as physically." He held up the sword, which flashed orange-golden in the afternoon sunlight, the flowing ceremonial script burned dark into the shining bronze. "Gods, does this sword not give you the biggest hard-on of your life?"

"It suits you, my...Yglind," Ardo said, squinting against the glint of the bronze. In this light, the hue of the blade was a near-perfect match for the coppery-blond hair covering Yglind's face.

"Doesn't it just?" Yglind stood up, swinging the sword in a tight figure eight, then held it up to admire it again. "I'll never tire of looking at it. Appearances matter, you know," he said, turning toward Ardo and Aene, though it was hard to tell who he was speaking to other than himself.

"I bet you got yourself Maerscaped for the Delve," Aene deadpanned. "Wouldn't want the Timon to think we're uncivilized."

Ardo covered his smile, having seen Yglind's freshly trimmed body up close on the trip.

"I did, I'll have you know, but not for that. It's simple self-respect. Always look your best, always feel your best, and you'll always be your best. Ardo, do we have any of that boar sausage left?"

"Working on it as we speak." Ardo laid a cloth on the stone and pulled out the last half-sausage, a bit of hard cheese, a handful of dried figs, and some unleavened flatbread he'd saved for the occasion. It would be nothing but sporecakes and jerky from here on out.

"That's a right proper picnic," Aene said through a mouthful of cheese, which she'd snatched off the cloth before Ardo had finished laying everything out.

"Not without a nice skin of berry wine." Ardo sloshed the wine into the three brass cups he'd brought just for this toast. He wanted everything to be special for Yglind's big moment.

"Now this is how you celebrate your Delve." Yglind held up his cup and clinked it with theirs, his wide smile warming Ardo's heart.

"May our time in the dark be but a brief and peaceful dream," Aene said. Yglind held his glass up, then blinked softly at Ardo as he drank.

The wine was sweet and refreshing, and the warm afternoon breeze carried the scent of pine and clean earth to his nose. Ardo shivered as a musty chill seeped up out of the crevice.

Once he had cleaned up the remains of their picnic, Ardo helped Yglind into his mail leggings, which were hell to get on because Yglind had insisted they be made to fit as tight as dancing pants. To be fair, they showcased his rounded, muscular ass and bulging legs to great effect, but they would have been more effective if cut a bit looser. Ardo helped him strap on his shield and lifted his helm, which was shaped like a stylized mashtorul head, but Yglind waved it off.

"I want to breathe free as long as there's fresh air to be had."

Ardo didn't argue, though Yglind's attitude worried him. There was no telling what would await them on the other side of the stone block. Four mines didn't go dark at the same time by accident.

"They're dead," Aene said as if that weren't obvious from the fact that the Timon guards' heads lay on the ground next to their bloated bodies.

Yglind lifted their faceplates with his sword, staring at them with disgust. Dull, desiccated eyes glared out of swollen faces frozen in shock beneath steel helms that had done them zero good. They had thick eyebrows, full beards, and mustaches, but no other hair on their faces and thick necks. They were bigger than Ardo had imagined, though it was hard to guess their full height in this condition; they might have been close to five feet tall with their heads still attached, their compact frames packed with muscle.

Whatever blade had removed their heads had been sharp enough to slice through the fine splinted armor they wore, which was a marvel of smithcraft.

"They've been dead at least a week," Aene said, still staring at the bodies.

Ardo scanned the ridges on both sides of the crevice, which were gilded by the setting sun. He felt suddenly penned in, like he'd never see the sun again, and they hadn't even entered the Deepfold yet.

"Someone's playing for keeps." Yglind's light tone was belied by a slight quaver in his voice as he stood. He pulled out his circlet and put it on his head. "I have no link at all; how about you two?" He adjusted the circlet, squinting in concentration, then let out a sigh.

"Not since we entered the pass last night." Ardo put on his circlet to check, but the Stream was dark, as if it had never existed.

"Well, now we know why." Aene motioned up at a hole chunked out of the rock above the square lines of the stone door. Twisted wisps of copper wire sagged out of the hole. "The Magni is gone." The Magni connected the mine to the nearest signal towers, allowing communication with Kuppham and the rest of Maerdom. Without it, if something went wrong, there would be no calling for help.

"*You'll still have the passive link to my circlet, of course, as long as there's not too much rock between us.*" Aene's mindvoice rang clear in Ardo's circlet, and he sent back a pulse in acknowledgment. Without the connection to the Stream, only Aene with her mage training had the skills necessary to speak through the local loop created by the circlets.

Yglind tore the circlet from his head and fluffed his hair.

"It'll be just like the Time Before," he said, tucking his circlet into a pouch. "No Stream, no distractions. Just Maer, metal, and mountains. This is starting to look like a proper Delve after all."

The afternoon shadows seemed to lengthen suddenly as the sun dipped below the ridge above, casting the crevice into near darkness. Aene absently flicked her wrist, and the bronze filaments snaking up the back of her hand fired up, bathing the area in golden light.

Yglind held up his sword in the glow of Aene's gauntlet, staring at it with hungry eyes that turned Ardo's stomach. Yglind had always been hot for a fight, but his expression took on a darker cast when he looked upon his Forever Blade. The sword would defend him against nearly any foe, but Ardo wondered if it could protect Yglind from himself.

Ardo examined the area around the entrance while Aene did some final preparations, scrolling through a series of lighted symbols hovering in the air above her gauntlet. He'd never seen a channeling gauntlet in action, and he wanted to study the symbols, but she turned her back to him, so he left her to her preparations. He stared at the rocky ground again, but whatever tracks might have once been there had been erased by time and weather.

Once she'd finished her preparations, Aene crouched near the entrance, her brass dice clacking in her cupped hands, which she moved in slow circles, shaking them each time they neared her body. She did this every night, always asking them to watch and remain close, though Ardo wasn't sure how their presence helped the dice. She'd inevitably make some vague pronouncement that didn't seem to mean anything, but the process fascinated him.

After what seemed like an extraordinarily long time, she released her hands and dropped the dice onto the stone. They quickly rolled to a stop, and she studied the runes, tracing glowing coppery patterns in the air with her gauntlet. Yglind took a step closer, tsk-tsking as he approached.

"And what do your mighty scrying dice tell you?" Yglind grumbled.

Aene scooped up the dice and dropped them into a pouch, rising slowly to face Yglind. Her face was hard with resolve, but her eyes were soft with regret.

"They say you're going to try your hardest to fuck this up."

"That's hurtful." Yglind's tone matched his words, and Ardo felt all the hairs on his body twitch. Despite his mockery of the dice, Yglind seemed to believe in them on some level.

"They didn't say you're going to die." Aene adjusted her gauntlet, turning to study the stone next to the door.

"No one's going to fucking die. Not as long as I hold this sword." He twirled it for effect, bringing it up to fighting stance.

"No one's going to die if you know when to keep it in your sheath," Aene muttered, moving to lay her hands on the stone. She closed her eyes, and her face tensed as her gauntlet glowed brighter, illuminating her beard like golden flames dripping from her face. Her hands formed into claw shape with her fingertips pressed against the rock. She held still for a few seconds, and a muffled *clunk* sounded, followed by a series of smaller *clinks*, like a great chain being unspooled. Yglind slid his helmet over his head and tightened the straps as an opening appeared at the top of the door, which began lowering with a deep grinding sound.

"You're welcome."

"Must you crow about it whenever you do your job?" Yglind said, though not without a touch of warmth.

Ardo stood by Aene, gripping his staff, as Yglind took a fighting crouch facing the growing opening. Familiar scents of mildew and rock reached Ardo's nose as the mine exhaled. A deep *clunk* ended the noise of the hidden machinery, and the only sounds were Yglind's huffing breath and the slight crackle of gravel underfoot as Ardo moved next to Yglind to stare into the mine's gaping maw. He tapped his amulet, and a beam of golden light penetrated the darkness, illuminating a wide, squared corridor. The beam from Yglind's amulet crossed Ardo's, and the immediate area was lit by the glow from Aene's gauntlet.

"Wait," Aene said, but Yglind strode through the entrance. Ardo turned to the sound of Aene's sigh, and they exchanged a brief, meaningful glance before stepping cautiously through.

To the right was a large steel lever affixed low in the wall, pointing down. Aene tapped on her amulet and shone the light on a spot in the ceiling where a copper wire dangled, torn from its moorings.

"That must be the one leading to the Magni they removed." Aene shone her light along the ceiling down the tunnel, where bits of wire dangled down in several more places.

"Somebody didn't want this to be repaired any time soon," Ardo said, almost to himself. He crouched, angling his amulet to study the floor. Bootprints crisscrossed a muddy area where water dripped from the ceiling. Most were small—Timon sized, he guessed—but several larger prints stood out from the rest. They were unusually shaped, longer but a bit narrower than most Maer's feet.

Yglind crouched beside him and lifted his faceplate to study the bootprints, his mouth twisted in a grimace.

"Look." He pointed along the lines of footprints. "These came from within the mine and returned, but there are none like this by the door." Yglind pressed his boot into the mud next to one of the prints, then moved it away. His print was wider in the middle but at least an inch shorter, and Yglind was one of the tallest Maer Ardo had ever met. "These don't look like any prints I've ever seen. What do you make of this, Aene?"

Aene crouched beside them, spread her fingers, and squinted with concentration as the bronze lines on her gauntlet pulsed several times. She clutched her hand into a fist and stood up, exhaling in a slow stream. Her eyes were dark behind the reflection from their amulets.

"These prints belong to humans."

2

Aene kept a good ten feet between herself and Ardo, who shadowed Yglind as he strode down the corridor much too fast for Aene's liking. Yglind was looking for a fight, but they needed to slow down and think.

Whoever had slaughtered the guards had taken measures to prevent news of the attack from reaching civilization and might still be inside the mine. It was hard to imagine humans venturing this far into the Silver Hills, but their presence in the Deepfold could not have been an accident, especially since several other mines had been hit at the same time. They had to be after the brightstone.

The Maer needed more and more of it for their automatons and gauntlets if they were going to have a chance in the war, and the humans must have learned that. Deepfold was the most important source of the stone, accounting for almost half of the Maer's supply, and there was little enough room for error even with all the mines operating at full capacity. She'd had to fight to get more than the five chips they'd tried to send her with, as she'd burn through them fast if they saw much combat. If the humans could shut down the Maer's supply, they would be at a huge strategic advantage.

Yglind stopped, squatting to examine a group of bodies on the ground next to an overturned cart. Four Timon lay sprawled across the corridor without armor or weapons other than the picks and hammers several of them still gripped in their lifeless hands. Two had been decapitated like the guards outside, and the others' faces and chests were scorched as if they had been hit by a blast of fire.

Aene stooped to inspect them, then recoiled at the smell of charred, rotting flesh. Unless the humans had some sort of oil-powered flame thrower, this was the work of a mage, and a powerful one at that. It would take half a brightstone chip to summon this kind of power through her gauntlet. The humans were not thought to use brightstone in their magic, but whatever the source, the mage who wielded such power was one to be feared.

Ardo leaned in close to one of the dead Timon and sniffed, wrinkling his nose slightly. "These bodies aren't more than a week dead."

Aene unlocked the History spell with a series of taps and held the gauntlet over one of the heads that still attached to a Timon body.

"Five days," she said once the timeline snapped into place. She saw only a blurred vision of the attack, colored by the Timon's fear and panic and dimmed by the decay of his brain. Several figures, three perhaps, one with a flashing steel sword.

"Humans?" Yglind asked, his bravado cresting through the slight tremor of fear in his voice.

Aene shook her head. "Maybe? I couldn't see. One of them had a steel sword—the Timon definitely noticed that."

"Are these magical?" Ardo traced the outline of the burns, which Aene now saw were jagged. More like a lightning strike than fire damage.

"My shield will eat their magic for lunch," Yglind snarled. "Let's find these skinfuckers and end them."

"No one's doubting your prowess or the craft of your armorer, but can we stop and think for just a minute?" Aene gritted her teeth at Yglind's unsurprising sneer.

"And let them roam freely and plunder all the brightstone from the mine? We need to move before the trail gets cold!" Yglind's voice raised, echoing off the stone walls, and he glared at Ardo rather than meeting Aene's eyes. "Back me up, Ardo!"

"As you prefer, Yglind..." Ardo paused in that way he had when he disagreed, and Yglind lowered his sword and sighed audibly.

"Ardo, are you siding with Aene now?" Yglind shot Aene a hot stare, which she deflected as best she could.

"No one is questioning your leadership, Yglind." Ardo took a step toward Yglind, his palms in the air. "By the Delve charter, you decide, and we support you, no matter—"

Yglind raised his hand, sighing. "Enough with the charter, Ard. Say your piece."

Ardo nodded. He leaned on his quarterstaff, glanced at Aene, and then at the dead Timon scattered across the corridor.

"It's just that, as Aene said, these bodies are five days old. I'm not sure if the trail is going to get any colder if we take a moment to consider the facts at hand."

"The facts at hand are that I have a coward for a squire and a touch-me-not flower of a mage who'd rather stand around examining dead bodies than go off to make some new ones with me." Yglind spat toward the corridor wall, but it fell well short. "Are we on a fucking Delve, or aren't we?"

"With respect," Aene said in a voice soft enough she knew it would piss him off further, "weren't we tasked with finding out why the Deepfold mine went dark and fixing it?"

Yglind opened his mouth as if to shout some more, but he glanced toward Ardo, clenched his hand into a fist, and breathed in through his nose, then loudly out.

"With respect, don't you think it likely that whoever, or whatever, killed these Timon and the guards outside were also the ones who ripped out the Magni and made a mess of those copper wires?"

"Of course, but—"

"And would it not be reasonable to assume that these same perpetrators might now be perpetrating further harm on the single most important source of brightstone in all the Maer lands?"

Aene sighed. She hated it when Yglind was right. "Which is exactly why we need to stop arguing and think, just for a moment. Let me throw my dice and see if they can offer any guidance."

Yglind turned away and swung his sword through the air several times. "Throw your fucking dice. I'm going to walk down to that intersection and check it out, then I'll come back and collect you. Ardo, with me."

Ardo held his hands wide, arching his eyebrows, then turned to follow Yglind down the corridor. Aene cursed under her breath. The dice needed more than just her energy to work properly, but Yglind didn't have to know that. As much as he derided the ritual, he gave her words more credence with the dice to back her up, which was half the battle anyway.

She pulled the dice from their pouch, rolling them around in her hands to warm them up. She narrowed her mind, pulling from her circlet for focus, and began the first rotation, thinking of their mission, the mine's broken link, and Yglind's pride. She shook the dice and began the second rotation, picturing the decapitated Timon and the closed gate, wondering how the humans had gotten through it and why the bodies in the mine were more recently dead than those outside. On the third round, she replayed the images from the dead Timon inside the mine, the flash of the human's steel sword, and the lightning burns. She watched Yglind and Ardo walking down the corridor during the fourth round and cleared her mind for the fifth.

The clatter of the dice as she threw them echoed off the cold stone, and they came up sun, moon, tree. She traced the patterns in the air with her gauntlet, suddenly wondering why the humans were still here after all this time. They hadn't been killed if she read the dice correctly, but neither had they entered or exited through the stone door. That meant they were still inside the mine, either trapped or busy with something that would take them almost a week to accomplish.

She saw movement out of the corner of her eye, a tiny flash of light, and something skittered toward her. She gave a little cry, snatched the dice, and jumped back just as a gray shape like an oversized slug flipped into the air where she had been standing. A thin beam of bright white light poured from its mouth as it raced toward her feet on a hundred tiny legs. She leapt to the side, activating the blast function of her gauntlet. Five points of copper light streaked out from her fingertips, converging on the creature and knocking it back. It writhed and twirled on the ground, flipping erratically for a moment, then lay still, steam rising from its twisted body. White light trickled from its open maw, which looked like a lamprey's mouth, with concentric rings of tiny crushing teeth.

Several more flashes of light blinked near the wall, and she turned to see four more of the creatures flowing across the floor like juiced-up centipedes. Footsteps pounded toward her, Ardo in the lead, and she double-tapped her gauntlet to armor up as she pointed toward the creatures, whose name she suddenly remembered.

"Brightworms—four of them!"

The bronze-shod end of Ardo's staff crushed one's head as another scuttled up his leg and two rushed toward Aene. She hopped and dodged, hoping the Force Shield would hold them at bay since the blast drained the chips too fast, and she couldn't afford to waste them on something this small so early in the Delve.

Ardo dropped his staff and swatted at the creature, which slithered between his fingers and latched onto his amulet. Yglind's sword flashed in out of nowhere, cutting the creature in half, its head still locked onto the bronze, its tiny jaws working even with its head detached from its body. Aene leapt over the scurrying worms, one of which changed direction while she was in the air and was on her boot before she knew what was happening. It flowed up her leg, and she hit it with a blast before it could get any farther, knocking it onto the floor and stinging her leg through her Force Shield. Yglind's sword cut it neatly in two, sinking a half-inch into the stone; then he stomped on the last one, which burst into a flash of light beneath his boot. Ardo pried the creature's slowing jaws off his amulet with his dagger, then flipped his staff up to his hands with his foot and used it to crush its severed head.

They all stood, breathing heavily, scanning the area for more points of light or slithering shadows, but all was still.

"Well, that was bracing," Aene said, dropping her Force Shield with a double tap. She touched the button on her gauntlet, which glowed two times, then went dark. She'd used up half a chip already, and they were barely inside the mine.

Ardo fingered his amulet, which had teeth marks on it, but its light still shone strong.

"Let me see that," Aene said, stepping closer and examining the marks under her light. The teeth hadn't penetrated the case, but a few more seconds, and it might have broken through and wrecked the whole thing.

"What the fuck is a brightworm?" Yglind asked, eyeing the creatures with disgust.

"The bane of the Timon. The name says it all." Aene knelt by one, using her dagger to pry open its smashed mouth, and a faint stream of light trickled out, weaker than before. "They eat brightstone, which is why they were after Ardo's amulet and why they came after me first. Skundir's balls! If I'd been a little slower, they might have destroyed every bit of my tech."

"Well, that's a bullshit creature to start our Delve," Yglind whined. "Didn't your dice, you know, warn you about them?"

"They don't fucking predict the future, Egg. I just get a sense."

"Quit fucking calling me that."

"Sorry, must be the stress of combat, *Yglind*. I got interrupted, but they got me thinking about these humans. They're still in here after at least five days."

"Well, maybe they're dead." Yglind sounded disappointed.

"It could be, but...I don't know." Images cast by the scrying dice flashed through Aene's mind. It didn't feel like the humans were dead. "I think maybe they're trapped somewhere. The Timon are known for their elaborate mazes, you know."

"But if they were trapped, wouldn't the Timon be out and about, cleaning up their dead and such?" Yglind's bravado had faded, replaced by a disarmingly thoughtful tone, and Aene was reminded that he was pretty smart for a knight once his penis-sword-brain deflated.

"Maybe..." Ardo made little circles in the dust with the tip of his staff. "Maybe they are trapped, but maybe there's something else in here the Timon are afraid of."

"Yes, and maybe it wiped out the Timon, or caused them to stay locked away behind one of their infamous stone doors." Yglind's eyes lit up, and Aene got a hollow feeling in her stomach. "I wonder what it could be?"

Aene shook her head. "The Timon are doughty fighters, and they have metal magic. It's hard to imagine anything they couldn't handle in their home territory."

"Well, I can only think of one way to find out, and it doesn't involve standing around with our thumbs up our asses, as much fun as that might be."

Aene closed her eyes and blew out a sigh. "I hate to say it, but I agree. Lead on, Eg—Yglind. And keep a sharp eye out for more brightworms."

3

Yglind reacted to the click a half-second too late, and the floor swung out from beneath him with a high-pitched squeal of metal. He braced for impact, but instead of a hard stone floor, he fell into icy cold water, which rushed into his lungs. He tried to force it out while struggling against the weight of his armor not to sink to the bottom. Two more splashes followed, and the light from his amulet showed Ardo and Aene treading water.

He fumbled for his sword, which had slipped from his grasp, and as he sank below, his foot touched bottom. He picked up the sword and pushed up to the surface, coughing and choking. He grabbed the end of Ardo's staff with his shield hand, and Ardo pulled him to the edge of a rough stone pool.

Yglind sprawled onto the rock, vomiting water and the remains of the picnic onto the slimy stone. He vaguely heard Aene and Ardo coughing and sputtering in between his own retching.

"You gotta admire the engineering of that trap," Aene said, rolling onto her back and staring up at the ceiling, which had closed back completely. Only the faintest outline of a square showed where they had fallen through.

"Fuck," Yglind croaked between dry heaves, "the Timon and their engineering."

"I told you to move slowly, Egg."

Yglind glared at Aene, wishing his stomach would stay still for long enough for him to hurl an obscene threat at her.

He dry-heaved again, then pushed up to all fours with his fists. He held the position for a moment, and a growl burbled up inside him, emerging as a belch that almost made him retch again. He felt better once that had subsided, and he pushed back to sit on his heels, then made his way to standing.

Ardo held out a hand to Aene and hauled her to her feet. With her hair matted to her face and her clothes plastered to her body, she looked even skinnier than usual. She rubbed her hands along her arms, twisting in a whole-body shiver. Yglind's soaked padding leeched the heat from his own body, and he sheathed his sword and shucked his gauntlets.

"Ardo, come help me out of this mail. We all need to shed these wet clothes as fast as we can."

"Of course, my lord." If Ardo was cold, he didn't show it as he moved behind Yglind and unbuckled his shoulder plates.

"Pants too," Yglind said as he shimmied out of his mail shirt and unlaced his padding. "Sorry about before," he said quietly as Ardo helped him remove his padding. "You're anything but a coward. I just—"

"You just think with your sword sometimes." Ardo stood with the mail shirt over one arm and the padding over the other, looking Yglind up and down. "Apology accepted."

Yglind's heart stirred at Ardo's forgiveness, which he surely did not deserve, but soon the cold shook him from his reverie. His body hair was wet and matted, and he shuffled from foot to foot, rubbing his arms, while

Ardo and Aene stripped down as well. Aene still wore her amulet, her circlet, and her gauntlet, which she was shaking and tapping.

"The dunk in the water drained the chip," she said, removing the gauntlet and the wires running up her fingers. "Give me a minute to replace it, and I should be able to use it to give us a little heat."

"At least the amulets are still working," Ardo said, shining his light around the space. They were in a low cavern whose floor was covered in water, though there were a few dry spots along the edges. "We could—"

He stopped mid-sentence, his light shining on a dark shape slumped against the wall not twenty feet away from where they were standing.

Yglind picked up his sword, turning so his light shone on the shape, which was a quadruped twice the size of a Maer, long and sinuous, and covered in gray fur matted with congealed blood. Its head hung half-severed from its body, a snout like an oversized wolf full of black teeth drooping awkwardly on the rocks.

"Fuck," Yglind said, letting his sword droop. "These humans killed all the good monsters and left us with fucking brightworms."

Aene crept through the shallow water along the shore toward the creature, slipping a fresh chip into her gauntlet and snapping it shut.

"Aene, don't be an idiot. There's no telling what—"

"Don't be such a fucking ballsack, Egg," she called over her shoulder. "It's dead."

Yglind splashed after her with Ardo following close behind. He had to hand it to her; she might be a little thing, but Aene was braver than a lot of knights he'd known. Definitely not a touch-me-not flower, as he'd said before.

He arrived as she crouched over the creature's head, golden light from her amulet shining into its glazed eyes. Yglind and Ardo stopped, scanning the water, but apart from the ripples following their movement, it was as still as glass. Aene closed her eyes in concentration, and Yglind glanced at Ardo, who watched Aene with burning curiosity in his eyes.

Yglind knew Ardo harbored dreams of learning the craft, though being low-born, he would need a pile of credit higher than the Great Tooth to be accepted into study. If Ardo finished his term of service, Yglind could put in a good word, but with war bearing down, Yglind was sure to be called to the front lines, and he couldn't imagine going into battle with anyone but Ardo at his side.

"It's been dead about five days," Aene said, flicking her gauntlet, which went dark. "Humans, I think. Shining metal, for sure."

"What is it?" Ardo crept in for a closer look at the beast, which had claws more like a cat than a wolf.

"Hulshag," Aene said. "A cave-dwelling carnivore. They eat rock crawlers and such." She shrugged.

"Well, I hope there's more where that came from." Yglind shone his light down the dark, watery passage leading out of the chamber they were in. His feet were growing numb from the cold, and his body wasn't far behind. He stepped out of the water onto the rock the creature lay on. Aene wrapped her arms around her torso, shivering in her wet fur.

"We need to get warmed up before we go any further," Ardo said, eyeing Aene, who nodded, teeth chattering.

"I can put up a force bubble around us, which gives off a little warmth, and if we set our clothes out against it, it should dry them, given time."

"In the meantime, we'll need to use body heat to stay warm, just like they did in the Time Before." Yglind glanced at Ardo, who flashed a weary smile.

"I'll be the big spoon," Ardo said, touching Yglind's elbow.

"Um, no. I'm not sleeping with anyone's cock pressed against my ass," Aene said, wagging her finger. "I'll be the big spoon, you can be the middle, and Yglind gets the inside. I'll put up a force bubble around us and set a motion alarm so we can all get a little sleep."

"Nobody here wants their cock anywhere near your ass, but fine." Yglind slid his hands under the heavy beast's back and rolled it into the water. It would have made a worthy opponent and definitely would have counted for one of the five kills to certify the Delve.

Ardo scuffed at the stone with his staff to scrape off a patch of dried blood with fur stuck to it. The stone was fairly flat and almost level, and more importantly, it was dry. It was the best they were going to get.

Ardo lay down, and Yglind snuggled into his warm body, which helped offset the cold of the stone. Ardo shifted as Aene lay down behind them. Yglind heard her tap her gauntlet, and a thin bubble of faintly glowing copper light surrounded them, tinting the cave sepia and giving off a faint warmth. Yglind pressed his ass against Ardo, smiling as he felt him grow hard despite the conditions. Ardo always got it up for Yglind, and while there wasn't much they could do about it with Aene there, it always felt good to be wanted.

Yglind nestled in against Ardo, who tucked his hand under Yglind's ribcage. Though the stone was cold and hard beneath him, Ardo's body heat and the faint warmth of the dome softened his mind enough that he drifted off to fight a pack of hulshag in his dreams.

"You two slept like a couple of babies," Aene said as she pulled her robe over her head. "I'm surprised your snoring didn't summon more hulshag."

Yglind barked a laugh. "I wish it had! I'm itching for a little action." He laced up his padding, which was still a bit damp, but his body heat would dry it out as they went.

"I'm sure you'll have your chance before too long." Ardo held out his mail pants, and Yglind stepped into them, wiggling as Ardo tugged them up. Yglind held still as Ardo helped put the rest of his armor in place and strapped on his shield, then tiptoed up for a peck on the lips before handing Yglind his helmet.

Yglind had just tightened the straps on his helmet when a low rumble echoed through the cave, the sound of rock shifting. He tensed for a moment, exchanging glances with the others, but he didn't feel any vibrations through his feet, and there were no aftershocks.

"What in the gods' shit was that?" he asked no one in particular.

"It wasn't an earthquake," Ardo said, ear cocked toward the watery passage ahead. "Maybe some mining operation?"

"More likely someone using magic to move stone," Aene said, studying her gauntlet and shaking her head. "Nothing registered, but...it doesn't feel natural."

"Well, whatever it was, if we're all warmed up, let's make our way down this passage and see if we can find a way out." Yglind hissed as he stepped into the icy, ankle-deep water, sword drawn, the light from his amulet illuminating the still surface and the irregular stone walls. "With any luck, there'll be a couple more of those hulshag kicking around down here."

4

Skiti turned the handle and pushed open the stone door as quietly as she could, listening for the humans' footsteps or voices. She wasn't sure what they'd done, but the rumbling she'd heard a little while before wasn't natural, and it wasn't anything mining related. She was pretty sure the keep was still locked down, as she hadn't heard the distinctive grinding of the gate opening. With the waadrech on the loose, they would probably hunker down until everything was safe. She'd heard the exterior gate open half a day before, which hopefully meant the Maer had sent a party to see why the link had been severed, though she wondered if the group they sent would be able to handle the humans, let alone the waadrech. With any luck, the waadrech would take the humans out, but after what they'd done to the Guard, she wondered if even a dragon could stop them.

Skiti's throat was parched, and her stomach groaned. She'd been hiding in the labyrinth service room for what she thought was four days, and she'd survived by licking condensation off the stone. With the humans running amok trying to break out of the labyrinth, she hadn't dared leave the safety of the locked room, but she was pretty sure they'd broken out by the same method they'd used to break open the chimney. Whether it was magic or some kind of alchemical explosive was unclear; their mage could throw lightning and crush stone with his mind, so who knew what they were capable of? Clearly, the legend that humans were uncivilized barbarians was at least partly false.

It didn't take long to find the source of the noise she'd heard; a passage in the labyrinth was filled with rubble, and the ceiling above looked like it had been blown open by a saltpeter bomb. Thinking back to the sound, it hadn't been loud enough to be saltpeter, and the hole was too even for that. They must have found a weak spot in the barrier, then blasted it with their magic. She doubted even the keep's hardsteel-laced walls could withstand this kind of power.

She considered using her Omni to climb up the way the humans had gone, but she didn't relish another encounter with them after she'd barely escaped with her life while the humans slaughtered four miners before her eyes. She made her way past the rubble into the main hall, following the deceptively simple 3-2-3-1 pattern of left-right-left-right turns to the dead end containing the hidden exit. She pressed the tip of the Omni against the crack and manipulated the little levers with her fingers until the key slid in and the door popped open with a groan. She made a mental note to have the hinges oiled when this was all over. As she closed the door behind her and looked around the circular room, a distant roar filtered in. The waadrech, there could be no doubt, though where it was and what the roar meant, she couldn't tell.

Skiti's gut wrenched with hunger pangs, and she doubled over, clutching the Omni with all her strength, until the pain subsided a bit, leaving her woozy and desperate. She shook her head, clearing the fog a little but not enough to think past her gnawing hunger. If she could make it back to the keep gate, she should be able to get them to open it by entering the code with the Omni, but it was two levels down and half a mile away. Between the humans and the waadrech, not to mention the brightworms they'd unleashed on the mine by breaking through the barrier around the chimney, she didn't like her odds. There should be some dry rations and water in the storage room by the main shaft on this level, which was a safer bet, though far from a safe one. It seemed like her only shot, so she smacked her dry tongue against the drier roof of her mouth, fiddled with the levers on the Omni to extend it into a trident, and crept out of the room.

She focused on silencing her footfalls as she crept down the empty passage. She paused before every intersection, listening for any sound, but the mine was eerily silent. She missed the familiar ping of the picks, which she could normally hear from almost anywhere, but she hadn't heard it since the humans had arrived. Given the overdue brightstone contract with the Maer, five days with no mining activity was a catastrophe almost as great as the dozen or more Timon the humans had killed.

There was a crater in the wall where the whisper cone should have been, so there was no way to communicate with the keep. She wondered how many of those the humans had destroyed. The damage they had caused was going to take months to repair and throw off mining operations even further. Luckily, the door to the storeroom was shut and locked, and she keyed it open with the Omni, wincing at the little groan it made as it popped open and the clank as she locked it behind her. The maintenance crews were going to hear about this. She stood with her ear against the door, listening for any indication that the noises might have attracted attention, but heard nothing. She shifted the key's shape, used it to open the food locker, and fell to her knees at the sight of the rows of sporecake tins inside. She opened a tin with trembling fingers and chomped one of the cakes in half, struggling to chew the dry, delightfully salty substance with her saliva-starved mouth. She unscrewed her empty canteen, her mouth glued shut with half-chewed sporecake, and turned the lever on the water tank to fill it. She poured a few drops into her mouth, turning the sticky glob into a thick, slimy paste whose subtle flavors bloomed on her tongue, more delicious than the most carefully seasoned frasti stew.

When she'd eaten the rest of the sporecake, downed her canteen, and refilled it, she stuffed a few more of the cakes into a pocket and plotted her next moves. She hadn't heard any further noises from the humans or the waadrech, or the other Timon for that matter. She couldn't risk the noise of the elevators, so she'd have to climb down two sets of ladders to the base level, which would be no small feat in her weakened state. She'd then make her way toward the keep gate, hoping that her presence would go undetected and that the gatekeepers would accept her code and let her in. The crisis plan would typically lock down even coded access, but they should be aware of her attempted entry and let her in. In theory, anyway, though the protocols were strict enough, she wasn't sure even that would work.

She pressed her ear against the door once more and heard only silence. She shifted her Omni into a trident, the weapon most likely to be effective at keeping a large-mouthed predator at bay long enough for her to make her escape, though she doubted it would phase a waadrech. She'd never seen one, but from the stories of the hunting parties, they could reach forty feet long, with teeth the size of daggers and scales like hardsteel shields. A waadrech would probably use her trident as a toothpick, but it gave her a small measure of comfort, and it might come in handy if she came across any brightworms.

The sudden presence of brightworms had given her much to think about during her confinement. There hadn't been any in the mine in recent memory, as the hardsteel-laced barrier had proven very effective in repelling them. She'd come to the conclusion that the humans had ripped a hole in the barrier when they'd destroyed the chimney, not only letting the waadrech in but also giving the brightworms a point of access. She'd managed to fend off three of them in the labyrinth by forming a net with the Omni and crushing them with it before they could chew their way out. She'd use that technique again if it came down to it, but the trident was a more versatile weapon, and there was no telling what else the humans might have unleashed in their brutish entry.

She opened and closed the door with minimal noise, and it was a short walk to shaft number two. She'd decided to avoid the main shaft, as it might be wide enough for a waadrech to slither down, and the side shafts were only big enough for one Timon at a time. With any luck, they would be too small for the humans to use, though no one knew for sure just how big they were. Some said they were the size of grosti, while others insisted they were only Maer-sized, in which case they could probably squeeze down the shafts.

She took her time descending the metal rungs, arriving at the bottom with trembling arms and heaving lungs. Another rumble sounded somewhere far away, similar to the one she'd heard before. The humans must have grown impatient with a door somewhere and used their magic to make their own opening. Or maybe they'd just destroyed another whisper cone. Assuming the humans and the waadrech didn't kill all the Timon before this was over, it was going to take an eternity to repair the damage.

Skiti moved as quietly as she could to the next shaft, where she paused, cocking her ear this way and that. She heard nothing other than the moan of the wind echoing through the shaft. She took a sip of water and a few deep breaths, then entered the narrow opening. She climbed even more slowly than before, pausing halfway down and wedging her body against one of the rungs to rest and have another sip. She wouldn't normally have had any trouble climbing, but she was still weak from her time in the service room. She thought she heard something from below, like the faintest splash of water, but she couldn't quite make out what it was. She looked up and down the shaft, knowing she barely had the strength left to climb the rest of the way down, and up was out of the question. Whatever the sound below her was, she had no choice but to continue.

When she reached the bottom, she heard it more clearly, though it was still faint: splashing, as if someone were walking through water. The only place she could think of that had enough water to walk in were the tunnels below the main level; maybe someone had fallen through one of their traps. Skiti slouched against the wall, extending the Omni back into trident form. She could barely walk in her condition, let alone fight, but with a bit of rest, maybe she could make it to the keep gate. She took a bite of one of the sporecakes and washed it down with another sip of her now half-empty canteen. The sound grew louder, and she struggled to her feet, trying to determine which way the noise was coming from. A faint light appeared down the corridor in the direction of the keep.

"Fuck," she muttered, staring back down the corridor behind her. If she walked in that direction, she would be stuck in a long, featureless hallway with no exits and no shafts for several hundred more yards at least. There would be no escape if the humans or the waadrech or anything else found her there. There was another storage room halfway to the keep, and if she could make it there, she could hole up again until whatever this was passed. She tucked her canteen into a pocket, gripped her trident, and crept along the corridor toward the light, which had a strange golden color, faint though it was. It seemed to emanate from the floor ahead, and as she approached, she heard voices, Maer, she thought. She breathed a sigh of relief. The Maer must have sent a party out to check why the mine went dark, and while a visit from the Maer usually meant extra hassle, in this case, it was a good thing. The voices stopped, and a tense silence filled the corridor. A low growl echoed from the direction she was headed, rising quickly into a roar that straightened the hairs on her beard. Shouts rang out, and the roar turned to a squeal, followed by more shouts and an agonizing bestial cry that ended abruptly.

"Another one," she heard a voice shout in Maer, and another angry growl sounded. She heard frenzied splashing, more shouting, and a high yelp of pain, then the sound of scrabbling on rock. She crouched, frozen in place, her trident pointed toward the light, which grew brighter, illuminating the corridor from below, where she could now make out a wide hole in the floor. A squeal erupted, then more scrabbling, and a great gray shape burst from the hole and came bounding down the hallway toward her. She'd never seen one alive before, but the size and shape of the creature left no doubt that it was a hulshag barreling awkwardly toward her as if wounded. It pulled up short as it saw her, baring its huge black fangs and uttering a sinister growl. It was twice her size, with blood glistening from several wounds and eyes glaring with rage. Shouting and scrabbling sounded behind it, but Skiti was too focused on the beast to notice what was causing them. The hulshag roared, crouched, then sprang, and she let out a roar of her own as she braced the trident against the ground and aimed it at the beast's terrible maw.

5

Ardo watched with his heart in his throat as Yglind leapt from the top of the rubble pile, sending a little avalanche of stones bounding down toward him. He dodged out of the way, almost running into Aene, who sidestepped a chunk the size of her head, which splashed into the water behind them. Yglind hung from the edge of the hole, his legs dangling, then with a great groan, he swung his legs up sideways and scrambled to his feet. A squeal of pain pierced the air, followed by frenzied growling and shouting. Ardo watched Yglind draw his sword and charge down the dark corridor, the light from his bouncing amulet slashing the walls like an errant blade.

"I'm going up," Ardo said to Aene, who nodded, fiddling with her gauntlet. Ardo studied the pile of rock for a moment, gripped his staff, and ran up the pile. He planted his staff on a large chunk of rock, which thankfully held, and vaulted up over the edge of the hole into the chaos of the corridor above. Snarls and shouts intermingled with the sound of hacking flesh, and Ardo could just make out Yglind standing with his sword buried in a large dark shape, his chest heaving. Beyond him crouched a squat figure holding a weapon pointed at Yglind, but they made no move to attack. Ardo closed the distance as Yglind yanked his sword out of the beast and pointed it toward the figure, stepping up onto the hulshag's body and jumping down to square off against the hesitant opponent, who stood a little over half his height.

"Drop your weapon, or I'll cut you in half," he shouted, pointing his sword toward the figure. Ardo was pretty sure it was a Timon female, carrying a steel trident with a long spear point in the center flanked by twin spikes on the side. She brandished the trident toward Yglind.

"I'll stick you like a salamander if you take one step closer," the Timon growled in nearly unaccented Maer, holding her ground. She was of sturdy build, though perhaps less so than the slain guards, and her face was covered with skin except for her dark mustache and beard, which framed a mouth curled into a snarl.

Yglind whacked the trident out of the way with the flat of his blade, but the Timon recovered quickly, thrusting it forward within inches of his face.

"My lord," Ardo said, easing up behind Yglind. "If I may?"

Yglind feinted toward the Timon, who took a step back, then Yglind relaxed, turning to stick his sword in the hulshag once more. The beast did not move, and Yglind wiped his blade on its fur. Ardo held out his palm toward the Timon, who stood her trident upright but kept her body tense.

"We were sent by the High Council to investigate after your link went down."

"Took you long enough." The Timon fiddled with something on her trident, and the tines snapped together, then the whole thing folded in on itself with a series of clanks. In the space of a couple of seconds, it was the size and shape of a club. She slipped it into a belt loop, staring down at the dead hulshag on the ground.

Aene padded up, bowing to the Timon, who raised her eyebrows and bowed back.

"Don't mind my idiot friend Yglind here."

Yglind made a face at her and handed his sword to Ardo.

"My lord," Ardo said, pulling out a fresh rag and wiping the blood from the blade.

Yglind crouched next to the hulshag corpse, lifting its bloody jowls with the tip of his dagger.

"You got him pretty good with that trident of yours," he said, looking up at the Timon. "What's your name anyway?"

"Skiti."

"Well, Skiti, you mind telling me just what the hell happened in here?" Yglind stood up, reaching toward Ardo, his eyes glued to Skiti. Ardo lay the pommel in his hand, and Yglind inspected the blade in the light from his amulet, then sheathed it.

"Humans," Skiti spat, squinting and holding her hand up against the light of Yglind's amulet until he turned it down. "Three of them, a big motherfucker with a sword, taller than you even, with some kind of powerful mage, and one other. Not really sure what their deal is, but they took out more than a dozen of our Guard, not to mention blowing holes in quite a few places, including the chimney." Skiti opened her mouth to continue, then cocked her head as if listening.

"What?" Yglind said, and Skiti shushed him with wide, annoyed eyes. She raised her index finger, and Ardo heard a strange sound, like the scrape of metal against stone.

"Oh, fuck," Skiti muttered through clenched teeth. "Follow me!" She turned and started running at full speed down the corridor. Aene sped after her, and Ardo looked up at Yglind, who rolled his eyes, clenched his teeth, and sprinted off, his sword glinting in the light of his amulet. Ardo hurried to catch up and found the group clustered around a steel ladder leading up into a narrow shaft.

"Come on!" Skiti hissed as she clambered up the ladder. Ardo heard the scraping sound again, followed by a heavy thump he could almost feel in his bones. Aene sprang up the ladder after Skiti, and Ardo gestured to Yglind.

"I'm not following this fucking Timon into that little tunnel! It's probably a trap or something!"

Ardo glanced up at Aene, who stood just inside the shaft, beckoning him with her hand.

A strange clacking noise echoed down the corridor, followed by another and more of the metal-on-stone scraping sound. Ardo turned his amulet to face the direction of the noise. A deafening roar erupted from the darkness ahead, where a huge black shape filled the narrow space. Yglind drew his sword, huffing in and out as he did when preparing to charge.

"Yglind, come on!" Ardo hissed, one hand on the ladder.

"You go," Yglind said through clenched teeth. "I've got some stories to make." It was just like Yglind to think about his legacy as he was about to get bitten in half.

The clack of claws on stone drained the blood from Ardo's face. As the dark shape emerged into the light from the amulets, he saw dirty black scales, yellow eyes the size of dinner plates, and teeth like jagged shards of broken pottery. The creature's mouth opened wide in a roar that vibrated the metal of the ladder, which Ardo gripped with all his strength as hot piss ran down his leg. Yglind let out a low growl as he stepped toward the creature, crouching low behind his shield with his sword held high.

"Get your dumb ass up here!" Aene screamed, and Yglind paused, his sword shaking slightly.

"Yglind," Ardo whimpered, "in this hallway, we have a tactical disadvantage. We need to—" The words stuck in his throat as the dragon charged forward, bounding like an oversized stoat. It was on Yglind before Ardo had time to react, and Yglind's bronze sword flashed toward the creature's head, bouncing off with a clang, sending several huge scales skittering across the stone floor. The beast's great maw clamped down on Yglind's shield, and Yglind whacked it in the neck with his sword. It whipped its head with a fearsome roar and sent Yglind's shield skittering down the corridor, leaving a bloody gash in the mail on his bicep. Ardo tethered his staff and scrambled up the ladder, stopping to angle his staff into the chute.

Aene hung in the entrance, her gauntlet glowing with power. A golden flash whipped past him, and a rope of coppery light wrapped itself around the dragon's head, lashing its jaws shut. Ardo glanced up as he hung just below the entrance next to Aene, who was fiddling with her gauntlet as if she were going to cast another spell. Skiti was climbing up at remarkable speed, seemingly heedless of their predicament. The beast thrashed this way and that, banging its enormous head against the ceiling as the rope of light strained, and Yglind darted in, jabbing at its chest with his sword. The dragon squealed as blood spurted from the wound, and it swiped at Yglind with its claw, sending him crashing against the base of the ladder, his sword clattering onto the floor.

"Egg, hurry!" Ardo shouted. Yglind shook his head, obviously dazed, and fumbled around for his sword. He sheathed the weapon once he was back on his feet, glaring up at Ardo as his hands found the rungs.

"Don't you fucking start with that Egg shit too!" he growled, taking a moment to find his footing before moving up with a bit more alacrity. The dragon roared as the rope of light snapped and dissipated into a thousand little sparks, and it bounded toward the ladder. Another flash of gold blinded Ardo, who just managed to hold on as he heard the creature roar in pain. Aene climbed quickly through the entrance, and Ardo followed, though he was half blind from the flash, and he heard Yglind huffing up behind him. A vicious hiss sounded from below, followed by the sound of scratching and scrabbling, then another deafening roar. Ardo's vision slowly cleared, and he looked down to see Yglind, who climbed slowly as blood seeped through the shredded padding beneath the torn mail on his arm.

The sound of wrenching metal screamed up the shaft, and Ardo felt the ladder swaying, straining, as the dragon pulled on the rungs from below. A great *snap* sounded, and the dragon tumbled to the floor, hurling the broken ladder end down the hallway and bellowing with rage. Ardo gazed down at it, and it fixed him with a huge golden eye, then it was gone with a clatter of claws and a swish of its impossibly long tail.

6

"Just a little farther, Yglind." Ardo's voice was cheery on the surface, but Aene could hear the tremor beneath.

"Don't...fucking...lie to me..." Yglind managed, gasping for breath.

Aene looked up past Skiti's thick body and saw nothing but a narrow, round tunnel with a rickety ladder going up into the darkness. She looked down at Ardo, who shook his head, worry engraved on his face.

"Skiti, how much longer til we get to the next level?" Aene asked.

"About five minutes normally; at least double that at our current rate."

Skiti had been moving slowly for their sake. Aene was sure of it. Yglind groaned from below, and Ardo let out a hissing sigh. There was no way Yglind was making it for ten more minutes, and she couldn't get past Ardo to heal Yglind in this narrow chute.

"How much time to get back down?" Ardo called up.

"About the same," Skiti said in a strangely loud whisper without slowing her climb, "but you should be asking how long it will take the waadrech to figure out which end we're coming out of so it can be waiting there for us."

Aene slowed as she noticed Ardo lagging behind, which meant Yglind was struggling even more than before.

"We've got to do something, Aene," Ardo whined, his voice cracking. "You brought some medic's balm, right?"

"Yes, though I'm not sure exactly how you plan on administering it in this fucking weasel chute!"

A series of clinks sounded above, then a pause, a deeper click, and the sound of grinding stone.

"Lucky for you, every shaft has a respite room halfway up." Skiti's hiss echoed in the chute. "It'll be a tight squeeze, but we should all fit. If not, I can just hang out in the shaft and listen for our scaly friend." Skiti climbed just above the opening to let them in.

"You're a lifesaver," Aene said, tapping Skiti on the boot as she shone her light through the doorway, which was more of a hatch. Inside was a cube-shaped room like an undersized broom closet.

"It's only fair since you saved mine first."

Aene slipped through the door and could stand, but with only a few inches to spare. Ardo was almost a foot taller than her, and Yglind was even taller than him, so it was going to be more than a little tight. She tapped her gauntlet to check the charge and saw only one pulse. She would have to change the chip if she did anything more than use it for a light. She didn't want to use up the medic's balm if she didn't have to, but when she flipped up Yglind's visor and saw his face, the ashen look in his eyes as he slumped down to the floor, she wrestled it out of her pack.

"Pull that padding aside and shine your light in there."

Ardo did as he was told, and Aene winced to see the squishy red padding all around the wound, brimming over with blood, which ran in thin rivulets between the seams of Yglind's armor. Aene stuffed a piece of clean cloth into the wound and eyed Ardo, who pressed down on it, getting no reaction from Yglind.

"Hey, fucko, open your godsdamned eyes!" Aene said, flicking the bridge of Yglind's nose.

"I'm not a-fucking-sleep," Yglind grumbled.

"Yeah, you're too tough to sleep. I know. Ardo, you ready?"

Ardo nodded as Aene unscrewed the cap of the medic's balm, dabbed two careful fingers in, and blinked at Ardo. He removed the rag, and Aene rubbed the balm into the wound.

"Ah, fucking skinfucker fuckstaff fuck!" Yglind cried, and Aene heard Skiti snort a laugh in the shaft outside.

Aene woke up from her little nap to see Yglind slumped in Ardo's arms, Ardo's lips pressed against his forehead. The blood on Yglind's armor had dried, and his breathing looked steady. Ardo blinked reassuringly, giving Yglind a gentle squeeze. Yglind snuggled further into Ardo's neck, his thick arm grasping Ardo's waist. She'd never quite understood why someone as kind and respectful as Ardo would want to be with Yglind, given how rude he was all the time, but they showed such tenderness in moments like this that she assumed there was more to Yglind than his exterior led to believe.

Skiti was not in the room, and Aene looked out the hatch-like door to see her wedged in the tunnel, feet propped against a rung of the ladder.

"Everything quiet up there?" Aene whispered.

"I heard a bit of a growl up above a little while back, but nothing since." Aene could hear the yawn in Skiti's voice.

"You want to switch places, catch a little nap while I stand watch?" Though she didn't love the idea of hanging on a ladder in a narrow chute, it seemed like the civilized thing to do.

"If you insist," Skiti said, her feet already untangling themselves from the ladder.

Aene hauled herself out the hatch and down a few rungs as Skiti slid into the room with practiced ease. She wrinkled her nose, which stuck out like a little brown berry from her neatly trimmed beard.

"No offense," Skiti mumbled. "You just smell different."

"We're none too fresh after our travels, no doubt. Have a nice rest."

Skiti seemed to fall asleep immediately, and Aene found a comfortable enough position, wedging her butt and lower back against the side of the chute opposite the ladder with her feet planted on one of the rungs. Other than the ambient light of her amulet, which she left on glow so she could see her immediate surroundings, it was completely dark in the chute, the silence broken only by the sounds of breathing and light snoring from the small chamber. After a time, she heard a distant roar and what might have been voices, though it was too faint to be sure. The commotion died out quickly, and silence returned once again.

Though she usually found the quiet dark of the underground peaceful, this was unfamiliar territory. Between the discomfort of the position, the uncertainty of the surroundings, and her growing need to pee, Aene had had enough after what she guessed must have been an hour, and she poked her hand into the opening, brightening the glow of her amulet a bit.

Yglind blinked and shielded his eyes with his hand, and Ardo sat up, rubbing his face and looking around in bewilderment for a moment. His expression softened as his eyes fell on Yglind, and he let his cheek fall atop Yglind's head. Skiti opened one eye partway but did not move.

"I heard the waadrech, I think, a little while ago, and maybe some voices, but it was all a long way off, and it's been quiet ever since. How's your arm, Egg?"

Yglind glared at her for a moment, then glanced down at his bicep, lifting the rag from the wound. "Doesn't feel too bad, actually. Good stuff that medic's balm."

"Think you can climb?"

Yglind made as if to stand up, then slumped back down again when his head bumped the low ceiling. He raised his arm and made a slow circle, wincing, then nodded.

"I'll be fine," he grunted. "Plus, I've gotta piss like an ox, and I'm afraid I'd fill this little chamber up if I went in here."

"Don't even think about pissing down the shaft." Skiti's voice shot out like a knife. "You're in civilization now. There are latrines at the top and bottom."

"Isn't there a policy for exigent circumstances?" Yglind was obviously feeling better since his natural chippy personality had returned.

"We have laws to punish those who foul public spaces," Skiti grunted, sliding through the hatch and starting up the ladder. "I'll go up first, so if you lose control, it won't be on me."

Aene followed Skiti, and she heard Ardo and Yglind argue briefly until Yglind gave in and squeezed out into the shaft and began climbing behind Aene, with Ardo following. Yglind's grunts showed he was in pain, but he kept up the pace, and within minutes, Aene felt a change in the air. Skiti stopped, emitting a soft '*psst.*' Aene wished the Timon used circlets, as that would have allowed them to discuss their plan without the use of words. Yglind wasn't wearing his anyway, but she sent a message to Ardo.

"*I guess we stop and listen.*"

Ardo pinged in response.

Yglind couldn't have heard her message, but he stopped too. They all remained perfectly quiet, and nothing in the mine disrupted the silence. After a full minute, Skiti crept up slowly, holding her hand down in a 'stop' gesture. Aene ran through a number of possible scenarios, including throwing a Force Shield around Skiti, using a flash to blind any opponents, and a few others, but Skiti emerged from the shaft, looked around, then motioned her up.

Though the air in the wide hallway was only marginally fresher than that in the shaft, Aene felt like she could breathe again for the first time since they'd begun their climb several hours before. Yglind emerged, sliding his sword noiselessly from its sheath, his face drawn with fatigue but alive with anticipation. Ardo climbed up after, his staff clanking awkwardly against the ladder as he did so, and the sound, small though it was, echoed down the hallway. Ardo winced, and Aene blinked in response.

"If you've got a trumpet, might as well blow it now," Skiti hissed.

Ardo mouthed 'sorry,' and Skiti waved him off.

"I don't smell the waadrech at the moment," she said in a low voice. "We should head this way, in the direction of the keep, though we'll have to go back down another shaft to get to the entrance." She glanced at Yglind, whose eyes darkened at her words.

"You think you're up for it?" Skiti asked Yglind in a tone that might have been mildly mocking.

"I'm fine," he said, rolling his shield arm, which was no longer burdened with a shield but looked fairly stiff.

"My lord can surely climb down the shaft," Ardo interjected with steely politeness. "But it would be better if we could find a secure place to properly treat his wounds first."

"I said I'm fine, Ard."

"There is a storeroom near the main shaft," Skiti said in a softer tone. "Just a few hundred yards this way. It's secure, and we can get a bite to eat and some fresh water, then head down. And with any luck, the whisper cone at the main shaft will still be operational, so we can communicate with the keep."

Aene wanted to ask what a whisper cone was, but Yglind spoke before she got a chance to ask.

"Fine. Whatever. Lead the way." Yglind stared at his sword, which glowed golden in the light from his amulet.

"I'll go a little ahead," Skiti said, holding a hand in front of her face. "Your light kinda fucks with my dark vision."

Aene angled hers down, and Skiti blinked thanks as she held out the metal rod on her belt, twiddled its end for a moment, and it shot out into the trident form they had seen it in before. Aene had never seen metal magic close up, though she had read about it. It almost looked purely mechanical, but she knew even the Timon were not capable of such feats without magic.

Skiti stopped next to a fortified door. Next to the door was a rough hole in the wall, which looked like it had been blasted out by saltpeter.

"This is the second whisper cone they've destroyed." Skiti picked at the rock, tossing a little pebble against the wall. "It's gonna take us forever to repair all the damage they've caused."

"We'll make them pay with their skinfucker blood." Yglind's voice had an unusually nasty undertone, even for him.

"Let's get you fixed up and back to the keep, and then we'll talk about payback."

Skiti's device reverted to its clublike form with a series of clanks, and she formed a key with the tip to open the storeroom, which was not much bigger than the cubicle in the shaft, but at least it was tall enough that they could all stand up. Skiti fiddled with the device again and the tip transformed into a fine key, which she used to open a metal cabinet filled with tins and jars. She opened a tin and handed each of them a circle of some dried brown substance that might have been a sporecake. Aene sniffed it—it was earthy and a little sour. She took a cautious bite, and though it was drier than the sun-baked sands of the Gray Valley, it had a pleasantly salty taste, maybe better than the ones they'd brought, which had been ruined when they'd fallen into the water.

"Sporecake. Not the best, but it does the trick. Water's in that tank," Skiti mumbled through a mouthful, gesturing toward a tank with a spigot.

When they had all finished chewing their sporecakes and washed them down with some rather stale, tinny water, Aene sat Yglind down and turned up the brightness on her amulet to get a better look at his wound. The medic's balm had done its work, and the surface was scabbing over nicely, but the muscle beneath would take more time to heal than they had. She tapped her gauntlet into life and flicked through the functions projected in the golden light. She traced the pattern of the Healing glyph and focused the light on the wound. She closed her eyes as the gauntlet guided her into the damaged flesh. Muscles began knitting back together, closing around the gap left by the waadrech's claw, and the little bits of disease it had delivered were scorched into oblivion, dissipating like dust motes in sunlight. As the wound was almost healed, the gauntlet's power faded, then blinked out.

Aene glanced up at Skiti, who was watching intently, brow furrowed.

"Need a new chip," Aene said, popping open the disc on her gauntlet, shucking the burned-out chip, and pocketing it. She fished out a fresh one and slid it into the slot, whose sharp sides scraped off the soot covering as it went in, and the gauntlet glowed strong and steady again.

"I knew you used brightstone for your tech, but I'd never actually seen it in action before. It's incredible." Skiti's voice was soft, almost reverent.

"It makes my job a lot easier. The gauntlet does most of the work. Your device seems pretty damned impressive, too, if you don't mind my saying. Works on metal magic, right?"

Skiti's face spread into a grudging smirk. "I guess you could call it that, in your tongue. It has a certain poetry in Timon. *Buidesta*. Mastery of iron would be a better translation. This Omni maximizes the inherent properties of the metal with a lot of engineering mixed in. The rest is the art and skill of the bearer." She held out the rod, manipulating little indentations around the base, and it spread out into a fan shape, with intricate mesh webbing forming fractal patterns between long, sharp spines.

"And some philosophy, too, if my studies told the truth?"

"You studied our philosophy?" The device retracted into its stubby form with a flick of Skiti's wrist, and Aene wanted more than anything else to hold it in her hands, to run it under her gauntlet's scrutiny.

"As much as I could. We have a few scholars of Timon culture and history on faculty at every university, but it's not the most popular subject, given..." Aene winced, and Skiti blinked understanding. The Timon were reported to have tortured and killed hundreds of Maer soldiers and spies during the wars, though Aene imagined the truth was probably more complicated than what she'd learned in school.

"Our history is fraught, to be sure." Skiti cracked a smile, and her voice turned lower as Yglind's whistling snore reverberated in the small space. "No one here knows much about your magic except that it relies on copper and brightstone."

"Among other things. Maybe when this is all over, we can do a little show and tell. Meantime, I'm going to catch a few winks, assuming the door is secure?"

"It'll hold up to a waadrech, though after seeing what the humans did to our tunnels, I don't know if anything would keep them out." Skiti closed her eyes and leaned her head against the wall.

"Ardo, you awake?" His eyes were closed, but he gave a thumbs up as he opened them.

"I got you." He shifted, propping Yglind against the food locker, stood up, and stretched his legs.

"Wake me in an hour, or if anything goes bad." Aene's mind buzzed with thoughts of Skiti's Omni, the metal mastery behind it, the waadrech's jagged teeth, and the humans' motives. She quickly realized she'd never get any sleep if her thoughts kept circling, so she summoned the Sleep glyph and gave herself a soft tap, and soon drifted off into a gentle, golden slumber.

"Wake up, sleepy face." Yglind's voice pierced Aene's sleep like the harsh light of morning peeking through the blinds, and she swatted away a tickle on her beard, her hand hitting something sharp and hard.

"Fuck you, Eggfuck," she said, scooting away from Yglind's sword point, which was dangling an inch from her face.

"What?" He held up his hand as if in self-defense, a shit-eating grin on his face.

"Why do you always have to do that?"

"Do what?" Yglind sheathed his sword, smoothing the hair on his face and touching up his mustache.

"Be an asshole."

"A what?" He blinked as if shocked.

"An asshole, Yglind. Why can't you just be you?"

"Sorry." He turned and took a drink of his waterskin, and he didn't turn back around for a long moment. When he did, his smirk had returned, but perhaps with a twinge of humility.

"Well, if you two are just about done, I think it should be safe to head down the main shaft. It's only about a hundred feet ahead." Skiti had been pressing her ear to the door. "I haven't heard a peep."

"All right then." Yglind unsheathed his sword and took a few huffing breaths. "Let's do this."

Ardo gripped his staff, and Aene ran through her standard lineup of combat spells so they would be fresh in her mind in case she needed to summon them. The gauntlet was almost fully charged, which always gave her extra confidence.

Skiti blinked her acknowledgment, shifting her device back into trident form, and flipped the lever to open the door. Yglind stepped out into the hallway, turning and posing his sword several times, then gestured them forward. Aene followed Ardo, and Skiti emerged and shut the door quietly behind them.

"It's this way," Skiti said, turning back to them but gesturing down the hallway.

Aene's breath caught as she saw the glint in the darkness, and a figure emerged from the shadows, crouched and draped in black, and placed something shiny on the floor. The object flashed for a moment, a pale, blueish light, and Aene could not move or breathe; even her thoughts felt frozen, unable to do more than simply watch the scene unfolding before her. The figure rose from his crouch, hurrying over to Aene and carefully removing her circlet, then unlacing her gauntlet slowly and gently as if he were undressing a doll. She was powerless to stop him, even almost to want to.

He glanced up from beneath his dark hood as he lifted the gauntlet from her hand, and green eyes blazed from a face covered in ruddy tan skin, except for a beard around the mouth and chin. She had never seen a human before, but there was no question that's what he was. A hint of a smile flickered across his mouth, and then he was gone, moving to Yglind, prying his fingers off his sword and tucking it awkwardly into his belt. He glanced back at the shiny object, which Aene could now see was shaped like a figure eight, filled with tiny sparkles that seemed to flow through its curves, faster with each passing second. He rushed over, removed Ardo's circlet, and tucked it into a shoulder bag along with the other items. He returned to pick up the object, turned his head away, and the blue light flashed again, but much brighter this time. Aene's hand flew to her eyes, which were imprinted with the splotchy shape of the light, a giant blue figure eight with ragged edges, slowly fading as the darkness of the corridor returned. She tapped on her amulet, which thankfully he hadn't taken, and a circle of light appeared around them, though it hurt her eyes to look at it.

"What the fuck was that?" Yglind said, shaking his head and looking around.

"Some kind of time spell, maybe?" Aene had read the theory, but no living Maer was known to have mastered this ancient magic.

"He took my sword." Yglind stared at his empty hand, still half curled from where the human had pried it from his fingers. "*He took my fucking sword!*" he shouted with sudden desperation.

"Egg, shut the fuck up," Aene hissed.

But it was too late.

A roar reverberated through the corridor, sounding both far and near, coming from all directions at once.

7

Yglind drew his dagger and tapped his amulet into life, but there was nothing to be seen beyond the range of his amulet except darkness.

"Ardo, give me your dagger." Ardo stared at him for a moment, dumbstruck, then shook his head and pulled out his dagger, flipping it to offer it grip first. Yglind took it, moving his arms around a few times to bring back the memory of the technique. His left arm hurt, but in the heat of battle, it would do. He had trained with dual daggers for many a long day, and he would plunge them both down into the space above the thief's collarbones as soon as they caught up with him. Nothing would stop him from getting his Forever Blade back.

The roar sounded again, louder and closer this time, but it was still impossible to determine what direction it had come from.

"Yglind, did he get your circlet?" Aene asked with a tremor in her voice.

Yglind felt the hard circle in his pocket and tossed it to Aene, who caught it with a glare.

"Hurry! This way!" Skiti said, already padding down the corridor. Yglind followed, letting the light from Aene's amulet guide his footsteps so as not to mess with Skiti's dark vision. As annoying as she was, she was their only guide. Without her, the waadrech would find them, and he didn't like his chances with only two daggers to defend himself, especially since Aene had lost her gauntlet to the human thief. Could the humans really stop time? If so, Yglind didn't see any way they'd stand a better chance the next time they met. But on the other hand, the thief hadn't killed them, which was perhaps the most confounding thing of all, not to mention the worst mistake of his skinfucker life.

They passed a large shaft with ladders on either side, and Skiti slowed enough to wave them forward.

"There's a smaller shaft about a hundred yards up ahead, where the waadrech can't follow. This shaft is too wide, and I'm afraid—"

Her words were swallowed by a deafening roar from the hallway ahead. Yglind angled his amulet down the hallway, and its beam shone on the creature, filling the corridor not fifty feet away in the direction they were heading. Its yellow eyes reflected the light from the amulet, glowing like golden fire in the darkness. He felt its stare, the hunger in its eyes, the hatred, and his legs trembled at the sheer size of it. He had hurt it, and now it wanted revenge.

He squared off against it, blocking the others with a wide stance, whipping the daggers in a jagged X through the air in front of him, despite the pain in his arm. The dragon huffed, then opened its mouth in another roar, showing hundreds of jagged teeth and a throat big enough to swallow him whole. Yglind felt Aene flinch behind him and heard a mechanical sound that might have been Skiti's strange device. Ardo stepped up beside him, staff in hand, his jaw set in a grim smile.

"Roar," Yglind whispered, then together they opened their throats in a dual screech that hurt Yglind's ears almost as much as his ragged throat. The dragon's head dipped for a moment, then it surged forward, bounding through the tunnel and closing the space between them in seconds, its forked tongue flopping out of the side of its mouth as it charged. Yglind crouched, preparing to roll under it and try to stab it from beneath, but as it neared them, Ardo stepped forward, bracing his staff against the ground and shoving the bronze-shod end right into the creature's maw. The dragon stopped, and its jaws snapped shut, chomping the staff in two and leaving Ardo with only a club-sized length of wood with a splintered end. Yglind leapt at the creature, his daggers flashing for its eyes, but it raised its snout and batted him sideways with it, sending him crashing into the wall.

The creature gave a roar that vibrated Yglind's bones, then pounced on Ardo, who whacked it with the remainder of his staff as he tumbled out of the way. Yglind scrambled to his feet, bringing a dagger up low and wedging it between two scales, hilt-deep into the creature's neck. A sound like a great bullwhip snapped in the air, and Yglind was stunned as the creature's tail clocked his helmet, nearly popping his head off his body.

"Down!" Aene shouted, and Yglind slumped against the wall as a flood of golden light rushed past him, swirling around the waadrech, which roared and swatted with its great claws.

"Quickly!" Skiti screamed, and Ardo tugged Yglind toward the shaft.

"Can you climb?" Ardo's voice was shaky, almost tearful. Yglind clapped him on the shoulder and swung his legs down, still dizzy from the blow to the head. He slipped and fumbled his way down the first few rungs until his mind cleared a little, and he looked up to see Ardo climbing down above him and Aene on the ladder across from him. Skiti slid over the edge and onto the ladder like a circus performer, and the waadrech's head appeared in the opening, half-lit by the erratic lights of their amulets. It roared, causing Yglind's grip on the ladder to falter, and it stuck its head down, snapping at Skiti, who slid down a couple of rungs just out of reach. Yglind climbed down as fast as he could as the creature gripped the ladders on either side with its claws and squeezed into the shaft. Skiti fiddled with the base of her device, which flashed as it formed a cross that spread out to block the shaft.

The dragon's claws latched onto the impossibly thin bars of the cross, which bowed upward, creaking, but somehow held. The dragon opened its jaws wide and blasted them with a roar that was amplified by the shaft, sending Yglind's head spinning again.

"Will it hold?" Aene asked in a small voice, her hands fumbling for the next bar down.

"It has to," Skiti said cheerfully, following her down. "Because if it doesn't, we're all dead."

"Egg!" Aene hissed, snapping Yglind from his stupor. "Get the fuck moving!"

He bared his teeth at her through his faceplate but started moving, finding the next rung down, then the next, and Ardo followed him as the dragon pulled on the crossbars again, and again they flexed and groaned but held. The Timon's metal magic was impressive. Yglind quickly found his rhythm, and his head cleared as they moved down together at a steady pace. The dragon rattled the bars a few more times and gave a final roar, then all was silent except for their labored breathing and the sound of their hands and feet finding the bars on the shaft's wall.

"I think it's gone," Ardo whispered, stopping momentarily and cocking his head.

"Either that or it's lurking right outside the tunnel waiting for us to come back up," Aene remarked.

"More likely, it's rushing to the next big shaft so it can climb down and intercept us below." Skiti glanced up the shaft, shaking her head. "You all keep going. I'm going to go up and listen, make sure it's not lurking up there, then remove my Omni and hurry down to catch up with you."

"And if it's waiting up there to pounce on you once you remove it?" Yglind said.

"Then you'd best start climbing faster because I'm not leaving that thing behind."

Yglind grunted and continued moving. Skiti's device was one of their few remaining advantages, and it had just saved all their lives, so he couldn't argue. Ardo had, too, stepping in with his staff, which had enough reach to at least distract the beast, but Yglind's attack had been a wasted effort. A dagger, no matter how well placed, wasn't going to do much to a beast that size. Until he found the fucking humans, murdered them, and took his Forever Blade back, he was going to need a better weapon to defend himself with.

The now-familiar clank-clank of Skiti's device changing shape sounded from above, and Skit began descending with remarkable speed. Yglind had mostly recovered from the blow to the head, but he didn't feel entirely confident in this awkward method of climbing, and Aene was struggling to keep up with even his slow pace. She was fit for a mage, but climbing clearly wasn't her strong suit. And without her gauntlet, she might prove to be a liability again before too long if they encountered the waadrech or the humans any time soon. He paused, waiting for her to catch up, and thought of the rush of golden light that had encircled the beast, slowing it down enough for him to shake off his dizziness and climb into the tunnel. How had she accomplished that without her gauntlet?

"Stop for a second," she said, heaving for breath as she hung onto the rungs opposite Yglind. "I need to put another chip in this circlet."

"Already?" Ardo asked. Yglind craned his head around to look at Aene, who had hooked one of her arms through a rung and had the circlet around her wrist. Chips usually lasted for months in a circlet, and Yglind hadn't used it since they'd first entered the mine, so it should have been fully charged.

"I drained its power to cast that spark storm," she said, placing the circlet's chip cover between her lips and fishing another chip out of her pouch. She popped out the old chip, which slipped from her fingers and ting-ed on several rungs as it made its way down the shaft.

"Fuck," she mumbled around the chip cover wedged in her lips. She slid the new chip into the tiny slot in the circlet, and a glow lined the rim of the slot until she replaced the cover and snapped it into place. She let out a slow, audible sigh, then smiled weakly.

"I didn't know the circlets could be used that way," Ardo said with a hint of pure curiosity that Yglind couldn't help grinning at. Even in these grim circumstances, Ardo's spark shone through.

"It's not ideal, and there are limits to what it can do, but anything light or heat-related can be channeled through the circlet, along with the usual mental stuff. But it sucked up an entire chip just for one spell, so let's hope I don't have to use it again too soon. I only have half a dozen left."

"Well, we are in a fucking brightstone mine, so with any luck, you'll be able to restock once we get into this keep. Right, Skiti?" Yglind raised his visor as he spoke.

"We mine the stone, but the design of the chips is proprietary. We couldn't make one if we wanted to." Skiti side-eyed Aene, who nodded, then shook her head.

"Tech keeps a tight lid on that stuff. The security to get into the production facility is unbelievable. And our first lessons in training are to never scrape off the coating and always return spent chips to the Guild. The fucking paperwork I'm going to have to do if I can't find that chip..." She stared down the shaft, heaved a sigh, and started climbing. Yglind matched her pace, and Ardo and Skiti followed close behind.

"Just another little bit, and we're there," Skiti whispered. Yglind stopped, his arm aching from the partially healed claw wound and his head sluggish in the aftermath of being whipped by the waadrech's tail. "And once we get down, it's only a couple hundred yards to the keep gate. Better if I go first."

Aene climbed down a few steps, then crossed over to hang beneath Yglind.

"Don't move until I give the word," Skiti hissed, putting a finger across her lips. "And turn those lights off if you don't mind." Yglind exchanged a worried glance with Aene and Ardo, then tapped his amulet off, and the other two blinked out shortly thereafter, leaving them in total darkness.

"Hang tight."

Yglind heard Skiti's movement down the rungs, much faster than the pace they had been keeping as a group. Living in the mines, climbing these ladders was no doubt second nature to her, and he had to admire her strength and stamina. Though Yglind exercised regularly as part of his training regimen, there was no substitute for the real thing. After a few moments, the sounds of Skiti's hands and feet on the rungs stopped, and the silence was as absolute as the darkness.

"One light only, and dim it if you can." Skiti's words carried through the shaft, somehow fuller than the average whisper but without vocalization. As Aene tapped her amulet into low light mode and they began climbing, Yglind wondered if the whisper was a special technique used to communicate without alerting potential predators, who might be drawn to the vibrations of normal speech.

"Oh, thank gods," Aene said under her breath as she reached the bottom and kneeled to pick up a tiny rectangle of dulled brightstone with copper filaments running up the sides. She slipped it into a pouch and stood up slowly, flashing a weak smile as she heaved for breath.

"Small victories." Ardo stood examining his broken staff end. Yglind knew he was especially fond of that staff, with its bronze-shod tips. He often spoke with reverence of the strength of the ironwood, which the dragon's jaws had snapped like a pine branch.

"The dragon will figure out where we are soon enough. Are you all ready to move?"

Yglind glanced at his companions, whose eyes showed reluctant agreement, and he nodded to Skiti. She turned and walked down the hallway at a modest clip, moving in near silence, which Yglind, with his armor, could not match. He softened his footfalls as much as he could, but he still clinked a bit with each step.

"It's right up ahead." Skiti stopped and spoke in a low whisper. "I'm going to go up and try the code and see if I can make contact. They might have changed it up since the humans arrived, but I can always try the emergency code if all else fails."

"Maer aren't allowed into the keep," Aene said slowly. "At least not according to my studies."

"Exigent circumstances should cover you. I think."

Skiti blinked, then turned and walked through the darkness toward what looked like a dead end, but with several squares of stone jutting out a few inches from one of the walls. Yglind heard the clanking sound of the Omni and could just barely see it fold in on itself, returning to the club-sized shape. Another series of metallic noises sounded, and Skiti pressed it against a square stone sticking out of the wall, fiddling with the other end. Nothing happened, and Skiti pulled the device back, fiddled with it a bit more, then pressed it against the wall again. Yglind turned as a strange scraping noise echoed down the corridor behind them. A click sounded from the wall ahead, then the faint grinding of stone, and a beam of pale light poured out of a crack in the wall. A roar filled the hallway behind them, and Skiti's eyes met Yglind's for a moment as she waved him forward with wide, terrified eyes.

8

Skiti stepped aside as the three Maer slipped through the half-open door. They stopped cold as they ran up against four members of the Guard, who formed a wall of full battle armor and bristling weapons. Another roar sounded, and Skiti heard the clacking thumps of the waadrech galloping up, its rear end sliding as its front claws caught the edge of the closing door. One of the Guard muscled past Aene and swung their wrist axe down on the dragon's claw, severing one of its fingers and clanging off the stone. The dragon's shriek reverberated in the small chamber as its claws slipped away from the door, and the gatekeepers cranked it closed with great alacrity. The dragon's roar was deafening, even through the thick stone door, and Skiti's ears were still ringing from its earlier screech.

The calm following the closing of the door lasted about three seconds until the four Guards raised their wrist axes and shields toward the three Maer. Aene put up her hands as she shrank against the wall while Yglind postured with his knives, though he held them in a defensive position.

"My Lord," Ardo said, touching Yglind lightly on the shoulder. "They are not the enemy. We are their guests."

Yglind lowered his knives reluctantly, shaking out of Ardo's touch.

"You are not our guests," one of the Guard said, lowering her weapon but maintaining an intimidating stance, or as intimidating as a Timon could be facing a Maer of Yglind's stature. Skiti recognized Diyari by her voice, which was higher than most. "Not until Laanda decides you are." Yglind had to be almost two feet taller than any of them, and though he lacked the dense musculature of her people, Skiti had to admire the sheer size of him, the girth of his limbs, the way he filled the space.

"Are we to be your prisoners, then?" Yglind spat.

"Nothing like that," Skiti said, stepping toward him, then stopping when Diyari fixed them with stern eyes glaring out of her faceplate.

"The Maer are under our protection," Diyari said, her stance stiffening as she sheathed her wrist axe. "But you may not pass beyond the upper level until Laanda gives her approval." One of the other Guard set down a large chest in front of Diyari, who opened it with a key she took from around her neck. "Please place your weapons in this box. And your circlet," she added, motioning to Aene. Aene's jaw clenched as she removed the copper circlet from her head, and Skiti dearly wished she could get a closer look at it. She'd thought it was a communication device since they'd all seemed to carry them, but the mage had somehow used it to channel magic after her gauntlet had been stolen.

Diyari turned and signaled toward the two Guard on the other side of the inner portcullis, which raised with a clanking of chains.

"Follow me," Diyari said, turning with squared shoulders and striding through the entryway. Skiti fell in behind the Maer. Though she wasn't under the same strictures as they, she didn't feel right leaving them alone with the Guard. Yglind was bound to get into trouble if left to his own devices, and as big of an asshole as he was, she couldn't help liking him a little. Plus, he had saved her life against the hulshag, and she had to respect a Maer who went toe to claw with a waadrech armed only with a couple of daggers.

The rest of the Guard flanked them as Diyari led them to the holding room, which was wide enough for them to spread out, though Yglind had to remove his helmet to duck through the doorway. Even inside the room, there were only a few inches of clearance between the ceiling and his tightly braided hair. The room was equipped with several benches, a table, and a water tank. Skiti studied Yglind's helmet as he set it on the table. It was an impressive piece of equipment, shaped like a mashtorul head and inlaid with realistic veins and warts. It was bronze, like his fine chain and scale armor, the knives he carried, and the sword the human thief had stolen. It seemed the rumors were true, that the Maer did not use iron or steel in any capacity. Ardo stood at Yglind's side as if bound by an invisible tether while Aene collapsed onto a bench, her eyes bloodshot and bleary.

"We will bring you food and wine, and Laanda will join you shortly." Diyari removed her helmet, tucking it under her arm. "Do any of you require medical attention?"

"What we require is weapons," Yglind snarled, "since the human stole my sword and the dragon ate Ardo's staff. And we'll need Aene's circlet back as well. We aim to go back out there, hunt them down, and drain their skinfucker blood onto the cold stone of this mine."

"In that goal, we have a common purpose." Diyari's voice was firm and grim. "The humans killed a dozen of our Guard, not to mention murdering another score of civilians. We have a crew out tracking them as we speak." Skiti felt a wave of angry tears rising up; though she didn't know who exactly had been killed, Diyari's words dragged her heart down like an elevator counterweight.

"Do they know the humans can stop time?" Aene asked, pressing into the table with both hands to stand up. "That's how they got us. Some kind of magic I've never seen before, based in a crystalline object shaped like a figure eight."

"It is a wonder they did not kill you," Diyari said. "I will speak with Laanda. Skiti, with me."

"I'd prefer to stay with our guests if it's all the same to you." She had grown unexpectedly attached to the Maer during their short time together, and she felt like she needed to protect them.

"Your preference is irrelevant." Diyari spoke in Timon, and her voice was cold, devoid of her usual confident cheer. "Laanda will see you now."

Skiti clenched her jaw, glancing at the Maer. Yglind's face was twisted with scorn and rage, Aene's with hopelessness, but Ardo's blink reassured her. His steady hand would keep Yglind in check and keep Aene from slipping farther down inside herself. Skiti gave them a curt nod and followed Diyari into the hallway. The stone gate opened as they approached, and the blast of warm air as she entered the keep proper almost brought tears to her eyes. It had been a long, cold five days outside its comfort and safety.

Laanda was leaning over her map table, watching as her advisors moved pieces around like children playing Search and Slay, maneuvering for the best tactical advantage. Skiti noticed a group of three Maer figurines standing just inside the lines of the keep while a lacquered black dragon and three human figures were spaced well apart on the map. A group of six Timon cloaked in black stood in a straight line heading toward the humans, each figure bent in the same deadly crouch. Laanda stood up as Skiti and Diyari entered, summoning them with the faintest tilt of her head toward the door to her receiving room.

"Have the Maer been fed?" Laanda asked, sitting down in front of a mirror and touching up her beard.

"As we speak," Diyari answered with a curt nod.

"See to it that they get only the best. If this is a *Delve*, that means at least one of them is of high rank."

"A what?" Skiti asked. She couldn't quite place the Maer word.

"It's an archaic ritual for newly minted Maer knights. They have to prove themselves on an underground quest of some kind and slay at least five worthy enemies. More than a few *Delves* were sent against our people before the Great Peace, which you'd know if you'd paid attention in history class." Laanda's voice was gently teasing; Skiti had needed Laanda's help to pass most of her non-technical classes when they were in school together.

"Only high-born Maer can be made knights," Laanda continued, "so we must treat them as we would ambassadors."

"They are somewhat lacking in the subtlety commonly found among diplomats," Diyari said in a gruff tone.

"Nevertheless." Laanda blinked reassuringly. "See to it."

Diyari gave a half bow, casting Skiti an inscrutable glance as she turned and strode out of the room.

"Come, Skiti." Laanda touched her on the shoulder, her eyes soft with concern beneath her veneer of control. "Sit. Have a dram of hotstone." Laanda's posture relaxed now that Diyari was out of the room, and Skiti felt for a moment that she was once again in the presence of her lifelong friend and sometimes lover. Laanda retrieved the silvered decanter and glasses from a shelf and poured them each a healthy splash. The aroma of the whiskey hit Skiti like a whiff of fresh air in the brightstone pits, and she held the cup under her nose as she gently swirled the crystal-gray elixir.

"To the Depths." Skiti let the whiskey wash over her tongue, lighting every taste bud on fire and flooding her throat with its smoky, silky burn.

"To the Depths." Laanda downed her glass, and her face grew somber for a moment.

"Another?" Laanda asked as she filled their glasses too quickly for Skiti to answer, as usual. Skiti raised her glass and took a sip, smiling as it spread through her mouth like liquid fire.

"Must have been rough out there," Laanda said, her voice level but one eyebrow slightly arched. "We'd almost written you off for dead. How'd you survive?"

"They got trapped in the labyrinth, as you probably know. I hid out in a storage room and waited until they found what I assume must have been a weak spot in the barriers. Had a sporecake in my pouch, thankfully, but I had to lick condensation from the walls for water. I heard them roaming around, arguing, trying to break through the barriers but having no luck. Then after a few days, I heard something like an explosion, and once I went out, I saw they had ripped a hole in the ceiling with their magic, just like they did to the chimney." Skiti shook her head. The Timon had nothing to match this kind of power, and without Aene's gauntlet, neither did the Maer.

"We've double and triple-checked every inch of the keep's barriers. We're safe here."

"Maybe. But between their stone magic and the time stop, if that's what it was, if they find a way in, they can do all kinds of damage."

Laanda tossed back the remainder of her glass, reached for the decanter, then let her hand fall to the table.

"The Guard have a bead on their thief. At last whisper, he was heading down the back passage leading to the old copper gallery. The passage is equipped with a Subtle Net, assuming it's still operational. With any luck, they might bring him back for a chat, assuming the waadrech doesn't muck everything up. But tell me of these Maer. Who is their leader?"

Skiti shook her head, a rueful smile growing on her face. "Yglind, I guess. He's the one with the sword, or he had it anyway. A beautiful bronze number, a bit too long for these tunnels, but he made short work of a hulshag and faced off against the waadrech twice and lived to tell of it."

Laanda stood up straight, turning away for a moment. "I must admit I'm a little jealous. In my position, I can't exactly put myself directly in harm's way, but I would dearly love to test myself against this dragon." She turned to face the table beside her, touching the points of her crown with her fingertips. It was made of long strings of gold and silver, woven together into a delicate swirl that jutted up like a wind-blown flower. It was nestled in a velvet-lined box, along with an elaborate necklace of copper studded with tiny brightstones, so it glowed orange-gold. Skiti had only seen her wear the jewels and crown a couple of times on high ceremonial occasions. "Tell me of the others."

"There's Aene, a mage, who uses their brightstone magic. She has what they call a channeling gauntlet, or had until the human thief froze us and took their most prized possessions. She can use it to do almost anything—shield, weapon, rope, shower of sparks. Their magical tech is fascinating. I was hoping—"

"I was hoping you could get to the point," Laanda said warmly but firmly. "Can we trust them?"

"Of course," Skiti said without hesitation. "They came here to help. When the Magni went dark. They came to investigate. You said something about a *Delve?*"

"A *Delve,* yes. They're mostly just for show these days, from what I hear, but if the High Council sent them, I suppose we can trust them. Anyway, tell me about his armaments."

"Well, the sword was a little long, like I said, but he swung it as if it weighed nothing, and it cut through the hulshag like raw liver. It made a serious dent in the waadrech, loosened a couple of scales, and even drew blood. Has these cool etchings all along the blade and an elaborate guard and pommel."

"So, he's definitely of high birth. And the armor?"

Skiti smiled at Laanda's serious expression. She'd always had a thing for armor. "Fine chainmail with scales around the chest and rigid plates on the shoulders. Very dense, excellent coverage, though the waadrech's claw did pierce it and give him a nasty wound. He had a shield, too, of similar make, but the waadrech ate it, I think. At any rate, he didn't have it anymore when he climbed up into the shaft."

"Very well. If this Yglind is on a *Delve*, he'll want to find and kill that dragon, or more likely, die trying, which we definitely don't want."

"Actually, he's hell-bent on killing the humans after they took his sword. His eyes are filled with revenge."

"Excellent. Hopefully, the Guard can catch the thief and bring him back to us, along with their gear. Then we can help the Maer find and take out the other two humans and maybe even chase the waadrech back outside. Those things are vicious but not stupid. It won't go up against a fully armed squad of Guard. Do you think the Maer have it in them to kill the creature?"

Skiti shook her head. "Maybe." It was very bad luck to kill a dragon, and it wasn't clear the bad luck would fall on the Maer alone if it happened in the mine. "Fully rested, equipped, and in the proper circumstance? Maybe."

"We'll just have to make sure that doesn't happen. Oh, wait—" Laanda held up a finger, moved to the wall, and put her ear to the whisper cone. Skiti was glad to see the humans hadn't destroyed them all. Laanda closed her eyes, nodding her head slightly, then turned her lips to the cone and hiss-whispered: "*Bring him back at once.*"

She turned back to Skiti, a smirk on her face. "Well, that's a nice piece of luck. The Subtle Net caught the thief, and they were able to block off the passage so the other humans couldn't interfere while they disarmed and removed him. He should be here in a couple hours. In the meantime, I'm going to go make nice with the Maer. Give me a hand?" Laanda raised the glittering necklace, holding the ends behind her head so Skiti could affix the clasp. She relished the sight of the delicate chain around Laanda's muscular neck, the contrast made all the more delicious by Laanda's mail shirt, which had the texture of silk, but even a dragon's tooth wouldn't penetrate it. Laanda set the crown on her head and turned again toward the mirror, tucking a few stray wisps of hair inside the crown.

"Take me to them."

Yglind was pacing around the small room when they arrived. Ardo and Aene slept, leaning against each other's shoulders in a corner. Yglind stopped when Laanda entered, and the anger drained out of his posture, replaced by a sudden poise Skiti wouldn't have thought him capable of. He bowed deeply and slowly, turning a surprisingly warm and enchanting smile toward Laanda.

"Queen Laanda, it is an honor."

"Laanda will do fine. We did away with the title decades ago. But you have me at a disadvantage."

"Yglind, of the House of Torl, your Grace."

"Torl, as in General Torl?" Laanda's demeanor hardened as an edge crept into her voice. Skiti didn't know much military history, but the context was clear.

"She was my great-grandmother," Yglind said with a timid bow. "I am pleased that relations between our people have improved to the point that we can put aside ancestral enmity to focus on our present mutually beneficial relationship." Skiti's jaw dropped at Yglind's subtlety of expression. Was this the same foul-mouthed brute she had spent the past day with?

"I appreciate the sentiment, and I welcome you into our keep." Laanda's voice softened a hair. "Diyari, have their weapons returned to them at once."

"You are too kind, milady."

"I'm not a lady, and I'm only extending proper courtesy to those who have come to our aid. I gather the humans have taken something of value to you?"

Yglind's eyes darkened. "Yes. Help us find our belongings so we can kill them. That is the only courtesy I require."

"Of course. The Guard are bringing their thief to us as we speak."

"Let me have a moment with him, I beg of you." Yglind's face was animated with hatred and desperation.

"Not until our inquisitors have had a chance to speak with him. But we will return your property to you if he has it on his person. In the meantime, if you wish for some rest and perhaps a bath, I'm sure we could—"

"I don't need rest. I need my sword back so I can run those skinfuckers through with it!"

"While I appreciate your enthusiasm, I would remind you that we are in a Timon mine, and the prisoner falls entirely under our jurisdiction. We will allow you to question him under direct supervision once we're done with him. Skiti, show them to their quarters and the baths, if they're so inclined."

Skiti gestured toward Yglind, whose scowl softened, and he bowed to Laanda. "I accept your gracious offer."

"A bath would do us a world of good," Ardo said, touching Yglind lightly on the arm. "Look your best to be your best. Isn't that what you said before?"

Yglind breathed out through his nose, nodding, and lay his hand on top of Ardo's. Skiti had sensed that the two were a couple, and she could see how Ardo was a good influence on Yglind.

Two Guard entered with the weapons chest, and the Maer collected their equipment. Aene inspected the circlet, then carefully placed it on her head and closed her eyes, smiling for the first time in a while.

"This way," Skiti said as she turned toward the door.

9

Ardo eased into the steaming bath, which was hotter than the ones in Kuppham, but as the heat worked its way into his bones, a smile grew on his face.

"They're trying to boil us into submission," Yglind groaned, but it was tinged with pleasure, and Ardo's cock twitched at the sound.

"This is absolutely the most perfect bath I've ever taken." Aene rubbed a cake of pinkish soap on her hands, then scrubbed the hair on her head and shoulders with the foam. She floated the soap to Yglind, who lathered up and passed it to Ardo. They sat in silence, heads and arms covered in slowly popping fluff, until Aene closed her eyes and went under, then emerged, her shiny hair running straight down her face. Yglind and Ardo followed suit, and Ardo had to rub his eyes to get the stinging, minty soap out.

"Gods willing, they get our stuff back from the thief, and he tells us what we need to know to go wipe the rest of them out." Yglind's anger was muffled, his voice soft and relaxed, as it became when he was anticipating a release. The stress of losing his sword and of the battles behind and ahead had no doubt taken their toll, and Ardo found himself deeply aroused, despite all they'd been through, or perhaps because of it. He found Yglind's ankle beneath the water and ran his foot as far up his leg as he could reach. Yglind did not flinch, though his face quirked into a quarter-smile.

"I'll break out the scrying dice as soon as I get done soaking in this divine lake of molten lava."

"It would be good to find out what they have to say." Ardo hoped Aene would take the hint. "We are at a bit of a crossroads."

"You two are so fucking predictable." Aene closed her eyes and went under once more, then rose suddenly, water cascading down her sleek form. Her matted-down hair showed her lean muscles and tight curves to great effect, and Ardo briefly wondered what it would be like, what she would be like. He loved Yglind, and Yglind was the finest specimen of Maer-flesh in all the Silver Hills, but something in Aene's I-don't-give-a-fuck attitude suggested a latent power that made his cock rise a little more.

"I'll need you two to be present for the scrying, so don't be too long." She flashed them an amused expression as she picked up one of the towels the Timon had laid out for them, wrapped it around herself, and padded out of the bath.

"Finally." Yglind scooted closer to Ardo, his eyes alight with hunger. He touched Ardo's cheek, then ran his thumb over his mouth, pulling his bottom lip down for a moment before grabbing his beard and pulling him in for a kiss that was much softer than Ardo expected. Yglind's hand found his cock beneath the water, and he gripped it loosely, too loosely, sliding his hand up and down without letting Ardo get any friction. If Yglind was in a teasing mood, that meant he wanted a blowjob. Ardo had learned that much by now, but the light touch felt so good that he let Yglind keep at it for a while before he reached down and grabbed Yglind's cock, which was as hard as a sword pommel.

Yglind let out one of his little gasps, the sound of someone having his cock touched for the first time, though in reality, it was more like the thousandth. Ardo smiled, leaning in to kiss him again, feeling Yglind's grip on him weaken as he took control of Yglind's cock, pushing down, feeling Yglind's hot head press against the inside of his wrist as he snaked his tongue inside Yglind's lips. The faint moan in Yglind's throat deepened as Ardo slid his other hand down Yglind's thigh and cupped his balls, gently at first, as if he were holding a clutch of eggs.

Ardo loved holding Yglind's pleasure in his hands, loved the little sounds he made, the tenderness of his kisses. His brash manner melted away when they were in each other's arms, and Ardo wished the world could see the Maer he knew Yglind to be.

Yglind's hands ran lightly up and down his arms and shoulders, gripping his biceps as Ardo squeezed his balls with slow but inexorable force, stopping at Yglind's first little squeak of pain and holding the pressure at that exact point. Ardo teased his cock with his other hand, still kissing Yglind, who was frozen in the moment and unable to kiss back. Just like Ardo liked him.

He pulled back from the kiss, staring hard into Yglind's soft, desperate eyes.

"Do you want to fuck my mouth?" Ardo whispered.

Yglind closed his eyes, breathing shakily through his nose. When he opened them, they were so full and vulnerable, the exact opposite of the way they looked with his sword in his hand.

"Ardo, I—" he paused, his O-shaped mouth forming an inchoate sound as Ardo tugged upwards with both hands, and as Yglind rose to stand, Ardo had to adjust his grip to keep hold of all the important parts while remaining kneeling himself.

"You were saying?" Ardo slid his hand down Yglind's cock, water beading on its shiny-hard surface, and swiped his tongue across the head.

"I want to make love to your mouth." Yglind leaned slowly forward, and Ardo guided his cock between his lips, his tongue curling and lapping as he took him in as far as he could bear without gagging. Yglind did not grab his hair or shove himself in further as he sometimes did; he moved gently in and out, running his fingertips around Ardo's earlobes, folding them over, slipping his pinkies behind his ear, and weaving them through his facial hair and beard. Ardo squeezed Yglind's balls as he knew he liked, working him over with his lips and tongue. Yglind soon stopped moving and let Ardo take control. Ardo teased him, alternating between slow, lapping strokes and bouts of frenzied motion, back and forth through the cycle they both knew so well. With each gasp, Yglind surrendered more and more until Ardo knew it was time.

Yglind strained toward him, and his nails bit into Ardo's cheek. Ardo slipped one finger back and pressed it firmly against his hole. Yglind gave a muffled cry and bucked into Ardo, his hands finally finding the back of Ardo's head, holding him in place. Ardo drained him, breathing heavily through his nose as he fought against the gag and swallowed. Ardo released his finger, then his hand, tightening his lips around Yglind's slowly diminishing cock, sucking the last few drops straight down. He lightened the pressure as he pulled his mouth away, and Yglind's cock flopped out, bobbing in his face for a moment before Yglind lowered himself back into the bath, staring at Ardo with hot, glassy eyes.

"You're too good to me," Yglind murmured. Ardo melted at the soft tone of his voice, the vulnerability he let slip in moments like this.

"I'm nowhere near as good as you deserve."

Ardo's eyes fluttered, and his heart along with it, as Yglind scooted closer, angling his lips for a kiss.

Aene sat cross-legged on the ground in the spacious room the Timon had offered them. Ardo knew the economy of underground space meant a room such as this would normally be reserved for important persons, and it seemed Laanda was extending them every courtesy. Yglind's facility with diplomacy always amazed Ardo, though he had observed it many times. Yglind *was* capable of thinking about someone besides himself. He *was* capable of learning. Of changing. If he could quit hiding behind his mask of uncaring toughness and show the world just a glimpse of the Maer he was in their private moments.

"Please, sit," Aene said without opening her eyes. Ardo sat down and crossed his legs, scooting back when Yglind joined them, sitting with knees wide. Ardo glanced from Yglind's legs to Aene's, noting that Yglind's were at least twice as big around and looked twice as long in this position. He shook his head to clear the creeping thoughts of Yglind and Aene's legs tangled together, and Aene began to clack the dice around in her hand.

"Bring your thoughts to what has transpired," she said in a low voice, opening her eyes and glancing at each of them. "Recall every detail, down to the smell and taste. Relax your mind and let yourself flow through the moments leading up to this one."

Ardo's mind tingled at her words, which recalled those of Cloti's wandering acolytes, who would visit his village and lead meditation sessions for all those who wished to join. They never asked for or accepted anything except a bite to eat and a roof if the weather was foul. His parents had never let him attend the sessions, but he'd glimpsed enough that he would sometimes find himself awake late at night, sitting cross-legged as they did, trying to open his mind, though he was never quite sure what he was meant to open it to. He wondered if Aene followed Cloti's teachings, though she probably wouldn't admit it even if it were true.

The dice clattered on the stone floor, and Aene studied them for a moment, her mouth twisting as her hands moved in circles above the assortment of symbols, which were unlike any Ardo had ever seen elsewhere. They looked ancient somehow, but their simple lines seemed to emanate power. He wished he'd had the opportunity to study magic, but his family had barely been able to afford squire academy.

"Well?" Yglind's voice was hopeful, though his face was tense. Ardo had managed to distract him for a few minutes, but he was sure Yglind's mind was now fixed only on getting his sword back and punishing the humans who had stolen it. When the Timon brought the thief back, they would have to keep Yglind far away if they hoped to keep the human alive long enough to get any information out of him.

"It's...not what I expected, nor what I asked." Aene stared down at the dice as if they had offended her somehow, then snatched them up and tucked them back into her pouch.

"That's even less helpful than usual," Yglind whined. "Tell us what they said!"

"I asked if we should go out and chase the humans or wait for them to come to us." She stroked her beard, her eyes fixed on a spot of blank wall. "What I got was they are divided." She shook her head, her eyes casting down as Yglind snorted.

"Well, no fucking shit they're divided. They sent their thief to steal our stuff, and now he's been captured. Did they say..." He glanced at the pouch at Aene's side. "Did they say if I'll get my sword back?"

"Not a peep. But if they bring the thief back, I think our chances of recovering our property are pretty good."

"And his chances of getting disemboweled and fed his own entrails are even higher."

Ardo wanted to touch Yglind on the shoulder, to shush him with a whisper in his ear, but the sword's hold on Yglind's mind was almost greater now than when he held it in his hand.

"The Timon won't let you anywhere near him until they've done their worst, which, as you know from your history, is pretty fucking bad." Aene's voice dropped with what sounded like pity, which was odd since she clearly valued her gauntlet just as highly as Yglind did his sword. Maybe she'd been drawn in by the human's eyes, which had struck Ardo as the thief had stolen his circlet. It wasn't just the vibrant green color; there was a depth to them, a flicker of apology as he'd lifted the circlet from Ardo's head. He was a thief, but he was no killer.

"If they don't kill him, I will," Yglind growled. "That's a promise you can take into hibernation."

Aene snorted. "I seriously doubt I'm headed for such a distinguished fate. I'm more likely to be relegated to teaching novices once my time in the field comes to an end until they find me dead at my desk, slumped over a stack of term papers."

"If we finish this Delve right, put an end to the skinfuckers, and slay that dragon, we'll have earned our way to the Time to Come. Mark my words."

"Yglind," Ardo started, but Yglind waved him off.

"Yes, I know, the dragon nearly killed us twice. But once was without my sword, and the first time I was fighting it *all by myself.*" He glared at Ardo, then Aene, who glared back.

"It would have killed you if I hadn't slowed it down." Aene's voice rose quickly. "And it wouldn't have hurt you and eaten your shield if you'd just followed us into the shaft in the first place. But you had to go charging into the face of certain death like a fucking *child* playing Search and Slay. This shit is for keeps, Yglind, and even if I get my gauntlet back, I can't save you if the waadrech cuts you in half or swallows you whole."

"Don't worry, it won't. I've found its weakness. It won't get away so easily next time."

"What did you see?" Ardo asked. He couldn't imagine any weakness on a creature as well armored as the waadrech.

"I saw enough. Leave the dragon-killing to me, and just be ready to do what I say when I say it."

Ardo stifled a sigh. Yglind was a master swordsman, and he had an uncanny knack for finding an opponent's weak spot. Combined with his reach, strength, and surprising speed, it made him one of the most respected knights in all of Maerdom, or at least the most feared. The gleam in Yglind's eye and the tight line of his jaw told Ardo there would be no dissuading him. Ardo would follow him, no matter how foolhardy the move. It was Yglind's Delve, and he called the shots.

A distant commotion tinkled through the hallways, and Yglind sprang up, strapping the sword the Timon had given him to his waist.

"That's not the sound of fighting," Aene said, still seated on the floor, cocking her ear toward the doorway. "More like arguing."

"They've brought the thief," Ardo said under his breath.

Yglind unsheathed his sword, glaring at its short, silvery length. It looked more like a dagger than a sword when Yglind wielded it, but the shine of the blade and the fine craftsmanship of the hilt suggested a weapon of nearly equal quality to Yglind's, and perhaps better, being made of steel.

"You can put that away, Yglind." Aene rose to standing, using the strength of her crossed legs and graceful balance to rise without pushing off with her hands. "Though it is a wicked-looking blade."

"It's fucking emasculating, is what it is," Yglind spat, sheathing the sword again. "That skinfucker thief better have my sword, or so help me gods, Timon or no Timon, I'll cut his fucking balls off and stuff them down his throat."

"As poetic as your words are, I hope you'll show a fraction of the restraint you demonstrated in your talks with Laanda."

10

Aene ignored Yglind's pacing and remained seated, stretching her fingers and thumbs tight to form a diamond framing a patch of bare stone floor beneath. She fixed the top point of the diamond in her mind, stretching her vision to encompass the bottom one as well, then pulled wide to connect to the sides. The shape tightened, and she exhaled slowly, recalling the breathing practice of her pre-tech training. It had been a long time since she'd worked without her gauntlet, but she hoped to draw upon that practice. She wanted to use everything the gauntlet had taught her to pull energy from the world around her and see what she could do without it.

Once the diamond was fully rigid, she moved her consciousness forward so her mind was held in its center, secured by the four points. She was drawn down toward the floor, the mass of cold stone pulsing with untapped power. She lowered her head until the diamond framed her nose to her forehead, then bent forward in this position until the edges of her hands touched the floor. A deep energy tingled through her fingertips, and she tried to channel it to the interior of the diamond, but it kept streaking away like blood trickling downhill.

She tensed with her mind, using the stability of the four points to anchor her, but they flexed as her head grew light, the energy pooling in her hands becoming suddenly slippery, stretchy. She choked on her inhale as it all drained away in an instant, and a great buzzing dizziness enveloped her. She wanted to sit up because the position seemed to make it worse, but her head was glued to the floor, too heavy to lift. She heaved a sigh and sank deeper, letting her forehead press into the cold stone, giving in to gravity, to exhaustion, to failure. She was no proper mage, just a channeler. Without her gauntlet, she was useless.

Footsteps sounded, distant and insubstantial, and she found enough strength in her arms to push up halfway and open her eyes. The footsteps approached, solid now, walking with purpose and speed. She pushed the rest of the way up to sitting, and her head cleared, though it took her a few more seconds before she was ready to use the edge of the table to pull herself up to standing.

Skiti stood in the doorway, holding Yglind's sword in one hand and Aene's gauntlet in the other. Yglind bounded across the room, taking the sword and holding it up to the light, his eyes wide with a love purer than ever one Maer had for another. Ardo stepped forward and unbuckled the Timon sword, then took Yglind's belt and scabbard and fastened them around his waist. His face was drawn, showing so little emotion it made his jealousy all the more obvious.

"I am in your deepest debt." Yglind sheathed his sword and kneeled toward Skiti, who covered her mouth but not before Aene spied a smirk creeping across it.

"And I as well," Aene said, eyeing the gauntlet, gleaming and elegant in Skiti's hand. She glanced down at her wrist, whose hair was worn almost bare in several spots where the gauntlet normally attached. It had been quite a while since she'd seen it any other way. She'd worn it even while sleeping during their trip, and she wondered how long the hair would take to grow back if she stopped wearing the gauntlet. But her wrist and hand felt unnaturally light, vulnerable without its sheath of ready power. Her mind tugged her forward, and she moved to kneel, but Skiti waved her back up, holding out the gauntlet. Aene took it, studying it as if for the first time as she laid it gently across her wrist. Its fine wires and intricately grooved bronzework were a marvel of craftsmanship, and she wondered about those who toiled in hot, sweaty forges to make such items for her and the other mages. She tapped the center, and the filaments laced up the backs of her fingers, anchoring themselves among her hair.

"I am glad we were able to recover your belongings. I hope everything is still in working order."

Aene smiled as she closed the final buckle, feeling secure again. Capable. Like herself. She pulled up the menu, which glowed golden in the air above her wrist, and flipped through the spells.

"Everything is working perfectly," she said, tapping the menu away, then double-tapping to check the power. It was half drained, though she'd put a fresh chip in it not long before it was stolen and had hardly used it afterward. "I think the thief tried to use it, though."

"Would he be able to?" Skiti moved closer, studying the gauntlet with wonder in her eyes. "I mean, how does it..." She paused, shaking her head. "I'm sorry. I know you probably can't tell me."

"I'll show you mine if you show me yours."

Skiti's face broke into a grin, and she pulled the Omni from her belt. "What do you want to know?"

"Well, mine runs on brightstone chips, as you know, specially cut and laced with copper filaments in precise arrangements. And no, the thief couldn't use it, nor could anyone else, though apparently, he could drain half the chip just by trying. It's attuned to me and can't be reconfigured in the field. What powers your Omni?"

Skiti gazed into Aene's eyes, seeming to study her, then nodded. "It's only fair since I know about yours, and besides, Maer don't use iron, right?"

"Not if we can help it. Though honestly, it's always seemed like a silly superstition to me. Iron and steel are objectively superior for many applications. It's just...a cultural thing, I guess you could say."

"Makes perfect sense. Iron is revered in our culture, and mastery of it in all its forms is the cornerstone of my practice. But to your point about the power source, part of it must come from the mind of the master. It takes a lot out of you, but it helps if you eat a lot before and a little after. The rest comes from this." Aene got a closer look at the device as Skiti unscrewed the tip. There were three cupped indentations near the base, each about the size and shape of a fingertip, with a narrow gap between the circles and the base of the device. Her eye was drawn to a bright blue light shining out of the tip where the cap had been removed.

"Don't look directly at it," Skiti cautioned, holding the glowing end just above Aene's eye level. "It can burn your eyes, and it is dangerous to be exposed to it for more than a few minutes."

"Is that hotiron?" Aene asked, wishing she could lower the rod and glimpse it just for a second. Hotiron, like hotsilver and a few other metals, emanated power, making them useful for fueling magical and mechanical devices, but their instability was what had pushed the Maer to develop their brightstone technology. Hotiron was still used to power the automatons, but for smaller items like circlets and gauntlets, brightstone was a superior power source, except for the extreme rarity of the stone.

"Spirit iron, we call it. It fuels the mechanism, and I provide the direction." She screwed the cap back on, then held the rod out, pressing her fingers into the three circles. The rod extended into a smooth, thin shape with a disced end, which then opened and spread out in an array of oddly curved fins with a webbing of fine metal thread woven between them like a parasol. Skiti spun the base of the rod, and as the fins spun, they wove silvery patterns in the air. The patterns bunched together like a bud, then slowly flowered, layer after layer of delicate petals, which peeled away one by one, fluttering about the whirling mass as if chased by a cold spring breeze.

"It's so beautiful." Aene reached out her fingers, not to touch the patterns but to feel the energy of the Omni, like a weak static field surrounding a core of deeper power. She knew the Timon were masters of metal, but she had always imagined weapons and clever tools, not performance art.

"Let me show you something." Aene pulled up the menu on her gauntlet and found the Meditation spell. "It works best if we sit," she said, lowering herself down. Skiti did the same, and Aene noticed Ardo crouching nearby, silently watching. She gave him a gentle blink, then pulled up the Meditation spell, the image of a waterfall, gorgeously rendered in ghostly golden light in the space between them, with mist rising from where it met the water. She brought in the sound, the pleasant roar of the water, the chirping of birds, the rustle of leaves in the trees.

"Is this one of Cloti's?" Skiti asked.

Aene gave a start, and the waterfall flickered out. "No, of course not. Those aren't allowed in the catalog." Mages had lost their gauntlets for much less. And how did the Timon know of Cloti?

"So, there's a whole catalog in there?" Skiti's voice was hesitant as if she couldn't wrap her mind around the idea.

"There are thousands of spells in the Archive, and we can choose a few dozen, maybe a little more, depending on your gauntlet. There are gauntlets that will hold over a hundred, but it takes a long time to reach the level of mastery required to wield them, and most never do."

"Can...can you put the waterfall back up, please?" Skiti asked in a small voice. Ardo sat down and scooted in closer, looking at Aene expectantly. She glanced over at Yglind, who was sitting on the bench with his sword across his lap, wiping it down with a rag, seemingly unaware of their existence.

Aene closed her eyes for a moment to clear her mind, then summoned the spell again, and the waterfall popped back into existence, and the sounds as well.

"The trick is to watch the water as it falls without letting your eyes be drawn all the way to the bottom. They say if you can maintain yourself in that balance, that clear mental space, you will see your place in the larger whole, and your path will come clear to you."

They sat watching the waterfall, which maintained itself without Aene's intervention, and she stared at the water rushing down, trying to fix her eye on one spot without being drawn down into the mist below. She found her balance between the competing tensions of gravity and hope, and for a time, she knew peace.

The sound of boots scuffing drew her attention, and she looked up to see Laanda standing in the doorway, staring at the waterfall with a hint of wonder piercing her stoic mask.

"I'm sorry, I can—"

"Keep it going. It's incredible." Laanda's voice was soft and breathy.

"It's just a trifle, really. The gauntlet does most of the work."

"But not just anyone could use it, could they?" Laanda said, her mouth hinting at a smirk.

"It's attuned to me and me alone. It would take a Master Artificer to bond it to anyone else."

"Well, no one else would be able to do much with this Omni unless they had metal mastery and plenty of time to learn." Skiti held it up, her face glowing with an almost maternal pride. "The controls take a lot of practice."

"As fascinating as this scientific and cultural exchange may be, I have come for another purpose." Laanda paused, and her gaze fell on Aene with the weight of a stone door. "The thief has asked to speak with you."

"With...with me?" Aene's heart hammered in her chest as she thought of those eyes beneath the hood, that sultry green color, like emeralds seen in a shadowed room. Eyes that pierced like hotiron.

"He says he will tell everything, but only to you. And since I don't intend to harm him unless he has committed crimes deserving of such a punishment, I hope you can help us avoid less...tactful means of persuasion." Her tone was light but with a hard edge beneath.

"Of course, anything you need. Is he..."

"He's not been harmed. Much. He still laughs, which has to tell you something."

"People laugh for a lot of reasons." Aene didn't know what the Timon had done to the prisoner, but the history books told of what atrocities they had once been capable. Many believed they still practiced torture, despite the continental ban that everyone, even the Islish Realm, had signed.

"He's fine, and he's ready when you are."

"Oh, gods, okay, just give me a minute to..." Aene ran her fingers through her beard and hair, checked her gauntlet, and took a swig of water. Yglind leered at her from his bench, but he said nothing. Perhaps he was cowed by the Timon leader, or maybe he'd suddenly taken his diplomatic skills to the next level. She gave him and Ardo a nod, then turned and followed Laanda out the door.

"He says his name is Feddar, and he claims he wants to help us stop the other two." Laanda gestured left before turning down a side hallway, walking at a brisk pace.

"Pretty convenient for someone caught transporting stolen goods to the very people he now says he wants to help us stop." Aene had to hurry a bit to keep up with Laanda's bold strides.

"I'd normally agree with you, but I didn't get where I am by being a bad judge of character, and there's something to his story. I'm inclined to believe him, but I want your take." They arrived at a dead end where two armored guards stood, shouldering their weapons and bowing as they saw Laanda.

Laanda said a few quick words in Timon, and one of the guards used a key around his neck to open a kind of access panel that glowed faintly blue inside. He pushed his fingers into a circular opening, and the stone wall behind him slid apart from the middle. The Guard ushered them toward it with a sweep of his hand. Laanda gave a curt response, possibly thank you—Aene only knew a few snippets of Timon from her introductory course. Every Timon knew Maer at least passably, so it wasn't really necessary to learn Timon, though she always wished she'd found room in her schedule to take more advanced classes.

They turned again, descended a small staircase, and came to another stone door, which Aene could now recognize by the hairline crack from floor to ceiling, flanked by two more guards, just like at the previous door. They opened it as before, and Aene followed Laanda into a large, almost cozy room with a table and chairs and a long, plush bench facing three purple velvet curtains.

"What are you going to do with him?" Aene asked.

"What we do with him depends on what he has done and how we think we can use him. If he has killed any Timon, his life is forfeit. If, however, we believe him, and I'll need you to weigh in on that, our artificers have a plan to convince him to help us."

Aene didn't like the sound of that, but she kept her thoughts to herself. She wondered what exactly the artificers had to do with anything. Would they equip him with some kind of control device, as the humans were said to do, to create spies who would be unaware of the devices until they were activated?

"Have a seat." Laanda gestured toward the bench, and Aene sat as Laanda pulled aside one of the curtains, revealing what looked like a flameglass window with an odd bluish tint. Behind the glass, the thief sat at a table, hands bound behind his back, his ruddy tan skin seeming to glow in the harsh brightstone light. His head was turned down toward the table, and except for the occasional movement of his lips, he looked to be asleep.

"Don't worry. He can't see or hear us. Is this the human who stole your gauntlet and Yglind's sword?"

"It is," Aene breathed, pausing as the human raised his head toward the glass, the green of his eyes burning low and dark. "What is the artificers' plan?"

Laanda raised an eyebrow and shook her head. "I can't share that information, but the human will not be harmed, provided he is innocent of the murder of more than two dozen of our citizens. And provided he helps bring the other two in."

The thief closed his eyes and began to sing a low, haunting melody, like a love song for one lost to the grave. It must have been Islish, which Aene knew only a little, but the tune made the sentiment clearer than any words, and the human's voice had an enchanting frailty to it.

"How can we hear him, but he can't hear us?" Aene asked.

"One-way whisper cones," Laanda replied as if it were obvious. "Just like the glass. Mechanical, not magical, if you're wondering."

"I was, actually I..." Aene trailed off as the human held a note for a long time, then seemed to repeat the same line several more times until at last, his voice trailed off, and he opened his eyes, which seemed to pierce the glass, fixing her with a pleading gaze. "Should I go in to speak with him?"

"In a moment. But first, tell me why Yglind so badly wants to kill the thief and you do not."

Aene shifted in her seat, staring at the thief's face, hairless from nose to forehead, with a deep bruise around one eye socket.

"Yglind loves his sword more than anything under the heavens," she said at last. "When the thief stole the sword, he created an enemy for life. Yglind will not know peace until the thief has paid."

"He stole your precious gauntlet, yet you have expressed no desire to see him pay."

"Have you ever met a human before?" Aene asked, still staring at the thief, who sat back in his chair, twisting his arms behind his back, then slumping down, a defeated look on his face. Laanda grunted, shaking her head. "Neither have I. We have been on the brink of war for more than a generation, almost since hostilities ended between your people and mine, and I've never so much as seen one. I'm curious."

"Are you sure it's got nothing to do with those piercing green eyes of his? They are quite striking. Even I can admit that."

"Don't be ridiculous," Aene said, feeling her face flush. "I mean, they are unusual, but that's beside the point. Think of what we could learn from him, about their culture, their language, their magic..." Her mind drifted to the device he'd carried, how it had seemed to stop time. The humans were thought to be far more primitive than the Maer. It was said that only their ferocity, their cruelty, and their sheer numbers made them a threat to Maerdom. Either the Maer had gotten a lot wrong about the humans, or those in a position to know had worked hard to conceal the truth from everyone else.

"Not to mention their intentions." Laanda crossed her thick arms across her chest, which was almost as big around as Yglind's. "Why attack this mine? The Timon are not at war with the humans. I'm surprised they even know we exist."

"It has to be the brightstone. Either they need it, or they know we do and are trying to stop us from getting it."

"Either way, they could have sent trade negotiators. But instead, they send this...hit squad, for lack of a better term. By the way, you do speak Southish, don't you?"

Aene nodded. Every educated Maer had to take at least four years of the language. "It's been a while, but it'll come back to me. I was top of my class."

"Good, because Feddar doesn't seem to speak a word of Maer, and none of us speak Islish. Why don't you go on in there, bring him some hotstone and bread, and see if you can get him to open up a little."

Aene sat across from the thief, watching him tear little pieces off the bread and pop them into his mouth with nimble fingers. Feddar did not look at her except when he took a drink of his water, but the spark in his glance made her look down at her gauntlet, which she had set to record the exchange. When he had finished the last crust of the bread and the rest of his water, he slid the whiskey close and raised it beneath his hairless nose. His mouth quirked into a smile, even as his eyebrows furrowed as if he were trying to solve a puzzle.

"Oak aged, I'm sure of it, with a nice smoky note from the char, but there's something else here I can't quite place." Feddar took a delicate sip, pursed his lips, and closed his eyes for a moment as he set the glass down. His eyes blinked open, and his smile widened. "Limestone, heated to leach extra minerals. I'd bet my life on it." His Southish was exquisite, almost native, Aene mused. Better than hers, for sure.

"I'm no whiskey expert, but they do call it hotstone."

A self-satisfied expression grew on his face. "I knew it! I missed my calling."

"And so instead, we find you terrorizing and murdering Timon and stealing from a party sent on a mission from the Maer High Council. Maybe you should have gone into distilling instead of thieving."

"I never terrorized or murdered *anyone*." Feddar's voice took on a strident, almost plaintive tone. "And yes, I stole your gauntlet and your friend's sword, which, by the way, are both exquisite pieces of work. I had no idea the Maer—"

"Would try you for your crimes and execute you if the Timon don't do so first? Well, now you know."

He shook his head, straining against the chair he was tied to. "I was sent to kill you, not steal your belongings. But after what Geni and Turu did to those miners, I couldn't go through with it. That was not what I signed up for, what we signed up for."

"And what did you sign up for?"

"I'll tell you if you promise to have me transferred to Maer jurisdiction. I had no part in what they did to the Timon, and I won't be judged for it." The tremor in his voice suggested the humans knew of the Timon's history of torture.

"Can you prove that?"

He closed his eyes and sighed, shaking his head. "Wait," he said, his face lighting up. "Yes, I can. I mean, more or less. They can check my blade. The only blood on there is from the hulshag. It was Geni's sword and Turu's spells that did all the damage."

"So why did they even bring you?"

"You know the Timon's reputation with traps. It's one of my specialties."

"And yet you wouldn't be sitting here if you hadn't been caught in their Subtle Net."

Feddar laughed. "I saw it on my way in and came back to it. I had to let my companions think I'd been fooled by the trap lest they realize what I was up to."

"Which was?"

He leaned forward, his eyes hot and serious. Whatever he was about to say, Aene believed it already.

"We were sent to disrupt the brightstone operations, nothing more. At least that's what I was told. But Geni seemed to have other plans. They killed the guards outside the mine before I realized what they were doing. Then when we couldn't get the gate open, Turu had to blast a hole through the chimney. Groups of Timon came at us from both sides, and Geni and Turu just went off. It was horrifying." His eyes dropped, and Aene could hear the regret in his voice.

"And now you want to make it right, is that it?"

"It sounds corny when you say it like that, but yeah." He looked up at her from beneath a stray lock of hair, the corner of his mouth raised in a smile. He was far more charming than he had any right to be, but that wasn't going to stop her from fulfilling her duties.

"I can request to assist in the Timon's investigation, and if you are not found guilty of any crimes, I will ask that you be released into Maer custody once this whole thing has blown over."

"About that." He winced, shaking his head a little. "If I don't show pretty soon, I'd bet on Geni and Turu blasting their way into this keep somehow to come looking for me. Laanda says it's all fortified and been double-checked, which, okay, maybe it has. Maybe it has."

"Well then, the more information you can give us, the better the chance we can make sure none of your friends gets killed."

"They're not my friends," he said, his face souring into a frown. "And it's not them I'm worried about getting killed."

11

Yglind paced the halls of the outer keep to the obvious annoyance of the Timon guards, but they had evidently been given orders not to disturb him. He moved freely through the claustrophobic hallways, whose ceilings were no more than four inches above the top of his head. The fingers of his left hand caressed the pommel of his sword, and he periodically swung his right across to grasp it, just to keep the motion fresh.

Footsteps hurried down the hall toward him, and Aene came into view, walking with grim purpose.

"What was he like?" Yglind tried to keep the snarl out of his voice with about as much success as usual.

"He seemed...sad," Aene replied quietly. "I don't think he killed any Timon. He says his companions went off and just started..."

"It's skin fever. I knew it!" Yglind spat. "Those fucking green eyes and that hairless skinface get you in a twist?"

Aene closed her eyes, breathing out slowly through her nose. She blinked, then fixed Yglind with a withering stare.

"I believe him. And at any rate, they're testing his blade and his hands for blood now. We'll know for sure before too long."

Yglind felt a growl rise in his throat, then a thought fluttered in, quieting the noise. "If the Timon find the human innocent of the deaths, we can request he be transferred to Maer jurisdiction. The espionage and sabotage are directed at us. The Timon just happen to be in the way."

"Way ahead of you, Egg. I promised that in exchange for him sharing information about his colleagues."

"And you believe he freely gave you information potentially harmful to his friends and companions."

"Like I said, I believe him."

"Because you want to fuck him." Yglind hated the words as they came out of his mouth, but he could never stop himself from doubling down.

"You know what? Sure, I want to fuck him." Aene's voice rose, then softened as she continued. "He's got pretty eyes and a soft voice, and he seems to actually care about other people. But I'm not an idiot, Egg." She shook her head. "I know what you're thinking; he's just a good actor, and he stole your fucking sword. I get it. And even if he didn't kill any Timon, he was part of the group responsible. He's a villain. But that doesn't mean I can't believe him when he says he's sad about the Timon his friends killed."

Yglind nodded, chewing on his knuckle for a moment. Regardless of whether the thief was pulling one over on Aene, he and the other humans were going to die for what they'd done, whether by his hand or the High Council's. Yglind was on a Delve, and he was going to come back with the requisite five kills one way or another. The brightworms didn't count, but the three hulshag did; even if he kept the thief alive, with the two humans and the dragon, that added up to six. Five was the minimum, but six was hero shit, and he intended his Delve to be one for the ages.

From the looks of the thief, he didn't have the strength or the weaponry to commit the kind of carnage they'd seen in the bodies of the slain Timon. Heads sheared clean off and faces melted with magic. This was the work of opponents worthy of Yglind's talents. One of the humans was a great warrior and the other a formidable mage. He was going to kill them both, slay the dragon, and bring the thief back to the High Council as his prisoner. That was how legends were made.

"What did he say about these friends, then?" Yglind asked, trying to keep the eagerness out of his voice.

"The leader's named Geni, a knight, and apparently a very bloodthirsty one. They carry a magic sword, a Quick Blade, which swings fast and springs back after every hit so it can be swung twice as often as any other." Yglind's hand found his pommel, which seemed to pulse beneath his touch. No skinfucker sword could match his Forever Blade. "Turu is the mage, what Feddar called a storm crow. Apparently, he can summon lightning, wind, thunder, that kind of thing."

"And blast huge holes in solid rock. I'm hoping you can help keep him under wraps while I deal with the fighter."

"Feddar gave me a few pointers. Between me and Ardo, we'll keep him occupied."

"Good. And what is Laanda's position on all of this? Will she let us go after them?"

Aene sighed, leaning against the wall and running her hand over her face. "You're not going to like this part."

"I suspect not. Speak!" Yglind strained not to grind his teeth.

"They plan to release him and track him back to the humans."

"Release him?" Yglind shouted, and Aene shrank back for a moment. He closed his eyes and took a deep breath, wishing he could channel Aene's meditative calm, but the blood pounding in his ears deafened him to reason. "Gods fucking dammit, they will NOT release him unless it's onto the point of my sword. I will slay that thieving skinfucker and anyone who tries to stop me!" His voice echoed down the hallway, and he sagged against the wall as he realized how ridiculous he sounded.

"Egg, you're not listening," Aene said in a near whisper, "which I suppose shouldn't surprise me. Their artificers are going to put some kind of tracker on him, something he won't be able to get rid of. He's going to lead us to them, and then you can do your worst. To *them*, not to him. Just think of the renown you'll get if you bring a human spy back to the High Council alive. Think of the intelligence they can get from him. Your place in the Time to Come will be secure."

Yglind took in a deep breath, ready to shout another denial, but as her words sank in, he realized she was right. The humans had been encroaching on Maer lands for some time now, and though they'd been able to track them on occasion using trained birds and flying automatons, they'd never managed to capture one alive. He would become an instant legend if he brought the thief back to Kuppham.

"The Timon promised I could question him," he said once his blood had finally cooled a bit.

Aene closed her eyes, her lids fluttering in obvious frustration. "They did, but don't be surprised if they won't let you in there with your sword."

"I wouldn't need my sword to snap his hairless neck, but I give you my word, on the Torl family name, I will use my words, not my hands. But I do want to get a little insight into these companions of his, so I might better prepare to wash the floors of the mine with their hot blood."

The human watched Yglind with fear in his emerald-green eyes. His face was gaunt from fatigue and stress, but Aene was right. There was a sadness in his eyes, too, a haunted look on his face that could not be faked. Yglind had always imagined humans as bloodthirsty, uncivilized, and uncaring, but this man who sat before him showed a subtlety of expression that almost inspired pity.

"Your death is all but certain," Yglind said, enunciating as clearly as he could. It had been a long time since he'd studied Southish, though he'd always been pretty good at it. "The Maer High Council will find you guilty of espionage." He paused, collecting his words. "The penalty is death. Why would you help us?"

"I don't know your laws, but is there not some provision for a criminal who assists in the prevention of greater crimes?"

"Perhaps." Yglind scratched the hair on his face. It was off-putting how eloquently this human spoke of laws, and he was correct. The Maer justice system allowed for clemency in such cases, though how the human could have known that was beyond Yglind's comprehension. "At the very least, you will spend the rest of your life behind bars."

"No prison you could put me in would be worse than the one I live in every day, having seen what my companions did to the miners." His voice quavered, and his eyes were glassy as he spoke. Something in the way he moved his brow reminded Yglind of Ardo when he was concerned for Yglind's well-being. He felt a faint stirring in his loins at the thought, and he cleared his throat and squared his shoulders. He would not be weak like Aene and fall prey to the human's wiles.

"But you would prefer not to die."

The man's laugh was faint but genuine. "My job is generally to avoid that very fate, so yes. And I'm willingly submitting to having a tracking device installed, though to be frank, I'm a little worried about where they might need to put it."

Yglind barked a laugh before he could think to stop himself. "The Tim-on are known to be great artificers. I am sure they will find a solution that leaves your..." He gestured with his hands as he searched for the words. "Your privacy intact."

The man smiled full-on now, and Yglind could no longer ignore the effects of his gaze. He could see why Aene was so taken with him. "Your word to the gods' ears, Yglind," the man said with a wink. "So, what do you want to know?"

Yglind's fingers found the top of his scabbard, and his heart fluttered for a moment at his sword's absence until he remembered and saw himself laying it on the velvet lining of the weapons box. He looked up at the man's soft eyes, imagining the look on his face when Yglind ran him through with his sword, blood pumping across his skin, one last desperate gasp for breath, and then the great leap into the void.

"Tell me about the one with the Quick Blade."

12

"You want me to do what?" Skiti shouted, pushing up out of her chair and stalking across the room.

"We both know you have the skill," Laanda said coolly.

"Skill's not the point, and you know it." Skiti stalked closer. "I thought those days were far behind us."

"So were the times of war, and yet here we are."

"No one's at war, Laanda!"

"The humans and the Maer are. Most of our economy derives from trade with the Maer. I'd say that puts us at war, too."

Skiti looked deep into Laanda's eyes, seeking some spark of her longtime friend, but in this moment, she found none. "And you think that justifies torture?"

"It's just a safety measure, not torture. It won't harm him in any way, assuming he doesn't try to run off on us. If your craft is up to the task."

"Like I said before, that's a non-issue. But I think you should have a full Council vote on this. You don't want this coming back to bite you in the ass."

Laanda nodded, frowning. "Thank you for your counsel as always, Skiti. You should begin preparations immediately. I will notify you once a final decision has been made. How long will you need?"

Skiti ran through the possibilities in her head, what she could repurpose and what she'd have to shape herself. "Couple of hours maybe. I'll have to take his measurements."

"Very well." Laanda gestured vaguely toward the door, and Skiti turned and left, rage burning deep in her stomach.

Skiti entered the prison cell along with two Guard to take Feddar's measurements.

"So, it's to be a collar, then," he said casually in nearly flawless Southish as she wrapped the tape around his neck. The Timon sometimes did business with the South, so she had studied the language, but it had been a little while. The thief must have lived there to speak it that well.

"Something like that. We're going to have to take your shirt off."

Feddar lifted his wrists, and Skiti unlocked the livesteel cuffs with her Omni. The two Guard stepped in closer, and Feddar raised his hands as she unbuttoned his shirt. He was a little less hairy than a Timon and quite a bit thinner, but his anatomy was the same, and she measured the distance from his first to his fifth vertebrae and made a note on her clipboard.

"You can put your shirt back on."

Feddar flashed a begrudging smile. "So, we're really doing this?"

"Look, I'm just an artificer. I make what I'm told, and I make it right."

"And if they told you to make something that was unethical? Would you still make it?" His green eyes looked so guileless, but they didn't work on Skiti. She knew what he was. What he had done. Even if he didn't kill her clanmates himself, their blood was on his hands.

"I'll see you in a little while."

His eyes dimmed, and his smile faltered, and she turned away, stepping between the two Guard and out the door.

Skiti hurried through the halls to the lab. Heuli slid his fine lens up onto his forehead as she entered, his hands still holding a pair of tiny picks.

"I've set aside what I think you'll need." He laid down the picks in a tray where one of the next-generation Omnis lay half-assembled. "On the big table." He turned, gesturing her to follow him as he scurried over to the wide, brightly lit table, where a selection of rings, tubes, wires, and clamps had been laid out, along with an array of tools.

"Did she tell you?" Skiti's face burned with the thought that Laanda had made her go through so much formality when her decision was already made.

"Not as such, but she said you might need to make a tracker of some kind, so I figured there's only so many places that could be attached without causing harm. I got you some neck-sized rings, though depending on his measurements, you might need to stretch or narrow them a bit." He gestured toward a set of steel bands of various diameters. "Or if you're thinking ear to ear, these rings might do the trick if you shape them just right and attach them with an ever-rigid band and some balled hooks." He gestured toward the smaller rings of rounded steel and hooks with a ball end in a variety of sizes. "Bracelets too, of course, unless—"

"We're making a collar with a spinal clamp." Skiti shook her head, and Heuli nodded somberly. Laanda had insisted, and she was their queen, whether she liked the title or not. "The clamp's trigger will be locked, so it won't go off except by my command, even if he leaves the barrier. And it won't actually harm him to have it removed, but he won't know that, so I doubt he'll run. I don't think he's going to want to go hiking for weeks through the mountains back to human territory with that thing on his neck." She shook her head, unable to believe she was saying these words out loud, but then she thought of the three dozen Timon being laid out for the furnaces, the lines of mourners paying their last respects, and her resolve hardened. The Council had agreed with Laanda's proposal, so Skiti would see it done.

"And you say the Council decided that's legal?" Heuli held up his hands and backed away from the table. "Anyway, I'm going to be working on the primary extenders on this next-gen if you need anything. The sleeves get stuck sometimes, so I'm trying to smooth out the edges of the cuffs a little and see if that solves the problem."

Skiti glanced down at her Omni, thinking of the tiny grating sound she'd heard the last time she'd used it. It needed servicing after the abuse she'd put it through with the waadrech, but she didn't trust anyone else to do it, not even Heuli, and she would be too busy with the collar to have time to work on it. She'd just have to hope it held up.

"All right, I'm going to get started, and I'll holler if I need any help."

Heuli gave a thumbs-up as he lowered the fine lens back over his eye and leaned in with his picks to the Omni, which lay like a steely broom wilted across the tray. Skiti tore out the page with the measurements, set it under the bright lights, and started sketching.

Feddar watched with hurt eyes as Skiti laid out the collar and tools on the table. She picked up the collar and held up the spinal clamp so he could see it clearly.

"This collar goes around your neck, and this clamp attaches to the skin only, just at the base of your neck. It's perfectly safe, and it can't harm you unless you try to remove it." She tried to keep the right mix of threat and reassurance in her voice. "I designed it myself."

"And if someone tries to remove it?"

"Tiny wires will shoot into your skin, and they will find and entwine the nerves that allow movement in your extremities." It was only partly a lie; the device was designed to do just that, but only if she unlocked it.

The man looked as if he were about to be sick, and Skiti wasn't feeling too well herself.

"It can be reversed here, of course. None but the Timon have the metal mastery required. It might be possible one of your human artificers could find a way, given time, but it wouldn't be any fun for you, I can tell you that."

"I guess what they say about the Timon is true then," he said with a weary glare. "You still use torture in violation of the continental ban."

"It's not torture if you agree to it." She tried to say it as if she believed it. "You have the choice to remain imprisoned and be tried for your crimes without the benefit of cooperation. I'll only put this collar on you with your consent. It's a guarantee that you'll keep your word. You'd hardly fault us for not believing you just because, apparently, you've got such pretty green eyes." The others all seemed to find him attractive, though Skiti could never really judge such things. "But it will go a lot better for you afterward if you help us find the ones who did the killing."

He fixed her again with his sad, disappointed eyes and blinked what looked like assent.

"Say it."

"I accept the collar, in exchange for consideration in sentencing, under formal protest. I want to see this in writing: under formal protest against this cruel and inhumane device, your use of which amounts to coercion and torture, in my layman's opinion."

"One moment." Skiti nodded to Heuli, who picked up a pen and ledger and scribbled for a bit, pausing to mouth the words before finishing.

"...in my layman's opinion. Got it. Anything else to add, for the record?" Heuli held his pen aloft. "You should know that our laws are quite strict that all official transcripts be maintained in duplicate, so there is no chance your words will be lost to history, should someone wish to read them, assuming they have the appropriate clearance."

"And they say you're uncivilized."

"They say a lot of things about a lot of people," Skiti broke in, eager to get this over with and settle the knot in her stomach at what she was about to do. "Your complaint has been registered. Are you ready to begin?"

He blinked and nodded, lowering his head to expose the back of his neck, which was red and mostly hairless, though a diminishing line of fuzzy hair extended halfway down his neck before giving way to skin as bare as the heel of a hand.

"If you'd like some soma beforehand, we'd be happy to oblige. This is not an invasive procedure, but I don't imagine it's going to be terribly comfortable."

"Soma, gods yes, please, and I don't suppose there's any more of that hotstone whiskey lying around?"

"Alcohol is counter-indicated for procedures like this, but once you've shown no adverse effects for at least an hour, I'll see to it that you get a drink." She held out a soma lozenge on a long spoon, and he opened his mouth and took it in, cracking it with his teeth and chewing vigorously instead of sucking on it. He smiled as he crushed, ground, and swallowed, and his eyes no longer looked quite so sad.

"One more for the road?" he asked, his smirk showing he knew the answer. She dead-eyed him for a moment before continuing.

"This part won't hurt. I'm just going to unbind the ring and re-bind it around your neck. You'll want to hold still, though." She positioned her thumbs and index fingers to frame the ring, letting her mind flow into the smooth steel like a marble down a toy chute. She crinkled her nose as she searched for the mesh point, then blinked it open and eased it around his neck. The two Guard closed in a little, but she stopped them with her eyes. Feddar's hands were bound in livesteel cuffs, and there was no way even the cleverest thief could get out of them. She re-meshed the ring, but it was a little loose, so she tensed her jaw and tightened it just enough. The man's breath caught, but he gave a gentle nod.

"Is the soma working all right?"

"Good enough, I guess. Whatever this is, believe me, I've had worse."

Skiti cocked her head. "I sure hope that's true." She stretched the tail and let the clamp dangle for a moment, then laid it gently over the protruding vertebrae at the base of his neck. She closed her eyes and visualized the interior of the clamp, the dozens of wires, neatly coiled, inert until activated. She ran through each wire one last time, just to make sure there were no kinks or tangles, but everything was perfect, just as it had been the previous three times she had checked. She narrowed her eyes to lock the trigger, breathing out slowly once she knew it was secure.

"This may pinch a bit." She pressed the clamp into his skin, hearing his wincing breath as the tiny barbs sank in just enough to hold it in place without drawing blood. "Almost there," she murmured, pushing out the final spark, and the clamp sealed flush to his skin with a faint sizzle. If he'd been Maer, she would have had to shave the area, but the human's skin was conveniently exposed.

"That really sucked," the thief said through clenched teeth.

"You were a real champ." Skiti loaded another soma lozenge onto the spoon and held it out. Feddar's piercing eyes stayed with hers as his lips found the spoon, pulling the lozenge into his mouth and sucking on it this time instead of crunching. His eyes softened almost instantly, and his mouth relaxed into a smirk.

"I won't forget this." He spoke in a soft voice, and it was impossible to tell if he was referring to the bonus dose of soma or the fact that she'd just installed a paralyzing control device on his neck.

13

Ardo swung the staff in a wide circle, careful to avoid hitting the oil lamp on the table. It was lighter than his ironwood staff, but the ends were weighted, so it should hit just about as hard and maybe a bit faster. The staff was a hollow tube made of some form of steel, which had taken a little getting used to, but once he had worked up a light sweat swinging and striking the air, he'd almost forgotten it was made of the accursed metal. He'd never actually handled iron or steel before, though he had seen it in science classes and museums. From what little he knew of metallurgy, a staff in this style made of bronze would be considerably heavier and less durable. The craftsmanship was impressive, and he had to admit, it was a better weapon than the one the waadrech had eaten. He wondered if its jaws could snap this one the way it had his wooden staff.

He lay down the staff and drew the steel sword the Timon had brought Yglind. It was also lighter than expected, and its mirrored surface was almost hypnotic. He gave it a few swings; it felt good in his hands, manageable, quick, deadly. He was competent with a blade but not as skilled as he was with a staff. Squires were required to train in swordplay, but they were forbidden from using them in combat unless their knights were incapacitated or dead, so most of his training was with the staff. He doubted he'd ever have a chance to use a sword for real, but it gave him a strange thrill to hold such a deadly weapon. He could see why Yglind was so protective of his Forever Blade, beyond the bond laid between him and the sword. With a staff, you could keep someone at bay or knock them out. With a sword, you could end them in an instant. He sheathed the sword and picked up the staff again and had just completed a set of practice maneuvers when he felt a presence in the doorway. He turned to see Aene watching him, a sly smile on her face.

"Where's Yglind?" she said, stepping into the room and looking around.

"He went off to tour the defenses with Laanda." Ardo leaned the staff against the wall. "Something to drink?"

"I wouldn't hate a glass of that bitterroot wine." She sat down heavily on the bed, flopping onto her back and spreading her arms above her head, exposing her tight, fuzzy stomach as her shirt rode up. "It's been a fucking day."

"No doubt." Ardo brought over a tray with two glasses and offered Aene his hand, which she accepted, and he pulled her up. She weighed nothing, but her grip was like iron.

"Here's to the fucking Delve," she said, clinking glasses with him and taking a large swallow.

"To the Delve indeed. Speaking of which, I suppose it's almost time to leave the Timon's excellent hospitality behind and go hunt some humans."

"They're releasing Feddar in a few hours, once they're sure the tracking device is working properly." She shook her head, then took another long drink. "It's fucking wrong to put that on him."

"Even if he killed two dozen Timon?"

"He didn't. They checked his sword and hands. The only blood on there is hulshag."

"Are you sure this has nothing to do with that smoldering gaze of his?" Ardo shouldered her gently, and she leaned into him. She was warm and smelled of alcohol and muskwood, and her presence was strangely intoxicating.

"If I'm being totally honest, there is something about him. It sounds ridiculous, I know, but it's not just the eyes. I feel like..." She turned suddenly, her hands facing each other in claw shape, her eyes alit. "I feel like he's a good person."

"Maybe. But admit it, you've wondered what he would look like naked."

"The thought had occurred to me," she said as her fingers ghosted across the hair on his thigh and peeled his tunic up. Ardo froze, unsure what to make of this sudden development. "Don't you wish he were here right now?" Her fingers traced the outline of his cock, which was suddenly throbbing with want, and she squeezed hard through his drawers, holding him tight as her lips moved into his ear. "Can't you just imagine all the things we'd do with him if he were?"

Ardo pulled back for a moment, struggling to catch his breath as Aene's wide eyes devoured his. "I can, and wow, I really want to, but..."

He pictured Yglind walking in on them in this instant, the burning silence in his eyes, the clenched jaw. Ardo's cock pulsed harder as Aene tightened her grip, and his resolve slowly crumbled.

"You and Yglind aren't exclusive, are you?" She stroked him slowly, never shifting her eyes from his.

"No. I mean, he—we're not exclusive." Yglind had been with scores of other Maer since they'd been together, and he never hid it, but Ardo hadn't been with anyone else since he'd joined Yglind. It wasn't a big deal, shouldn't have been a big deal, but...

He lost his train of thought as Aene's hand slid inside his drawers, and she squeezed him tight, stretching the skin of his cock until he feared it might burst. She lightened her grip, tracing delicate lines up and down his shaft with her fingernails.

"I know we never have before, but I've seen you looking a few times. I know you find me attractive. You can't hide that." She gripped him tighter, and he clutched the covers, straining to keep it together. "If it's not too much trouble, I really need a release, and I was hoping you might not hate helping me?"

Ardo's hand slid up her back and over her shoulders, fine and birdlike beneath her downy hair. She took his other hand and moved it to her breasts, which were small and soft, her nipples erect beneath his fingers. As she braced against him, he could feel the muscles in her body coiled tight and ready to spring. She kept one hand on his cock and slid the other behind his head, gripping him tightly by the hair and pulling him in for a kiss that quickly became wet and sloppy as she crushed her mouth against his and caressed his tongue with hers. Ardo's mind was spinning with the kiss, her taste, the unfamiliar softness of her body. She put both hands on his chest and pushed him down onto his back as she swung her leg over to straddle him.

Ardo had only been with females a handful of times, but as Aene's lithe body ground against his and their lips danced together, his desire rose so quickly he feared he would spill before he was even inside her. He lifted her hips for a moment to relieve the pressure, amazed at how light she was. He could just pick her up and throw her around if he wanted, but when she wrenched his hand away and put his fingers between her legs, he was powerless to stop her. She moved his fingers across her cunt, a little wetter with each stroke, until his fingertips slipped in. He explored the silky terrain, letting her movement and the little groans in her throat guide him. She moved his fingers forward, pressing them into her clit and moving them in slow circles as she huffed hot breaths onto his face. She moved his hand with increasingly frantic gestures, and he followed her guidance as best he could until he felt every muscle in her body tensing at the same time. Her eyes closed as she came, and he imagined she must be thinking of the human thief, his green eyes, the intensity of his gaze, and he swelled anew with the thought.

She fell upon his chest, spreading the hair away from each nipple before licking and sucking, leaving space between his throbbing cock and her body as if she could tell how sensitive he was. Her fingers pinched his nipples as she gripped his chest and pushed herself back up astride him, wiggling her wet cunt over his cock. She rose up, moved her hands down to grip him, and before he knew what was happening, she had slid down onto him and was rocking back and forth.

"Hold still," she whispered, clutching the hair on his chest as she ground against him, her eyes still closed. "Be like a rock for me." Ardo closed his eyes and let his focus return to his cock, which was being swished and squeezed, stretched, pulled, and caressed with infinite softness. His mind flashed to Yglind riding him in this position, his strained grimace as he approached the precipice, but when Ardo opened his eyes, he saw Aene looking down at him, her eyes bright and hot. His hands found the tight curve of her hips, and he lay them gently there, feeling Aene's muscles move beneath his fingers, his head growing light as the pressure built within him. He kept his body stiff and still, like a rock, just like she'd said.

Aene moved like a being possessed, and Ardo felt a moan rise from deep inside himself and he framed her hips with his fingertips, careful not to squeeze. She bore down on him one last time, pushing out shaky breaths as she held their bodies tight. He felt her pulsing from within, squeezing out his last resistance, and he released, pressing up into her as she held him firmly in place, with no movement except for their mutual throbbing, which slowly subsided, and her head fell to his chest.

Footsteps sounded in the hall, long, hurried strides. Yglind.

Ardo wiggled out from underneath Aene, jumped up, and slipped his tunic on. Aene had just sat up and turned toward the door, half swaddled in the blanket, when Yglind burst into the room, eyes hot and sword drawn. He looked down at Aene, then turned his gaze toward Ardo, and his eyes softened for a moment with confusion or hurt—Ardo couldn't tell which.

"Time to gear up. The fucking humans are headed this way, and it looks like an attack."

"An attack? How?" Ardo pulled his leather jerkin over his chest and strapped on his knife belt. "I thought they couldn't penetrate the Timon's steel barriers."

"Well, they're headed this way in a hurry, and it seems they've brought company."

"What kind of company?" Aene tightened the straps on her gauntlet, then pulled on her robes.

"Apparently, they've got a half-dozen hulshag with them. Don't ask me how. We're to spread out, one of us on each level." He pulled his circlet out of his pocket and affixed it to his head. "These things will still connect with each other down here, right?"

Ardo was surprised since Yglind had been so excited about the prospect of going without his circlet on the Delve. He fished his out as well.

Aene nodded as she put her own circlet on. *"The entire keep is copper-wired, so the signal will be boosted, but you still won't be able to talk since we're not connected to the Stream."* Aene's mindvoice rang clear in Ardo's head. *"Two pings if you make contact, three if you need help."* He felt Yglind's ping, and he added his own.

"I'll be by the keep gate." Ardo recognized the bloodthirsty gleam in Yglind's eye as his sword took over. "Let's hope they try to break through there first. Ardo, I want you on the main level with the civilians, and Aene, you go with the artificers, see if you can cook anything up together. That level also houses the prisoner, so if there's any trouble, call us right away."

Aene nodded. A distant boom vibrated the ground, and Ardo tightened his grip on his staff.

"Follow me. I'll get you to the lift, and you can go your way from there." Yglind locked eyes with Ardo for a moment, and Ardo felt excitement, anger, and jealousy swirling together in Yglind's gaze, which he withstood as stoically as he could, given the angst and guilt coursing through his veins.

14

A ene followed an apprentice named Vee, a sprightly girl who was taller and thinner than most Timon, through the twisted passageways of the lower level. Her mind spun between the terror of the impending attack and the chaotic memory of fucking Ardo. She'd needed the release, and she'd gotten it, but her emotions were tangled from the encounter. Ardo's eyes were so soft and his body so hard, just as she imagined Feddar's would be. She shook her head to chase these thoughts away and focus on the very real danger ahead.

"The prison is that way," Vee said, nodding toward a hallway whose entrance was flanked by two armored Timon with wrist axes. "That hallway is trapped, by the way, so don't go down there without an escort. It's a long fall into a livesteel net, so not a deadly trap, but it's a pain getting disentangled. This way." She nodded and sped off down another side corridor until she came to a metal door with two wheels set in it with protruding knobs. She put both hands on the wheels and spun them this way and that with precise, almost jerky movements until the door popped open.

"Welcome to our lab." Vee ushered Aene in with a flourish of her long, thin arm.

Several Timon were hunched over tables under bright light, tools in hand, working with steady precision. One of them appeared to be assembling a device like the Omni Skiti carried. The base was a plain cylinder with the same three fingertip-sized indentations in it, but the other end was an array of metal tubes and wires splayed out on a tray. A faint blue light shone out from the top, illuminating the wires, which pulsed with subtle movements as the Timon fiddled with a mechanism at the base. He wore a pair of smoked goggles, presumably to protect his eyes from the hotiron rays. He made another small adjustment, herded the wires and tubes carefully into a straight line, and fiddled with the three indentations. The wires flowed into a cylindrical shape, which smoothed and closed at the other end until it looked just like Skiti's Omni, a plain steel rod the size of a club.

"Skiti said we could trust you around our tech." Vee sounded a little skeptical. "This is primary master Heuli, second only to Skiti in seniority."

Heuli pulled the goggles up onto his head and flashed Aene a tight smile, which softened as his eyes fell on her gauntlet.

"Gods is that..." he rose from his chair, approaching slowly, with something like reverence on his face. "That's a hand channeler, isn't it?"

"It is," Aene said with a nod. "Not the finest one out there, but a recent model."

"I've heard about them, but I never thought I'd—"

He stopped as another boom shook the ground, this one louder and closer than before. He cocked his head, seeming to count silently, then shook his head.

"That sounds like a saltpeter charge, and a big one, too," he said, his face grim. "One or two more of those might be enough to break through the barrier."

"Sounds like it's at the upper ventilation pipe," Vee said, and Heuli nodded.

"Whisper up to Laanda and have her send the Guard to engage them. Quickly!" Heuli shooed her with one hand as he turned his gaze down to the Omni, his brow furrowed in confusion. Vee stopped and turned halfway back around.

"That pipe's not big enough for a human to get through," Vee said slowly. "Not even an adult Timon."

"But you know what can squeeze themselves through really tight spaces?" Heuli leveled a heavy gaze at Vee, who nodded, her face solemn.

"Hulshag," Aene said, and the others nodded. It made sense; most underground predators had mobile joints. Aene tried to imagine a hulshag popping its shoulder out of joint to cram itself teeth-first into a pipe, propelling itself with its back legs, hard claws scrabbling along the metal as it inched its way toward them.

"Go!" Heuli said, raising his eyebrows, and Vee scurried off, leaning into a whisper cone at the other end of the room and making that distinctive hissing whisper Aene had heard Skiti make. Heuli picked up the Omni, maneuvered the buttons with his fingers, and the thing squealed as it extended, its head splitting into three tines, the center one significantly longer, the exact shape of the trident Skiti favored.

"The sleeves are still too tight," he said with a grimace, shaking the trident. "But its form is tight as a drum."

"Why tridents?" Aene asked, wondering at the functioning of the device, which seemed part mechanical, part magical.

"Anything with teeth that big, you want to keep at a distance until help arrives. It's the favored weapon among civilians who aren't trained to use wrist axes. Which, training or no, I wouldn't want to get close enough to use against a hulshag. I can get you one if you like. A trident, that is," he added with a wink. "I'm afraid Omnis are off the table."

Aene shook her head, holding up her gauntlet hand. "I have everything I need right here." Another boom sounded, followed by some rumbling. Heuli closed his eyes, seeming to count silently, and shook his head. "They've broken through. I always said it was a weak point, but the engineers assured us it would hold. And they were wrong, as usual."

Vee dashed across the room, her eyes bright with the excitement of the moment. "Laanda has sent out the Guard to intercept the humans, and the Maer warrior went with them...What's your friend's name?"

"Yglind," Aene replied, not bothering to correct Vee on the word friend, given the circumstances.

"Right. Apparently, the squad that's been tracking them has been out of communication, and...she fears the worst."

"As should we." Heuli stroked his beard. "The Guard will have the shafts blocked, and we need to put the lab on lockdown. Go make sure the hallways in this sector are clear, then lock the door." Vee nodded and darted out the door.

"What about the prisoner?" Aene said, trying to block out the vision of his hot green eyes. "They'll most likely come for him first. Maybe I should go help the Guard protect him."

Heuli looked her up and down, raising his eyebrows skeptically. "The Guard are very good at what they do. They can deal with a couple hulshag. We need to just hunker down."

"I can handle myself," Aene said, though she wondered if that would be true without Yglind and Ardo by her side. She'd done well enough in their early encounters based on her training, but she couldn't imagine standing shoulder to shoulder with unknown Timon, however heavily armed and armored they were. Yglind might be a giant, gaping asshole—definitely was, in fact—but he was a giant, gaping asshole who had faced down a dragon twice without being killed.

"They could be coming after our Omnis," Heuli said, staring at the trident in his hand with an almost maternal gleam in his eye. "It may not seem like much next to your hand channeler, but I bet the humans would kill to get their hands on one."

"Your tech is amazing," Aene said, eyeing the Omni, wishing she could hold it, fiddle with the fingertip buttons, and see what it could do. "Ours is next to useless without brightstone or the Stream. Speaking of which…" She tapped to check the power level, which was still at half after whatever the thief had done to it. If things got bad out there, she'd want a full chip just in case. She popped open the face, slid the chip out, and put it in the little pouch she kept for partials, then slipped a new one in place and closed it up. She looked up at Heuli, whose eyes were wide with admiration. A distant clamor filtered in, tinny and echoey as if it had come through the whisper cone rather than through the heavy door.

"You'll have to tell me more about your gauntlet after this is all over, but if you're going out there, now is the time. We'll be locking down as soon as—"

Vee burst through the door, her eyes bright with more fear than excitement this time.

"At least one hulshag is inside, and the Guard should be engaging with the humans any second."

Aene's stomach roiled, and she glanced back at the lab, at Heuli, pausing to consider whether she should stay to protect them or herself. But Yglind would never let her live it down if he found out she'd hunkered down to keep out of harm's way, and Feddar had to be protected at all costs.

"Go with the gods," Heuli said as he closed the door behind her.

15

— • —

Yglind jogged behind the squad of eight Guard, who moved with steady if unimpressive speed with their heavy armor and short legs. The shield the Timon had lent him was smaller than what he was used to, but it was lighter than his bronze shield, which he hoped he could find once they'd dealt with the humans. With any luck, whatever damage the dragon's jaws had done to it could be repaired. It chafed him to be carrying a shield that didn't match the rest of his armaments, but his sword felt hungry, and the weight of it in his hand, the perfect balance, helped him forget the unfortunate mismatch and focus on the task ahead.

The lead Timon held up her arm, and the group stopped so suddenly that Yglind almost tripped over the two in front of him, as dark as it was. They'd agreed to let him keep his amulet on glow while they moved, and he could turn it up with a tap if he needed more light. He briefly wondered if the humans would need light to see, like the Maer, or if they could see in the dark, like the Timon. The lead Guard exchanged a few short words with the others in their language, and Yglind heard footsteps, surprisingly quiet for one so heavily armored, and a shadow passed into the darkness ahead. The Timon armor was both stout and silent, with thin strips of leather padding the rows of scales. A few moments later, they returned, shaking their helmeted head and murmuring low words he could not understand, but Yglind caught the meaning even before the lead Guard spoke to him in Maer.

"Six of our Guard dead, four from sword, two from magic. That was the whole squad."

"What kind of magic?" Yglind asked, thinking of the burns he'd seen on the dead miners from before.

"Something that burned through the holes in their faceplates but left the metal mostly intact. Your shield may be of some use." She turned to the rest of the Timon and spoke in their language, then spoke to Yglind in Maer. "I told them to throw axes at the mage first. Once he's down, we can gang up on their fighter." She shook her head. "But those who lay dead are just as trained as we are. These humans are fearsome indeed."

"You take out the mage and let me handle the skinfucker knight," Yglind snarled. "No offense," he added, realizing the Timon had no more hair than the humans.

"If you can take care of the human fighter, nothing you say will be held against you." She paused as a low growl echoed down the passage, and the Timon all tensed at the same time. She hissed something in their language, and Yglind made out the word 'hulshag' among the syllables. The Timon sank into fighting stance, and two of them, including the leader, pulled out devices like Skiti's Omni and extended them with a series of neat clinks into a shape like a boar spear, a long blade with a cross guard to keep the stabbed beast at bay. Yglind tapped his amulet once to give him a little more light, but hopefully not enough to bother the Timon.

He heard faint clacks on the stone, and the two Timon with spears took several steps forward, points facing the shadows. A roar erupted, followed by another a half-second after, as two huge shapes burst into view, crashing into the two Timon. One shrieked in pain as he was flattened by the creature, whose jaws snapped and dug between his helmet and his neck guard, and his shriek died as a gurgle.

The leader stood, bracing her spear against the other hulshag, which thrashed at the metal blade sticking into its shoulder, and with a great roar, it wrenched the spear from her hands. It shook its body several times, and the spear clattered to the floor just as two axes came hurtling through the air, one bouncing off its thick, gray fur, the other lodging itself in its chest. It gave a yelping shriek, crouched, then leapt, landing atop one of the Timon in the front row, where it was immediately assailed by the wrist axes of the two behind it. They hacked into the flesh on the back of its neck. It jerked to the side, knocking the other Timon in the front row into the wall, then collapsed. The Timon recovered just in time to raise his wrist axe in defense as the other hulshag leapt at him, jaws wide. He screamed in pain as the black teeth clamped down on his arm, and the hulshag bulled forward, pinning him to the wall, heedless of the wide gash in the corners of its mouth from the axe blade. It raked the injured arm down, then its teeth found his throat, gnashing and gnawing, and the Timon sank in a spray of blood even as two axes clocked the hulshag's head.

It turned to them with a deafening roar, which knotted Yglind's bowels, but he could not get past the Timon in front of him, so all he could do was watch. The bloodied beast sprang at the leader, who had picked up her spear and was angling it for a strike, but the hulshag swatted it away with its paw. Its jaws found the Timon's shoulder with a sickening crunch that was drowned out by her desperate scream. She fell under the creature's weight, and the two Timon in front charged with their axes, but the hulshag's hind legs flashed out, sending them sprawling into the other two Timon, who stumbled. Yglind seized his moment, pressing through the tumble of bodies, and raised his shield just in time to deflect a staggering kick. The hulshag whipped around, gore flying from its gruesome teeth, and Yglind lunged with his sword, which sank deep into its chest. The creature's jaws snapped at his cross guard, its yellow eyes wild and bright in the light of the amulet. He bashed its head with his shield and twisted his blade, and the creature crumpled as blood gushed from its chest and pooled on the floor beneath it.

One of the Timon rushed to the leader, who was groaning like one holding in a death shriek, and removed her helmet. Her eyes were wide with shock, and the circle of blood forming beneath her left little doubt as to her fate. The Timon whispered frantically among themselves, and Yglind stuck his sword into both hulshag, just to be sure. The creatures had taken out three of the Guard, and the morale of those remaining had evaporated.

"You, tend to your leader," Yglind said to the one crouched by the expiring body. "You four, come with me." They hesitated for a moment, their expressions inscrutable behind their faceplates, and he did not wait for a reaction before turning and stalking down the hallway, the light from his amulet swaying with each step. He slowed as he approached an intersection where he thought he saw a faint light. He tapped his amulet off, holding a hand up toward the four Timon, who had apparently decided to follow him. Low voices sounded from around the corner, and though he could not be sure, he thought they might be speaking Islish.

He turned to the Timon and whispered, "Step around the corner and throw your axes if you see a human not wearing armor, then duck back into this hallway while I charge. If you hear me call for you, come and back me up."

The Timon nodded, or he thought they did, though it was hard to see in the dim light filtering in from around the corner. He stood leaning against the wall, sword and shield at the ready, his heart pumping, and nodded to the Timon, who moved in sync to the intersection, throwing axes in hand. Only two of them hurled their axes before a blast of bluish lightning filled the hallway, forking to strike each of the Timon, who stiffened, then fell. Yglind gritted his teeth, ducked low behind his shield, and charged around the corner.

Two figures stood about forty feet down the hall next to a circular opening in the wall, which had melted scraps of steel dangling from it. One wore tight-fitting clothes in purple and blue, and he leaned over his knees, gasping for breath. The other stood a full head taller and was covered from head to toe in shining armor, carrying a two-handed sword that would be even more difficult to wield in this narrow hallway than Yglind's blade. The armored one stepped forward, bracing against Yglind's charge, and as Yglind closed the distance, he felt power surge in his sword, its thirst to drain the skinfuckers' blood. A flash exploded in the tunnel, and Yglind crashed into a wall of greenish light that appeared suddenly like an impenetrable window, wrenching his shield shoulder and sending his Forever Blade clattering to the ground as he staggered with the force of the impact. He shook his head and scrambled for his sword, then stood glaring through the glowing membrane at the armored figure, whose smirk he could almost feel through their faceplate.

The man in the blue and purple clothes, for Yglind could clearly see now it was a human male, knelt on the ground, looking as if he were about to throw up. He wiped his mouth on his sleeve, then produced a small vial from a pocket, uncorked it, and drank. The armored figure approached the glowing barrier, looking Yglind up and down. They wore a full suit of elaborately decorated steel plate armor, and they moved as if it did not encumber them at all. Their sword shone in the light from Yglind's amulet, and he could see intricate patterns etched into it, not unlike his own blade. The figure sheathed the sword and slowly removed their helmet, revealing a beardless face, more pink than tan, in contrast to the thief, with hair lying in tightly coiled braids atop their head. Their full lips quirked a mocking smile, which was reflected in their light brown eyes.

Yglind sheathed his sword and removed his own helmet, trying to project the same level of calm confidence, but he felt his anger surging through his head, and he bared his teeth and slammed his fist against the barrier. The human's smile widened, and they pressed their lips to the barrier, then winked and turned away. Yglind felt a growl creep up his throat and emerge as a roar, but if the humans heard him, they showed no sign of it. The mage pointed toward the open pipe, and the two discussed for a moment. The mage formed his hands into claw shape, and the rock around the pipe started crumbling. The two were soon obscured by a cloud of dust or smoke, and Yglind heard footsteps from behind him. He turned to see the Timon who had stayed to look after his leader crouched over the bodies of the four who had been hit by the mage's blast. The Timon spoke in his tongue, words that sounded like the encouragement given to a dying soldier, to ease their passing.

"How many are alive?" Yglind asked.

"Just one, and not for long if we don't get him some help."

"And your squad leader?"

The Timon shook his head slowly.

"They've blocked the passage with their magic. How long will it take us to get to this spot using another route?"

"We'd do better to go back the way we came," the Timon replied. "It would take almost as long to get to that spot, and by that time, they'd be gone anyway. What are they doing?" The Timon stepped to the barrier, touching it tentatively with his gauntlet.

"The mage seemed to be crumbling the rock around the pipe. Where does that lead to?"

"The upper level, where the barracks are. And the armory."

"Can you get word back?"

The Timon nodded slowly, seeming to snap out of a reverie. "Yes, there's a whisper cone just back this way. I'll get a message through, and we can carry Boorn back to the main entrance."

"You can stay with him. Tell the gatekeepers to expect me. I need to get there while the fucking humans are still inside." Visions of the fighter's smirk swam in his mind, and his sword felt hot in his hand.

The Timon glanced at his fallen companions, then gave a weary nod.

"Go to the end of this passage, turn right, and go up the second shaft. It'll put you just a couple hundred yards from the gate." He paused, wrenching his helmet from his head, showing a face stained with blood and tears. "And if you find the humans, I hope you fuck them in the ass with your sword."

Yglind touched him on the shoulder, then turned and strode down the passage where they had come in but got only a few steps in before he stopped cold. Up ahead in the shadows, a dark shape filled half the passage, hunched over something on the floor. It shook its head vigorously from side to side, and a grisly tearing sound echoed down the hallway.

The dragon raised its head, juggling the bloody hunk in its jaws until it found the right orientation, then gulped it down. Sharp yellow eyes glowed in the light from Yglind's amulet, which he tapped twice for maximum brightness, tightening his grip on his sword. The creature stood no more than thirty feet from him, and it crouched low at the light, its pupils dilating, its forked tongue slithering in and out like a whip. Red slime dripped from the corner of its mouth, and Yglind saw the body of a hulshag beneath it, a heap of thick gray fur with a crater of red in its flank from the dragon's jaws.

Yglind glanced behind him at the Timon, who had frozen in place, his eyes locked on the beast. With the invisible barrier behind them, there was only one way out, past the waadrech crouched there like a frasti defending a found kill. But it had not attacked, despite its strong position. Yglind, alone in a narrow hallway, would be hard-pressed to get behind it or underneath it to attack the rear of its leg joints, where its scales were smaller for flexibility. This was not his fight to win, but he prepared for it, nonetheless, imagining how he might use a well-timed shield smash to keep its jaws at bay while he slipped past far enough to sink his blade behind its shoulder, hopefully crippling it before it had a chance to tear a chunk out of him. But the creature was too big, too strong, and too fast to let itself be outmaneuvered in such a small space. If it came for him, he would be lucky to make it out alive. But as they stood, staring each other down across the body-littered hallway, the dragon blinked, then lowered its snout and nosed in for another bite. Bone crunched, and the waadrech braced with its front legs to tear a long strip of red and white, which it tossed down its throat in three quick movements.

"Nice dragon," Yglind whispered, taking a tentative step forward. The waadrech watched him intently, then blinked again and went in for another bite. Yglind took two more steps, and the creature continued its meal.

"You might want to come with me," Yglind whispered over his shoulder, and the Timon stood up quickly and walked on soft feet toward Yglind, wrist axe in hand but lowered.

"How do we know it's not just waiting to attack us when we get close?"

"We really don't. But I'm thinking it's got an easy meal right there, with zero risk, as long as we're not around. You see those missing scales on the side of its head and that wound in its chest?" He lowered his sword so the Timon could get a closer look at it, but also as a sign to the dragon they were not about to attack. "This blade put those scars on it, and you can bet it doesn't want another taste." The Timon blinked in disbelief.

"And if it decides the opportunity is too good to pass up?"

"If it does, you go for the eyes, and I'll try to maneuver around to its flank." The sword warmed in his hand, and Yglind found himself hoping the dragon would test its luck. He hugged the wall opposite the creature, and the Timon did the same. They walked sideways with slow steps, and as they approached, the dragon flattened its body along the opposite wall, keeping its jaws closed and its head low, though its liquid yellow eyes watched their every move. As they passed, it shifted its body, and Yglind tensed until he realized it was moving to face them from the opposite way but not advancing. After they got another twenty feet further, it dug its head back into the hulshag corpse and started gnawing.

The Timon let out a huge sigh when they rounded the corner, then climbed quickly up into the narrow shaft, where Yglind knew from experience the waadrech could not follow.

"They're never going to believe our story," the Timon muttered, then let out a crazed giggle. "We faced down a dragon and lived!"

16

Skiti checked the prisoner's collar and livesteel cuffs, all of which were in working order.

"You should be really proud of these things, by the way," Feddar said. "These cuffs especially are much more comfortable than the ones we use, all rough edges and rusty chains. I believe you call it livesteel? Marvelous technology. I'm sure Geni would love to take a sample back to the Realm."

The floor rumbled again, and shouts echoed in from somewhere. The two Guard inside the door tensed, staring at the door as if it were a hulshag crouched and ready to spring.

"You humans don't know how to knock?" Skiti tried to hide the tremor creeping into her voice by speaking more loudly.

"All Geni and Turu know how to do is slash and blast until there's nothing between them and what they want."

"Don't underestimate our defenses."

"I wouldn't dream of it. But isn't the very reason I'm here that these same two lunatics slaughtered two dozen of your people? Do you really think it's safe to keep me here?"

Skiti paused, listening to the muffled sounds of distant struggle, Timon and bestial cries rising together. The humans had released four hulshag into the upper level; they must have been controlling them somehow. At least a dozen Guard should be waiting for them, armored and ready for battle. A chorus of shrieks pierced the distance, sending shivers across Skiti's scalp.

"Take me to them." Feddar's voice was animated, his green eyes sparkling. "Turn me over and let them take me out of the keep. It will buy you some time to figure out what to do next, and you said this collar can track me anywhere in the mine, right?"

"As long as you don't try to leave. If you do, you just killed yourself."

More shouting dribbled in, and a high-pitched yowl that stopped suddenly, followed by silence.

"They'll tear this place apart until they find me," Feddar said.

Skiti shook her head, then moved to the whisper cone as she heard Laanda's pitch.

"The humans are headed your way," came Laanda's whisper voice, sounding a little harried. "They've put up some kind of invisible barrier so we can't follow them. They'll probably find the shaft down, and from the looks of things, they won't be slowed by our gates for long. Put the Guard on alert."

"Maybe we should release the thief to the humans." Skiti could hardly believe she was uttering the words. A silence followed. "Maybe they'll leave if we do. The collar will keep track of him." The cone was silent for a long moment.

"Make it so," came Laanda's low reply. "Get Aene to help protect you. The Guard alone won't be enough."

"I'll see it done." Skiti stepped away from the cone and had opened her mouth when she heard Laanda's voice again, so faint she could hardly make out the words "Be safe."

"Rise and shine, Feddar," Skiti called, then turned and told one of the Guard to fetch Aene. "We're going to take you to your friends."

"I told you, they're not my friends. I just work with them." He glanced down at his cuffs, which they had affixed in front of him in case he needed to be moved quickly. "And with you, of course. If I do as Laanda asked, do you personally swear you'll take this collar off me?"

"It has been agreed upon and recorded. No further attestation is required."

"I require it, Skiti. I want to hear the words." His face was strained, his voice urgent. She didn't know whether to believe him, but if it was an act, it was a very good one.

"I swear to you, if you deliver your companions as agreed, I will free you from the collar."

"And relinquish me into Maer custody, correct?"

"Those are Laanda's words to swear, not mine, but as I said, it's all been recorded and put in the archive. It's law."

Feddar shook his head, smiling ruefully. "You put so much faith in your laws."

"Laws protect us from the whims of the powerful."

"In my experience, the only ones the laws serve are the powerful."

"Your society must be an unhappy place to live."

Feddar chuckled. "I can see they have you pretty well ensconced in your place in this hierarchy. I'm sure your queen has only the best interests of her people in mind."

"We don't use the word queen, but yes, she absolutely does!" Skiti found her voice rising, and the Guard by the door looked away when she caught them staring. A series of clicks sounded from the door, and Skiti nodded to the Guard, who opened it. Aene stood in the doorway, flanked by two Guard, and two more stood in the intersection beyond. Aene stared at Feddar for a long moment, then turned her tired eyes to Skiti.

"I figured you could use a little help."

17

—— • ——

Aene followed the two armored guards, with Skiti and Feddar behind her and two guards behind them. Her mind cycled through the spells she had stored on her gauntlet, and she pulled up the Force Shield so it would be ready in case the human mage took a shot at them. She hoped it would be enough.

"The main shaft is just around this corner," Skiti said. "They'll probably come down through there unless they can figure out how to make the lift work."

"And if they come down here, how are they going to get him out?" Aene asked, wondering if the humans would simply take the thief and leave. If they had come here to disrupt the mining operations, what better way than to kill everyone in the castle?

"It might be easier if you take these cuffs off me in case they need me to climb." Feddar's voice was surprisingly chipper, given the circumstances.

Skiti sighed and muttered a syllable in her language, and the guards in front stopped. Aene turned to see Skiti raise her Omni, eyeing Feddar with a grim frown.

"Since you're so big on promises, I'll take the cuffs off on one condition."

A blast sounded from ahead, like the release from a pressurized forge, followed by the sound of debris falling.

"Fair's fair," Feddar said with a bow. "What's your price?"

"Convince them to get the fuck out of here. I'll show you the waste chute on this level, and you can lower the ladder and climb down and out."

Feddar wrinkled his nose, then nodded. "I accept." He held out his hands, and Skiti's eyes narrowed in concentration as she manipulated the buttons on the Omni and touched it to the cuffs, which uncoiled and dropped to the floor like a dead snake. Feddar rubbed his wrists together and flashed Skiti a genuine smile. "Thank you, milady."

"I'm not a lady," she grumbled, picking up the cuffs. She looked like she was going to continue, then she cocked her head. Aene didn't hear anything, but Skiti's heavy expression fell over her like a lead blanket. "They're coming down. You two in the back, front and center. Crossbows ready."

The two guards behind them scooted around to the front, forming a wall in the corridor with the other two. Aene heard a scuffing sound, then clanking footsteps approaching from around the bend.

"Let me do the talking," Skiti said through clenched teeth as she held the Omni above her head. Its tip opened, and a dozen shining filaments emerged like willowy steel worms, waving gently in the air. The footsteps stopped, and whispered voices echoed down the hall.

"Release our friend, and we will leave without killing anyone else," said a voice in accented Southish.

"Show yourselves," Skiti called, her voice strong and steady. Hot sweat dripped down Aene's underarms, and her jaw clenched as she brought the Force Shield to the fore of her mind.

The figure who stepped into the corridor was as tall as Yglind, covered from head to foot in dust-covered plate armor, carrying a huge two-handed sword. They eyed the group for a moment, then tilted their head, and another figure emerged, human, or so Aene guessed, clad in dusty blue and purple finery. His face was all skin, save for a thin line of a mustache that ran down to his jawline and back up toward his ears, connecting to the hair atop his head. He held his hands in claw shape, and his face bore an eager sneer.

"Notice the collar around your friend's neck," Skiti said, raising her Omni a little higher. "One flick of my wrist, and he dies."

The armored figure cocked their head, and the mage's eyes burned dark.

"If you let our friend go, you will not be harmed."

"What about the Guard upstairs?"

"We only killed the ones who got in our way," the mage sneered. "We could kill you and just take him."

"One false move," Skiti warned, raising the Omni higher. Aene wondered if she really would do what she said, if she even could do it. She wasn't sure how the tech worked, but Skiti had said it wouldn't harm Feddar unless he tried to remove it, that it had failsafes built in.

"I could drop you before you have a chance to blink." The mage tightened his fingers so they pointed like closed flower buds. The armored one held out a hand toward him, and he relaxed his posture slightly, though his face still bore the same rictus of disdain.

"Release Feddar to me," said the knight, "and you have my word we will leave without killing anyone else who doesn't try to stop us."

Skiti spat loudly at her feet. "Your word?"

"My word as a knight of King Uimer. It is a sacred vow, and no knight would ever betray that word. Surely you have similar traditions."

"We hold law above tradition. Laws such as don't murder the innocent."

"There are no innocents in war." The knight's grip on their sword tightened, and the mage lowered his body as if tensing for a spell. Aene kept the thought of the Force Shield swirling beneath the surface of her mind like the iridescent sheen on a bubble, ready to pop at the slightest disturbance.

"I give you one last chance. Release the prisoner, and we will leave."

Skiti uttered a few curt words, and the wall of guards parted, though their crossbows stayed trained on the mage. Feddar bowed slightly toward Skiti, who grimaced in return.

"I trust you to keep your promise," he whispered to Skiti. "Aene," he said, turning his emerald eyes toward her. "You too."

"But I didn't—"

He stopped her with a soft blink that stirred Aene more than it should have. "See you soon." Aene's face flushed with anger at his confidence and at herself for being moved by his words, his gestures, his eyes.

The Timon guards closed formation again, and Aene moved to stand just behind them, setting aside whatever Feddar might have meant to focus on the enemies before her. The knight's body language was calm, but the mage remained twitchy. It might have been his facial hair, but she didn't trust him for an instant. When Feddar reached them, the knight clapped him on the shoulder, but the mage furrowed his brow and his face tensed into a malicious grin. Aene just had time to get the Force Shield up and in front of the guards when the lightning hit, jarring her mind and body as if she'd been shield-smashed. She strained to retain her focus, soaking up an extra charge to keep the barrier in place.

The knight's hand shot out almost as fast as the lightning, gripping the mage's neck and shoving him back into the wall, where his head hit with an audible thump. He stumbled, woozy, and began to raise his hands toward the knight, but Feddar intervened, holding him up and turning him away, speaking soothing words into his ear, and the mage slowly calmed. The knight stood silently watching him, their sword erect, the index finger of their other gauntleted hand pointing toward the mage. They remained locked in a staring contest for several seconds, then the mage twisted out of Feddar's hands, rubbing his neck and stretching out his arms.

"Go straight to the end of this hall, and you'll see a door with a lever," Skiti called. "There's a rope ladder coiled in a box next to the chute. Make haste, as the rest of the Guard will be here any moment."

The knight nodded, then turned away and started marching down the hallway without looking back to see if their companions were behind them. The mage flashed Aene a toothy grin before following, and Feddar gave a quick, gentle bow, then turned and hurried to catch up.

"Fucking humans," Skiti spat.

Aene nodded, but her mind replayed Feddar's words, *You too*, and the soft, knowing look in his eyes. She hadn't promised him anything, had she? Not with words, at any rate. But her heart tingled with the thought of seeing him again, then crumpled as she realized the only way that could happen was if he were her adversary or prisoner.

Skiti found the nearest whisper cone and hissed into it, waiting for a moment, but there was no response. Aene heard the sound of boots landing on stone, then footsteps moving in unison. Two Guard emerged from the side hallway, looking in both directions before motioning the others to join. Soon there were seven more, including Laanda, decked out in full splinted armor, only her more elaborate helmet and armor distinguishing her from the rest of the Timon.

She rushed forward, speaking quickly in her language and saying Skiti's name. Skiti responded, and Laanda nodded, closing her eyes for a moment, then fired off a long string of words. She sounded relieved, frustrated, and furious, all at the same time.

"Aene saved us all," Skiti said as the guards in front of them parted to let Laanda through. She took off her helmet, sheathed her wrist axes, and took Skiti by the shoulders. Laanda turned to Aene, her eyes bloodshot and wet.

"Thank you."

Aene nodded, still lightheaded from the shock of the mage's lightning. She wondered, if they met again, what she could possibly do against such raw power.

18

Skiti observed Laanda carefully over the days that followed the assault on the castle. Watched her construct her mask of stoicism moment by moment, then rebuild it when it cracked. When she spoke to the kin of each of the nineteen Timon the humans and hulshag had killed inside the keep. When she gave her blessing to send the bodies to the incinerator. When she sat in her room holding a glass of hotstone, listening to the days-long dirge filtering in through the whisper cone. When she trekked down to the training room, cold resolve etched across her features. Skiti studied that face she knew so well, tracking the changes, the number of times her mask crumbled and reformed. It was brittle still, and it needed to be harder, or perhaps more supple, if she was going to join the Maer and take her just revenge on the humans.

After the third night of mourning, when the halls of the castle rang with silence once the last notes of the dirge had faded, Laanda called the remains of her Council together and invited the Maer as well. She greeted them in full armor, with her visor pulled up to show the grim determination on her face. All those present joined in her steadfast silence, even Yglind, whose incessant pacing and grumbling had echoed through the corridors for the past three days.

"The time for mourning has ended." Laanda's words, spoken in Maer, were laced with hardsteel like the castle barriers, sending shivers through Skiti's bones. "The time for justice has come." She paused, running her thumb over the wrist axe in her hand, testing the sharpness of a blade that had been honed a dozen times since the attack. "The humans seem to have holed up in one of the old copper galleries. It has only one entrance, which they seem to have blocked with their magic. We presume they have exhausted their attempts to remove the collar, else they might have left or attacked again. They have not moved, or should I say the thief has not moved, except to break into one of the nearby storage rooms for food and water. We do not know what they are planning, but they have no doubt been preparing their next move and trying to anticipate ours."

All stood in silence, erect and attentive, eyes glued to Laanda's stern face.

"We will not wait for them to attack again. We will go after them, dig them out of their cowardly refuge, and end them without hesitation or remorse."

"What of the thief?" Aene asked in a small voice. "He was promised to the Maer."

Laanda closed her eyes, and Skiti could see them twitching beneath her lids. "If he cooperates fully and stays out of our way, he may be spared and delivered to what I am assured will be full justice." With those words, she eyed Yglind, who nodded, baring his teeth in a vicious grin. "But if he interferes in any way, I will cut off his treacherous head myself."

"Help me comb my hair?"

Laanda sat in her robe, smelling of muskwood soap and hotstone whiskey, retying the braids in her beard. Her voice had that soft edge to it, like she had already begun the transition but was hesitant to ask. She could never give up control all at once; control was all she had, and she'd lost most of it when the humans had invaded. All her efforts thus far had failed, resulting in many deaths she had been powerless to prevent, though Skiti was sure it hadn't stopped her from blaming herself.

"Of course." Skiti pulled up a chair behind her, collected her damp hair from her neck, still pink from the warmth of the bath, and began teasing the knots out of it with a pick. "That helmet has wrought havoc. We should put you in some tight braids."

"That sounds lovely, but I don't have the patience for braids tonight." There was a catch in her voice, and Skiti worked the pick deeper into her hair, scraping the tines lightly against her scalp and working her way from forehead to neck. Laanda remained silent while she worked, and Skiti saw her posture relaxing, her shoulders rounding, her breath deepening.

"It's been a long couple of weeks," Skiti said, laying down the pick and running her thumbs up and down Laanda's neck, pushing into the thickly corded muscles, smiling as Laanda emitted a low hum.

"Next little while's going to be rough too." Laanda leaned into Skiti's thumbs, and Skiti dug as deep as she could, using the dampness from Laanda's hair to help her thumbs slide up and down a few more times. She worked her way down along the tight muscles of Laanda's neck to her thick shoulders, kneading with her fingers and rubbing in circles with her palms. She felt Laanda relax even further, and she squeezed her biceps, massaging the hefty muscles, then running her fingertips lightly over the callouses on her elbows.

"Do you want me to keep going?" Skiti asked timidly, in the way they had evolved over the years, though Laanda rarely wanted to be restrained anymore. She was always too busy.

"Yes, please. If you don't mind."

"Your pleasure is my pleasure," Skiti replied, completing the formula. "Let me just get the bed ready."

Laanda grasped Skiti's hand, craning her head around to show her eyes, whose usual hardness had been subsumed by soft, earnest want. They would set out in the morning with the Maer to face what might well be their death. This could be the last time they were together, and if so, Skiti intended to make it count.

Skiti grabbed a stack of towels from the washroom and put three of them down on the bed, leaving another to the side. Laanda turned to watch her, drinking a large gulp of water and dribbling a few drops into her beard. Skiti opened the wardrobe where Laanda kept her tools and weapons and retrieved the dusty leather bag. She opened it and surveyed the contents, which lay gleaming in their places as if she'd just cleaned and replaced them yesterday, though in reality, it had been over a year.

She met Laanda's hungry eyes as she pulled out the mesh and cuffs, the suction cones, and the joy stick, laying each one on the bench in the order she hoped to use them. She picked up the herbal oil off the bedside table and added it to her layout, along with a pitcher of water and two cups. She blinked and patted the towels, and Laanda stood up, shedding her robe, showing her powerful body, so capable of wreaking destruction. In the three steps it took her to reach the bed, her strut softened, and she lay down on the bed with the delicacy of a patient in the healing room.

"You know my word," Laanda said, her fingertips grazing Skiti's thigh as she looked up from where she lay.

"Say it."

"Waadrech."

Skiti smiled, gripping Laanda's fingers in hers. "We'll make a dragon out of you yet."

She ran her fingers up Laanda's arm, pushing it over her head when she got past the elbow, then leaning over the bed to move the other arm up. Laanda held still as Skiti ran her fingertips down the delicate skin of her armpits, raked her nails through the hair there, and kept going across her breasts, letting her pinkies drag on Laanda's nipples a bit as her hands moved down along her ribcage toward her tight hips. Laanda closed her eyes, and Skiti cupped her hands over her strong thighs, letting her thumbs slip between her legs for just a moment before running her hands slowly down to her feet and back up again. She made little circles with her fingernails in Laanda's pubic hair, then lifted her hand as Laanda started to lean up into her touch.

"May I restrain you now?"

"Yes," Laanda breathed, one corner of her mouth quirking into a smile.

Skiti took a set of livesteel cuffs and activated them with a thought, feeling the metal go soft and supple beneath her fingers. She coiled them gently around Laanda's wrists, then stretched the end up to loop through the iron ring in the wall above the headboard.

"Cold," Laanda whispered, and Skiti warmed the metal with a long touch until it was body temperature.

"Better?"

"Much."

Skiti bound her ankles next, warming the livesteel before wrapping it around each ankle and attaching it to the sturdy rings built into the corners of the bed frame. She touched up each cuff until it was secure enough to prevent unnecessary movement but not so tight as to cause distress. Laanda's beatific expression told her what she needed to know.

"The mesh. Please," Laanda said in a voice not much more than a whisper. Skiti unfolded the mesh and lay it across Laanda's body, covering her from collarbones to toes. She took her time tucking the edges under Laanda's sides and legs, wrapping her feet, then pulled a circular opening between her legs.

"Are you ready?" Skiti asked, leaning over Laanda's face to look into her eyes. She saw exactly what she needed to see: desire, trust, and submission.

Laanda took a deep breath and let it out slowly. "Yes."

Skiti lay her hands on the mesh, concentrating for a moment to make sure she warmed it and used the right amount of pressure, and the mesh tightened beneath her touch. It shrank to fit Laanda's body, enwrapping every bulge and curve like a second skin, showing even the nubs of her nipples and the individual muscles of her thighs.

"Tight enough?"

"A little tighter."

Skiti touched the mesh again, and it pulled taut, shiny. She eyed Laanda, who blinked her assent. Skiti spread her fingers across the mesh, closed her eyes, and felt it harden beneath her touch into a smooth shell, like molded steel armor. She put one palm on the metal covering Laanda's chest and touched her cheek with the backs of her knuckles, then leaned in and kissed her. Their beards tangled, and Laanda's lips opened, taking Skiti's upper lip in hers and sucking gently. Though Skiti didn't care much for kissing, she let Laanda play for a bit until Laanda's face flushed and her breath deepened. Skiti removed herself slowly from the kiss and lifted the blindfold, holding it up with a questioning look in her eyes. Laanda nodded, and Skiti kissed her again, then lifted her head off the pillow to affix the black velvet over her eyes.

Skiti crawled onto the bed, drumming her fingers over Laanda's shell, moving them slowly across her stomach and down to where the thick brown hair poked out of the circle she had made. She continued drumming down Laanda's cunt, lightening her touch, then put two fingers together and tapped three times. Laanda's muscles tensed, and Skiti cupped her hand between Laanda's legs and held it firmly in place, slowly increasing the pressure, feeling Laanda strain toward her touch, but the shell allowed no upward movement.

"I'm going to apply a bit of oil," Skiti said, dipping her fingers in the pitcher and rubbing the oil gently over Laanda's cunt. She tapped three more times with her fingers, smiling at Laanda's sharp intake of breath, then picked up the joy stick, which came alive at her touch. She felt the spirit iron inside it, raw, hot, bottled-up power, and she let her mind flow into the metal, warming the stick and sending a pulse into it. The joy stick vibrated slowly in response, and she squeezed with her mind to increase the speed just a bit, then touched it to the shell around Laanda's leg. Laanda's breath caught, and Skiti could see the shell vibrate ever so slightly around where she had touched it. She rubbed a bit of oil over the end, then ran it slowly up Laanda's thigh. It slid effortlessly across the shell, and she moved it up over Laanda's stomach, across both breasts, then slowly back down, stopping just as it reached the edge.

"Please," Laanda whispered.

"As you wish." Skiti pressed the joy stick into Laanda's hairy mound, then slid it slowly up and down. Laanda licked her lips, and Skiti continued moving the stick as she crawled over her metal-encased body to kiss her. Laanda's lips were not greedy this time, and Skiti kissed her softly over and over as she pushed out another pulse, increasing the joy stick's vibrations. Laanda's lips opened with a short huff as Skiti pressed the tip gently against her clit.

Skiti touched her forehead to Laanda's, feeling the sweat pop out as Laanda grew close, then pulling her back by slowing the vibration.

"Please," Laanda said in a low whine.

"Not yet," Skiti whispered, kissing her again, enjoying the feel of Laanda's desperate lips on hers, the texture of her, the taste of her need. "We have some work to do first." She sat back on her heels, straddling Laanda's metal-encased thigh, and sent a pulse into the joy stick, which vibrated with a lower, more powerful hum. She edged the tip of the thrumming device into Laanda's cunt, pushing with the gentlest pressure so it slid in one hair's breadth at a time. Laanda's breath grew irregular, and Skiti stopped. She left the device halfway in, letting go with her fingers, eliciting a deeper whine.

"Skiti, please. Please!" Laanda's voice had taken on a soft, desperate quality. She had a way to go yet before she was ready.

"You need to let go of the idea that your entreaties will change the outcome. There is only one word that will do that. Do you have something to say?" Laanda shook her head gently.

Skiti pushed the joy stick all the way in, and Laanda sucked in a hissing breath as her muscles clenched. Skiti sent another pulse into the device and held the connection, sensing the device swelling up inside, Laanda's breath growing shorter. She stopped just as the throaty growl began, then removed her hand, leaving the thrumming device in place.

"Just breathe now. I won't be moving the joy stick, and you won't be moving either." She slid up to lay her head on the pillow next to Laanda's, watching the movement of her lips, the flare of her nostrils, listening to the pace of her breath. "You will stay on this edge for as long as it takes." She ran her fingers through Laanda's beard, toying with her braids, scratching her fingernails against the underside of her chin.

"I want," Laanda panted, and Skiti lay a finger across her lips.

"Don't want. Just be." She let her head fall against Laanda's, her fingers splaying across her cheek. Laanda blew out a slow breath, then took in another one, and Skiti fell into a sympathetic rhythm with her, surprised to feel a tinkle of arousal herself, as if Laanda's excess were bleeding into her. She could take care of that on her own later. This was Laanda's moment.

In time, Laanda breathed slowly and steadily, and Skiti with her. They lay, breathing in sync, for a long while until Skiti was sure Laanda had accepted the edge. It was time to push her over.

Skiti ran her fingers over Laanda's lips, then down to her neck, which she squeezed with gentle pressure as she pushed up and hovered over her face.

"I want to see your eyes," she whispered into Laanda's mouth. Laanda nodded, and Skiti removed the blindfold slowly to give her eyes time to adjust. Laanda's eyes were deep, glassy, all-consuming. Skiti leaned down and pressed her lips against Laanda's, maintaining the gentle pressure around her neck. Laanda kissed her with languorous abandon, and Skiti played along, her lips and tongue trying to find the rules to this mysterious game. When she heard Laanda's breath speeding up, she sat back, touching the shell around each nipple, and the metal shrank to form two perfect circles opening around each stiff nub. She wished she could bottle the expression on Laanda's face as she lay the livesteel suction cones in place and activated them so they pulsed lightly every half-second. Laanda's eyes were hot with barely restrained yearning, her stoic mask precarious and fragile like an egg wobbling toward the edge of a table.

Laanda's groan rose to a surprised shout as Skiti placed the third cone on Laanda's clit, focusing for a moment to link it to the cycle of the other cones. Laanda's throaty growl quickened as Laanda doubled the speed of the pulses, then gripped the joy stick and returned it to its normal state, with only the bulbed end wider than the shaft. She pulled it out slowly, leaving only the tip inside Laanda, then concentrated, sending the cones and the stick into a slowly increasing cycle of vibration. She stared into Laanda's eyes, which burned hot and dark as Skiti slid the joy stick all the way in, then pulled it back out, teasing at her entrance for only the briefest moment before pushing in again. She increased her force with each stroke, stopping to change her grip so she could climb across Laanda's metallic shell, grabbing her by the beard and stretching for a kiss. Laanda devoured her lips, a low hum rising from deep within as Skiti fucked her with the joy stick so hard and fast her muscles ached with the strain. Laanda's lips froze as she let out a series of increasingly desperate moans that would surely be the talk of the castle while they were gone. Her voice died, and her breathing seemed to stop as she came, as if she were choking. She took in a wheezing gasp, then let it all out with a deep, moaning sigh.

Skiti concentrated on slowing the vibration in the joy stick and the cones gradually, pulsing ever more gently, until at last the pulse stopped. She pressed into Laanda's lips as she pulled the device out and laid it on the soaked towels, then deactivated the suction cones and removed them one at a time. She tapped the shell, which softened back into silky mesh, then removed it with care, folded it, and placed it on the bench.

Laanda watched her with soft, almost glowing eyes as Skiti touched each of the livesteel cuffs, releasing them. Laanda stretched her body taut, then rolled over on her side, and Skiti slid out the wet towels and put a dry one in their place. Laanda patted the bed beside her, and Skiti shed her robe and snuggled into the spoon of Laanda's body, pulling a blanket over them both.

"I'm so lucky to have you," Laanda whispered, laying a hand on Skiti's hip. Skiti reached down and patted Laanda's hand.

"We are all lucky to have you, my Queen." No matter how much Laanda hated the title, in Skiti's eyes, she would never be anything else.

Laanda nuzzled into her neck, her hot breath caressing the fine hairs there, but did not make any further overtures. When they were younger, Laanda sometimes tried to reciprocate, and Skiti had gone along with it a few times and even sort of enjoyed it, but she'd always felt strange about another person touching her intimately. Once she'd finally gotten up the courage to tell Laanda how she felt, Laanda apologized and never asked again. She was one of the few people in the castle Skiti had been able to truly open up to, and she found herself on the verge of tears as she realized how seldom they got to be together like this. She snuggled deeper into their shared warmth, wrapping her arm around Laanda's, and managed to send away the dark thoughts of tomorrow and lose herself in the peaceful security of Laanda's embrace.

19

A rdo rose when Yglind entered and closed the door softly behind him. Yglind stalked over to Ardo, seized him by the shoulders, and leaned in close, lips less than an inch apart, their beards and the hair on their faces tangling together.

"My love," Yglind whispered, pressing his hot lips against Ardo's, sliding his hand down Ardo's back, then to his buttocks, which he squeezed with maddening gentleness. Ardo's hand gripped Yglind's ass and jerked him closer, pressing their already hard cocks against each other like crossed batons. They kissed for a while, softly at first, then harder as Yglind's hands slid up and around to rake across his chest, their lips and tongues pushing, sucking, pulling, exploring. Ardo gasped as Yglind's hand found his cock and squeezed it softly.

"We might die tomorrow," Yglind whispered in his ear as he ran his fingers lightly up and down Ardo's length.

Ardo pulled back for a moment, fixing Yglind with a hard stare.

"No one's going to die, Yglind."

Yglind kissed him again, with such gentleness it made Ardo's balls ache.

"We might," Yglind said between kisses. "This could be our last night together on this earth." Ardo's chest tightened at the words, and a wave of tears surged, stopping just short of bursting forth.

"Stop saying that! Just kiss me." Ardo nipped at Yglind's lips, then pulled back just a hair, watching Yglind's eyes go from soft to hard in the space of an instant. Yglind crushed Ardo against his body, and Ardo moaned into the kiss as Yglind's hands found his ass and squeezed tightly. They kissed with abandon, their bodies grinding together until Ardo was so close, he had to pull back lest he spill before they even had a chance to begin.

"Yglind?"

"Yes, my love." Yglind toyed with Ardo's cock, then held it gently as it throbbed against his hand.

"I'd like you to fuck me now."

Ardo lowered to a crouch on the bed, his heart leaping as Yglind eased in behind him, running his hands all over Ardo's body, his cock hard against Ardo's ass. It felt so good to be wanted like this, to be needed. Yglind kissed up and down his back as he applied the oil, his fingers plying Ardo with such delicacy it sent shivers through his core.

"Please, Yglind. Please."

Yglind pressed his cock against his entrance, and Ardo relaxed to let him in, pleasure flooding his body as Yglind pushed in slowly, filling him completely, their bodies molding together. Yglind took it slow at first, reaching around to tease Ardo with his fingers as he pressed in with strength and control. Yglind let out a little grunt each time he smacked against Ardo, whose voice joined his, louder as Yglind's speed increased. Soon there was no holding back, no pulling away from this brink. Ardo's legs trembled, and his body arched into Yglind, whose hand found Ardo's cock and squeezed it tight as they moved in a final frenzy. Ardo clenched around Yglind, uttering a series of breathless moans as he gushed onto Yglind's hand and all over the sheets, smiling as he felt Yglind spill inside him.

Ardo slumped to the side, and Yglind stayed with him, cradling his body and breathing into his ear.

"Gods, I love you, Ardo. I don't say it enough, but it's true."

Ardo craned his head around, looking into Yglind's soft eyes.

"I love you from now to the Time to Come."

Ardo helped Yglind into his armor, securing the straps and adjusting each joint with care. Yglind remained oddly silent, his eyes soft and distant. When Ardo had finished, he stood back and admired his handiwork. Yglind looked positively majestic, standing with shoulders erect, encased from neck to foot in burnished bronze with his family's mashtorul crest. The Timon had even recovered his shield, which the waadrech had spit out after their first encounter, and repaired it so Ardo almost couldn't see where they'd patched the bite marks and painted the steel to match the bronze. Yglind stood with his mashtorul helmet under his arm, looking Ardo up and down with a wistful gleam in his eye.

"When this is all over, I'm going to pin you down and fuck you into the Time to Come," he said in a low voice laced with a hint of menace, sending shivers of delight straight to Ardo's core.

"I will hold you to that, my lord."

"But first, the fucking humans need to die."

"Except for the thief, you said." Ardo grew sad at the thought of those pretty green eyes open in the vacant stare of death. He worried what Yglind might do and what Aene was prepared to do to stop him.

"We'll see what happens when we get there. One way or another, I'm going to get my five."

Ardo hesitated, doing the math. Yglind had killed two hulshag, and if he managed to kill all three humans, that would make five. But they had decided to take the thief back alive, and he wasn't sure if that would count. And even if it did, Ardo didn't see Yglind passing up the chance to add a dragon to his list.

"You know five is not a codified number," Ardo said. "There's nothing in the charter that says—"

"Have you read any of the classic Delves? Jarold? Quintin? The Great Wyrm of Fellhole? A proper Delve is five kills. Five!"

Ardo opened his mouth to retort, but Yglind's expression stopped him cold. Yglind wore a fierce, faraway look as if he could see directly into the Time Before. When he spoke again, his voice was softer but still firm.

"I know the godsdamned charter, Ardo, and my family has connections. If we stop the humans and bring back the prisoner, I'm in. But what will people say when they hear I got three or four? What books will be written, what songs sung about the knight who faced a dragon three times and ran away?"

Ardo gazed into Yglind's steadfast eyes. There was no arguing with him on this. He was right, and even if he wasn't, he was Yglind, and there was no way he would ever let this go. It was part of why Ardo loved him.

Ardo stepped to Yglind, untucking his beard, which had become trapped under his collar, and adjusting his shoulder plate, though there was nothing wrong with it. He raised up on his toes just a bit and laid a soft kiss on Yglind's lips. They lingered in that kiss, barely moving, until the voice of a deep horn echoed in through the door.

"You're going to be amazing," Ardo said, squeezing Yglind's shoulder as best he could through the armor and padding. Yglind bared his teeth in a smile.

"I really am." He slung the helmet atop his head, adjusted it with a few quick touches, and turned toward the door. "Today, we not only make history—we make the future."

The group crowded into the gatehouse, which was barely big enough for them and the half-dozen Guard who stood near the gate. Laanda studied each of their faces, glancing at Skiti, then Yglind, Aene, and finally Ardo, who nodded as her gaze fell upon him. She studied him for a moment, the lines around her eyes crinkling, then her expression hardened. She uttered a string of commands in her language to the guards, who stood up straighter as she spoke, then nodded, almost in unison.

"They know our plan," she said in Maer, looking directly to Yglind, "and they'll have a squad of six ready at all times if called upon, but I don't intend to send them out except in the direst circumstances, given everything that's happened." She turned her eyes to Aene, then again to Ardo, then back to Yglind. "This is all on us. Skiti has made some modifications to her Omni, which we hope will help minimize the effects of the human mage's power, but they've had several days to prepare for us. We must be ready for anything." After seeing what the humans had done to the Timon, Ardo doubted they'd ever be ready.

"We are beyond ready," Yglind said, puffing his chest out. "Aene has been working on her own solutions as well. Keep the mage in check but a moment, and we will end him."

Laanda flashed a grim smile, then lowered her helmet onto her head. It was a work of art, sturdy and perfectly fitted to her armor to leave no weak spots but adorned with delicate swirls of gold and silver, almost like a crown. She carried a spiked axe, longer and heavier than the wrist axes most of the Timon seemed to favor, though she did have two of those strapped to her side, along with two smaller throwing axes, a long knife, and a crossbow slung across her back. She was carrying enough weapons to supply a small army.

Skiti smiled weakly at Ardo, then moved to Laanda's side. She was outfitted with a leather jerkin, like Ardo, and her trusty Omni, which she held in trident form. She hovered close to Laanda, though whether from a desire to protect or be protected, Ardo could not tell.

At a word from Laanda, two guards cranked the wheels on the wall, and the stone door slid open with a grinding squeal. The six guards poured silently through the gate, forming a line blocking the corridor. They stared into the darkness for a moment, then one of them gestured, and Laanda strode out, followed immediately by Skiti and Yglind. Ardo joined them, and Aene walked out with him, sticking close to his side, flashing him a nervous smile.

"It's four hours' walk to the old copper gallery, including some climbs." Laanda spoke like the military commander she was. "We'll want to go slowly in case they've left us any little surprises. Skiti, be ready to deploy the dome." She glanced at Skiti's trident.

"I've tweaked my Force Shield, so I think it will withstand his blasts better," Aene said, "so between us, we should be able to buy a little time."

"Yes. We've all got nice toys," Yglind grumbled, gesturing forward with his sword. "Can we get on with this?" His voice bore the edge of one too long denied release. Ardo had taken care of Yglind's sexual needs, but he could not slake his thirst for blood, nor that of his Forever Blade.

Laanda turned to face Yglind, and while Ardo could not see her eyes through her visor, he felt their heat. Even Yglind shrank a little from her, though she stood two heads shorter than he.

"Let me make one thing perfectly clear." Laanda's tone was so crisp and dry it parched Ardo's throat just to hear it. "We are in a Timon mine, pursuing enemies of the Timon, who have killed dozens of our people and done untold damage to our operation. You are our guests, and we appreciate your assistance. But don't think for a second that I'm going to let your thirst for blood and glory jeopardize our chance for justice." Her voice never rose, her tone never sharpened, and her body did not waver as she craned up to glare at Yglind through their visors. "I am in charge here, and we go where and when I say."

Laanda punctuated her speech by whirling around and stalking down the corridor. Skiti hurried after her, and Yglind paused for a moment, holding his sword close to his faceplate to study it, then strode to catch up.

"Laanda handled him pretty good," Aene murmured as they hurried to follow the group.

"Or so she thinks." Ardo knew that when Yglind grew silent, unpleasant things tended to happen. He hoped he could be there to help temper Yglind's worst instincts and shine like the bronze sword he seemed to prize above all else.

20

— • —

Aene watched Yglind's body language as they walked but did not see any sign of trouble. Laanda had put him in his place, and he seemed to have accepted it. Or perhaps he had swallowed his pride for a chance to puff it up later if he could get the five kills he was so obsessed with. Ardo stayed near Yglind as always, leaving him space while remaining close enough to assist if need be. Aene hadn't seen Laanda in action, but the way she carried herself, the strength of her body and the force of her personality, left little doubt she was a formidable fighter, and her barely cloaked desire for revenge made her doubly dangerous. Aene wondered which one was more eager to spill the humans' blood and if either really meant to spare Feddar. If it came to it, she would do what was necessary to stop them herself.

Aene stayed focused as they walked, pulling the Force Shield up to the tip of her mind, then bringing the blinding cloud to the ready. She hoped to use it to distract the mage long enough for them to close on him. If Laanda or Yglind could hold off the knight for a little while, they could kill the mage, then double up against the knight. As long as Feddar didn't intervene, she liked their odds.

After a time, they stopped at a whisper cone, which the humans must have missed in their hurry. Laanda held a short hissing conversation, then turned back toward the group. "No movement from the humans, as far as they can tell. Not the thief at any rate, or Heuli would have seen it on the board." Aene tried to imagine this board, how it tracked the collar. She had gathered that the walls were laced with a magical steel barrier, which carried a signal when the collar was moved, but the Timon's metal magic was hard to fathom. She sometimes wondered if it was magic at all or more a combination of technology and training, as some would argue her own magic was. Without her gauntlet or circlet to channel through, she couldn't do much, as she'd discovered when her gauntlet had been taken.

"...go up the shaft first, with me following behind, as we can move fastest up the ladders." It took Aene a while to process what Laanda had said while she'd spaced out. Laanda nodded to Yglind. "You and Ardo come next, and Aene, you stand watch at the bottom, just in case."

"I'll throw my scrying dice while I wait," Aene said, pulling them out of her pouch, feeling their weight in her hands, the tingle of a message they were eager to deliver. She hadn't rolled them since before the attack, so they should have solid energy built up by now.

Skiti leaned over to stare at the dice, which Aene held out on her palm to show her. Skiti reached out tentative fingers, then jerked them back when Laanda barked at her in Timon.

"You can pray however you like while we climb," Laanda said, casting a glance that felt scornful though it was impossible to read through her helmet. Laanda muttered something in Timon, and Skiti nodded, glancing back at the dice once more before giving her Omni a quick shake, and it slid back into its club form with a series of metallic clicks. She tucked it into its belt loop, then took hold of the rungs and began climbing up with practiced grace and speed.

Laanda watched her for a moment, then put her hands and feet on the lowest rungs.

"Let me climb a hundred feet or so before you head up. We need to be spaced out in case there's any trouble." She turned and muscled her way up, disappearing into the shaft above.

"While you wait, lend me your focus," Aene said. Ardo lowered himself down immediately, but Yglind stayed where he was, staring up the shaft.

"Yglind, please? You know it works better the more people—"

"Spare me," he said, and Aene could almost hear his sneer.

"You don't have to sit. It wouldn't kill you to give me a few seconds of your attention. It might even save your life."

Yglind's sigh was muffled and tinny through his helmet, but he turned, lifted his visor, and looked down at the dice. Aene closed her eyes and concentrated, bringing to mind the dragon's jagged teeth, the mage's lightning, the knight's sword, and the quirk of Feddar's eyebrows. The dice clacked extra loudly in her hands as she moved them through one circle, by which time they were practically buzzing with energy. She released them, and they rolled several times, then seemed to freeze in place on the stone. She stared at the symbols, burning them into her mind, then closed her eyes and let them float as bright copper shapes against a pitch-black background, swirling and rotating like leaves in the corner of a windy courtyard. They spun faster and faster, becoming a blur of fiery orange that began to take on shape and texture. Yglind on one knee, his left arm hanging limp, holding his sword overhead as the knight bore down with theirs. The mage's face, contorted with malice as he cupped a ball of crackling energy in his hands. The inside of the dragon's mouth, teeth dripping with blood. Feddar's eyes, wide with terror, his face contorted in a scream.

Darkness without end.

Silence.

Nothingness.

Aene blinked against the light from Yglind's amulet as she pushed herself up on her elbows. The back of her head throbbed, and her mouth had a coppery tang in it. She touched her tongue, but there was no blood.

"...all right?" Ardo's voice echoed as if from a long, twisted tube, and she could only make out the last words.

"I'm...fine, I think. I just...wow." Her thoughts cleared a bit, and she realized she must have passed out and hit her head, which would explain why she was lying on the floor instead of seated in lotus position. Pain spiked through her forehead as the images from her vision returned in a flash. She pressed her palm against her temple as if she could root out the offending sensation.

"You don't look fine." Ardo knelt by her, holding her hand in his, and pulled her slowly up to sitting.

"I'm getting there." She shook her head a little, and the fog began to lift.

"What did you see?" Yglind crouched above her, his eyes wide with almost boyish curiosity. Aene smiled; it was always a joy when Yglind's façade slipped for a moment. As much as he loved to mock the dice, she wondered if he didn't believe in them more than she did.

"It's...hard to explain, but I saw you fighting the knight and losing rather badly."

"The dice lie!" Yglind punched the ground with his metal-encased fist. He turned as a hissing sound echoed down the shaft. "Gotta go." He stood up and flipped his visor down. "Ardo, I want you right behind me, no matter what Laanda says. Aene, will you be able to climb up when we call?"

She waved him off, collecting the dice and slipping them into her pocket. "No problem." She reached out for Ardo's hand and let him haul her to her feet, only feeling dizzy for a moment.

"Are you sure?" Ardo asked in a soft voice as Yglind disappeared into the shaft.

"Absolutely. I just...the dice had a lot to say, and I'm still processing it."

Ardo touched her gently on the shoulder, and she felt a little spark from the touch and the soft look in his eyes. She remembered those eyes locked on hers as she hovered over him, the gentle touch of his hands on her hips, how he stayed still and hard as a stone for her. She blinked and touched him on the cheek, and he turned away quickly and stepped toward the ladder.

She saw the shapes out of the corner of her vision just in time to tap her gauntlet to armor up. They were on her in an instant, knocking her to the ground and clamping their jaws around her neck and limbs. Four lizards the size of full-grown Maer pinned her beneath their weight, mouths full of tiny teeth gripping and shaking, chomping again, but unable to break through her force armor. She ripped one arm free, grabbed the dagger from her belt, and stabbed the one that was trying to crush her neck, and it thrashed away, dislodging one of the others off her arm. One still held onto her foot until a dull silvery flash struck its head, and it released as it flopped over sideways, then reared up, hissing and baring its teeth like a miniature waadrech.

Ardo pivoted as one of the creatures leapt at him, and he whipped his staff around to knock it out of the air, then drove the tip straight into its eye as it lay stunned on the ground. Its body trembled and shook, then went stiff. Another one clamped its jaws around his calf, and he let out a pained grunt as he adjusted his grip on his staff, then popped it between the eyes with the end. It let go, flopping around awkwardly on the floor. Ardo drove the tip through the top of its head, and it collapsed.

The remaining two flung themselves at Aene, and she dug deep into the gauntlet's power to shoot off two full blasts, hitting both of them and sending them twisting backward, their skin blistered by the force of the blasts. Ardo leapt between the writhing creatures, finishing off one, then the other, then moved next to Aene, his back to her. He turned in all directions with his staff held out sideways to ward off any would-be attackers, but none came.

"What in the gods' shit was that?" Yglind called down, and they could hear his boots clacking down the ladder.

"Rock crawlers, I think," Aene said, studying the creatures.

"Pretty big for rock crawlers," Ardo commented, prying one of their mouths open with the tip of his staff.

"Pretty aggressive, too," Aene said. Rock crawlers were common enough, though they seldom got this big, but they were usually so shy they were only glimpsed. Stories told of babies being carried away, but for them to attack a full-grown Maer was unheard of.

"You got attacked by rock crawlers?" Yglind said in a crestfallen voice. "Why do you get all the fun?"

"Ardo killed all four by himself," Aene said, immediately regretting it as she realized what that meant for Yglind. He would only become more desperate now, more reckless, which might easily lead to scenarios like the one the scrying dice had shown her.

"I'm not sure if rock crawlers would have counted toward your five," Ardo said, wrapping a bandage around his calf, which was bleeding from numerous tiny punctures.

"They wouldn't, but I still would have liked to get my blade wet before the big event. I wonder why they attacked you." He jabbed at one of the rock crawlers with his sword, then poked at each of the others in turn. He lifted his faceplate and turned to Ardo, looking from his staff to his eyes. "You got four, eh? Nice work!"

Ardo waved him off, but there was a hint of an embarrassed smile on his face.

"They were just rock crawlers, my lord. You'd have dispatched them in seconds without taking a scratch."

"Speaking of which, let me get some medic's balm on there." Aene knelt by Ardo, digging the jar out of her backpack and opening it. "No telling what kind of nasties you might get from that bite."

"Ow, ow, OW!" Ardo whispered as Aene quickly removed the bandage and rubbed a thin layer of the balm all around the area.

"Can you climb?" Yglind asked.

"Of course. It's just a scratch."

"Good." Yglind's face lightened for a moment, then he turned as Laanda's whisper echoed down the shaft, strangely clear, despite the low volume.

"What's going on?"

"Rock crawlers," Yglind hissed as he started climbing. "We took care of it. On our way back up now."

Ardo touched Aene on the shoulder, looking both ways down the hallway, then followed Yglind up the shaft. Aene did a few deep breath cycles staring at the opposite wall and keeping her focus on her peripheral vision in case anything else came creeping up on her. Everything was quiet. The rock crawler carcasses caught her eye, and her mind spun off to the hulshag the humans had sent into the castle. She realized in a flash that the mage must have been controlling them and the crawlers too. Perhaps he was more of a generalist; human mages were said to have limited areas of focus, but controlling subterranean creatures was about as far removed from lightning as she could imagine. Ardo's *psst* snapped her out of her reverie, and she looked up to see him inside the chute, gesturing at her to climb. She glanced down the corridor one more time in each direction, then took hold of the clammy iron and started climbing.

Though she thought of herself as fitter than the average mage, she was slick with cold sweat and trembling with exhaustion by the time she reached the next level. The others stood, barely winded, talking in whispers.

"Skiti's going to go in front of us and keep an eye out for any traps or surprises," Yglind said, his voice strained with impatience. "We have two more shafts to climb, apparently. They say it's too risky to use the lifts."

Aene sighed, nodding. She would have liked to see how the Timon's lifts differed from the Maer ones, but that would have to wait. Climbing one shaft had been a struggle, and she wasn't sure if she was ready to do two more. She might have to draw a power-up from the gauntlet and use a Strength spell to boost her, but she would make it.

"Makes sense."

"We should have a bite to eat and some water," Ardo said, offering several of the Timon's gray sporecakes and a waterskin.

"I can always count on you to bring the picnic," Yglind said, lifting his faceplate and grinning. He cracked off a corner of the cake and chewed thoughtfully. "These really aren't too bad." He twisted his mouth sideways, chewed some more, then swallowed. "Better than the ones we lost when we fell into the water. Color me impressed."

"They're better than nothing," Aene said through a mouthful of the pasty substance. "I could eat the hell out of some flatbread right now, though."

"Don't talk about food." Ardo sighed, chewing and staring at the corner of sporecake in his hand.

Laanda appeared beside him, faceplate up, and flashed a warm smile. "Once we rid this mine of the human pestilence, we'll treat you to a feast such as you have never imagined."

"I hope you like it spicy," Skiti added with a smirk.

Yglind's mouth twisted into a snarly smile. "What's the point of living without a little spice?"

Aene stifled a giggle and had raised the waterskin to her lips when she noticed something out of the corner of her eye, floating in the air in the shadows just beyond the low light of their amulets.

"What in the gods' shit is that?" She tapped her gauntlet to armor up, then turned up the light on her amulet, and the others turned toward the direction she was pointing. An eye-sized globe of what looked like clear glass twinkled in the yellow light, hovering in the air at eye level. It started floating away from them, and Aene followed it with her light, but it moved fast enough that it would be out of eyesight in seconds. She glanced up to the others, who stared at her expectantly.

"We follow it," she said, hurrying after it at a fast walk.

21

Yglind caught up with Aene and touched her shoulder, but she kept walking fast enough that Yglind had to work to keep up.

"What is that thing?"

"I don't know exactly, but I'd bet a dozen brightstone chips the human mage is using it to spy on us."

"Fucking humans," Yglind spat. "I will take great pleasure in running my sword through their hairless bodies."

Aene stopped and stood facing Yglind, her eyes bright and hot. He shone his light on the receding ball, then lifted his faceplate and turned to face Aene.

"Not Feddar," she said in a steely voice.

"What?"

"The thief. Not the thief. You swore."

"I never swore. I just said…" Yglind looked back down the hall, and the ball had all but disappeared. "Aene, we need to—"

"Swear it, Egg. Fucking swear it!" Her voice rose, as did the fire in her eyes. Yglind found her terrifying when she had her mind set on something like this.

"Fine, I swear, on the Torl coat of arms, I won't kill the thief except in self-defense." He tapped his breastplate, which showed the stylized mashtorul figure that was his family's logo. "Now are we going to follow that floating orb or what?"

Aene's eyes narrowed for a moment, boring into his, then she turned and took off running down the hall. Yglind sighed and jogged after her, clanking with every step. He had almost caught up when a burst shot forth from her gauntlet, forming a meshy net of golden light. It collapsed into a ball, then floated back toward them.

Aene held the tangle of light suspended above her hand, and Yglind saw that the glass ball was in the center of it. Aene's face tensed with concentration as she moved her fingers in strange patterns and the golden threads vanished one by one. She raised her hand and took the ball between her thumb and forefinger.

Skiti edged in between them, eyes wide as she stared up at the ball.

"Is that—"

Aene nodded, holding the ball close to her face, staring into it. "I see you, skinfucker. You can throw all the tricks and beasties you want at us, but I'm coming for you. Take a good look because the next time you see me, it'll be you I do this to."

She closed her hand into a fist around the ball, then flung it against the wall, where it burst into a cloud of glass shivers and dust. Skiti looked up at Aene in horror.

"Good," Yglind snarled, clapping Aene on the shoulder. She spun away from his touch, glaring at him again. "Sorry," he mumbled. That's what he got for invading her boundaries. Sometimes he forgot.

"Well, at least they can't watch us anymore," Laanda said. "But we might want to take a different route, as they'll be expecting us this way."

"We could double back and go up through the bat caves and around," Skiti said, trailing off a bit at the end as she looked Yglind up and down.

"It might be a tight fit for you two." Laanda eyed Yglind and Ardo. "But I think you'll manage. It's as good a plan as any, though it does involve considerably more crawling through guano than the other ways."

"The humans won't have paid much attention to the bat tunnels." Skiti ran her fingers through her beard. "If we can keep quiet enough, we just might sneak up on them without their noticing us."

"Ah yes, more sneaking and subterfuge." Yglind flipped up his faceplate, suddenly hot with irritation. "Why can we not simply head directly to this copper gallery and end the skinfuckers?" He held out his sword for emphasis, and it felt right in his hand, solid, perfectly sized, and weighted just for him. A sword like this deserved to be put to good use.

"I appreciate your enthusiasm," Laanda said coolly, which had the opposite effect on Yglind, but he bit his tongue as she continued. She was a queen, after all, and he was representing the Torl lineage. "But surely you can appreciate our intimate knowledge of the mines of our own jurisdiction." She put an irritating level of emphasis on the last word. "And the humans have had ample time to prepare for our arrival. It's safe to assume they have a few surprises planned for us. Why not return the favor?"

"She's right, my lord." Ardo leaned forward to touch Yglind, who jerked his arm away. Ardo ducked his head a little and held up his hands in deference for a moment.

Yglind turned to Aene, who was doing a poor job of stifling a smirk.

"Fuck both of you," he muttered, then blinked hard and looked down at Laanda. Though he towered over her, her sturdy frame and grim demeanor told him she was not only a formidable fighter but a determined leader as well. "If you say we go through the bat tunnels, then through the bat tunnels we go."

Yglind cocked one shoulder sideways as he tried to bend his elbow at an unnatural angle to squeeze through the narrow crevice, but his shoulder plates just wouldn't fit through, no matter what he tried. He'd already left his shield behind after he'd had to crawl through a space that was just the wrong shape. He sighed, trying not to panic as his shoulder got caught on the way out.

"I'm backing up," he grunted, bracing with his other arm and pulling until his shoulder plate popped free, sending him tumbling to the ground at Ardo's feet.

"Perhaps if we remove your shoulder plates entirely?" Ardo held his hand out, and Yglind snarled at him as he let himself be pulled up, but he felt it stretching into a smile as he saw the concern in Ardo's eyes.

"Feeling guilty for siding with them?"

"I wasn't siding—You know I'm always on your side."

"When you're not beneath me." Yglind chucked Ardo on the cheek with his gauntlet, and Ardo turned his face away with a smirk, but not before Yglind saw what he needed to know. Ardo may have fucked Aene, but at the end of the day, he'd always come back to Yglind's arms. Gods knew why Ardo tolerated him, but Yglind felt it with every misstep, every verbal blunder. Ardo always forgave him. Ardo loved him, warts and all. Ardo made him want to be a better Maer. Yglind's heart swelled at the thought, and as Ardo's fingers made quick work of removing the shoulder plates, Yglind leaned into him, though he could not feel his warmth through his armor and padding.

He just fit through the crevice without his shoulder plates, which Ardo had tied to his belt, so they jangled against the rock at every movement. They weren't going to be sneaking up on anyone like this.

"Just a few more tight spots, and then it opens up a bit," Laanda said as they paused for breath in the next open space. "I think you can put your armor back on there, and you should be good for the rest of the way."

"Where are the bats?" Aene asked, staring up at the ceiling.

"This time of year, they're closer to the surface." Skiti chewed a corner of sporecake. "We'll see them when we get up a little higher."

"I've always found them fascinating." Aene's eyes grew soft, dreamy. Yglind smiled despite himself. "They fly around in these tight spaces at top speed without using their eyes. That's incredible."

"Well, let's get moving, and I'll show you some." Skiti led the way, climbing up to a small ledge and crawling through a hole in the ceiling. She moved smoothly, but with care, her fingers and toes finding holds with the ease of a mountain goat. Yglind sighed and followed, struggling to find the holds he'd seen Skiti use, and it took him five times as long to climb up, though his reach was almost twice hers.

They passed through a series of chambers and passages, heading ever upward until they entered a large cavern with hints of natural light filtering in from somewhere. Skiti held out her hand to stop them, creeping out into the room with her eyes on the ceiling. Yglind looked up and saw that large segments of the cave were darker than the others, covered in an almost endless swath of tufted brown fur.

"Holy shit, are those—" Aene ended in a hissing gasp.

"Bats," Laanda said in a low voice. "Lesser brown mountain bats, to be precise. Found throughout the Silver Hills, especially in places with access to deep tunnels. Not to be confused with—" She slid her axe into a loop at her side and slung her crossbow around, backing toward them and staring up into the darkness above. Skiti was frozen in place, staring up at the same spot. Yglind held his sword out in front of him, looking up at the shadowy ceiling beyond the reach of the light from his amulet but seeing nothing. Ardo moved a few feet away, holding his staff out sideways, and Aene moved back into the entrance.

"What in the gods' teats is it?" Aene hissed.

"Springers," Laanda whispered. "At least half a dozen of them. They mostly eat bats, but sometimes they get frisky."

"What the fuck are springers?" Aene's whisper sounded angry.

"Hulmar," Yglind said over his shoulder. "Big weasels that can climb like squirrels. But they don't get over three feet long, right?"

A dark shape sprang from the shadows above and flew through the air toward Skiti, whose Omni formed into a latticework dome covering her. A jagged bolt of fur, claws, and teeth crashed into the dome, bounced off, and was hit immediately by a bolt from Laanda's crossbow. Skiti flicked her Omni, and the dome unfurled into a whiplike shape with many tentacles, which wrapped around the thrashing creature. It had to be as long as a Maer was tall, though considerably thinner, with sharp teeth gnashing at the wire net it was encased in. Skiti darted forward, pulled her knife, and jabbed it into the creature several times until it stopped moving.

Yglind's sword pulled him forward, even as Laanda called out "No!" from behind him. He glanced up in time to see a dark shape hurtling toward him, and he swung his sword by instinct, cutting the creature in half as the front end of it crashed into him, knocking him to the ground. Its teeth clacked against his neck guard, even as its life flooded out of its body, soaking Yglind's padding with its warm, sticky blood, which reeked of musk. A great burst of light shot up from Aene's hand, illuminating a twenty-foot-wide swath of the ceiling above. As the light moved across the rock, it revealed a dozen or more long brown shapes, which launched themselves down like a hail of great furry arrows. Thousands of bats took flight at the same time, filling the air with the low rumble of their collective wings.

Yglind sprang to his feet just in time to sidestep one that was headed straight for him, only to find himself faced with two more that sprang out of graceful tumbles, launching themselves at either ankle. He cut one down before it reached him, but the other latched onto his shin guard, pressing against his boot with its paws as it jerked its head side to side, loosening the plate. He swung his sword around to strike it, but his elbow was caught in the vice grip of another set of jaws, weighing him down and bringing him to one knee. He swung his pommel around and smashed the one on his leg, which let out an eerie shriek as it twisted away from him, looking equal parts dazed and furious.

He shook his elbow to try to dislodge the other creature, whose four feet were clawing at him, the front two digging into his elbow joint, its rear feet ripping at the shin guard. It writhed but stayed latched on, and Yglind let out a snarl as its claws raked his leg where his armor had been pulled back, slicing into his flesh through the mail. Something flashed out of the corner of his eye, and the creature went limp, an axe sticking out of its spine just below the neck.

Yglind sprang to his feet, bracing in all directions to make sure there were no unseen hulmar ready to spring. He saw Ardo keeping a pair of them at bay with his staff while Laanda sank her big axe into the head of one that lay writhing on the floor. Two long brown shapes scurried down the wall directly above Aene, who stood oblivious, staring down at two steaming corpses in front of her.

"Aene! Above you!" Yglind shouted, and Aene jumped back inside the entrance just as the two hulmar dropped to the ground. One popped up and raced into the entrance, obscuring Aene from view, while the other lay motionless with an axe bisecting its head. A bright light flashed in the tunnel, followed by a heavy thud. Laanda blinked and rushed into the entrance, and Yglind leapt forward and sliced clean through the one remaining hulmar, whose jaws were wrapped around the steel end of Ardo's staff. Its two halves plopped to the floor in quick succession, and all was quiet except the distant whisper of the bats flying out of the cave.

Ardo and Yglind exchanged a relieved glance, and Ardo's smile faltered when his gaze fell on Yglind's shin, which was bleeding through his mail from several scratches from the hulmar's raking claws.

"Yglind, you're hurt." He knelt to examine Yglind's wound, which was starting to throb now that the heat of battle was waning. Yglind felt jittery, hollow inside, at the suddenness of the fight, especially its end. No sooner had he gotten fired up than it was over, and his hot blood had nowhere to go, so it pooled around his heart.

"It's nothing. Let's keep moving."

"It's not nothing, Yglind," Ardo said, his voice softening as he dug bandages out of a pouch and started dabbing the wound. "Gods know what fetid disease lurks in those claws of theirs." He took the medic's balm Aene offered him, smearing it on, and Yglind hissed at the sharp burn.

"He's not wrong," Skiti said, crouching to examine the wound. "Is that medic's balm?" she asked, her voice high with wonder.

"It's standard equipment on a Delve," Ardo said as he tightened the bandage and worked to reattach the shin plate.

"Along with that fancy sword and armor?" Skiti stood, eyeing Yglind's sword as he wiped the blood from it. He held it up, letting the light from his amulet reflect off its shining surface like a disc of pure sunlight off a lake.

"This is my Forever Blade. It will see me through this life and the Time to Come." He gave it one last wipe and slid it into its sheath. His mind flashed to a childhood vision of this nebulous future, which he had always imagined as a great playroom full of mechanical soldiers. The sound of their gears clicking smoothly as they moved with a grace too perfect to be real. The faint smell of oil and fresh solder. The soft glow of polished bronze.

Skiti nodded, staring at the hilt, then turned serious eyes up to meet Yglind's.

"I sincerely hope you make it there."

— · —

22

Skiti smelled it before she saw it, a rotten-meat putrescence, no doubt from the shreds of Timon and hulshag gore plastered around its mouth. She stood before the tunnel leading out of the cavern, not daring to move a muscle as she stared at the dark shape lurking just inside the entrance. Its eyes glistened like huge glass beads, and its grotesque size was rendered all the more horrifying by its perfect stillness. It could lurch out and snap her up before she'd have time to raise the Omni in defense, but it just sat there, a silent mass of hulking menace, staring at her. She held up one hand toward the creature and took a slow step backward. It shifted in the shadows but did not bolt out and crush her skull with its huge jaws full of jagged teeth.

"What's the holdup?" Yglind hissed.

"Waadrech," Laanda whispered, sounding as calm as if she were identifying a species of common bird. Skiti took another step back and another until she nearly bumped into Yglind and Laanda, who held their weapons at the ready. Yglind's eyes glowed with a hunger she had seen too often among the Guard, and Skiti flashed Laanda a worried look as she slipped between her and Yglind.

"Why isn't it attacking us?" Skiti whispered.

"It doesn't want us," Yglind muttered, half-turning his head around and lowering his visor. "It's here for the hulmar."

"Which it's most welcome to," Laanda said. "Let's give it some space and see what it does. If it attacks—"

"Then it's mine," Yglind said, his body tensing. He was a beast of a Maer, six and a half feet tall, with impossibly broad shoulders and hands the size of crevice spiders. With his armor and sword and a little luck, Skiti wondered if he might not stand a chance against the creature.

"*If* it attacks." Laanda stared at Yglind until he turned his gaze away from the dragon to meet hers.

Yglind said nothing. No one spoke or even seemed to breathe as the creature emerged from the tunnel, placing one foot in front of the other with a kind of heavy grace. Skiti's breath escaped, and she struggled to inflate her lungs again as its body kept coming, easily forty feet long, thick and powerful, covered in gray-black scales. It paused, raising its heavy head to look in their direction. Its nostrils flared, and it showed half its jagged teeth before turning away from them and walking deliberately toward the closest of the hulmar bodies, which were scattered across the cavern floor.

They watched in silence as it snuffled around the body for a moment, then pinned it with one clawed foot and split it open from neck to tail with the other. It locked eyes with Skiti, then lowered its snout into the mass of entrails spilling out of the hulmar carcass and began tearing out reddish-purple organs with its teeth. Skiti turned away in time to see Ardo brace his hands on his knees and puke on the floor, take a step back, then puke again. The sound and smell of his retching, combined with the horrid tearing and gobbling sounds of the dragon as it snapped and gulped down its meal, almost pushed Skiti over the edge as well, but she ground her teeth and kept it together, albeit barely.

"We should leave while it's busy," Laanda whispered.

"I agree," Yglind replied. "Ardo, you good?"

Ardo gave a thumbs up, wiping the puke from his beard and looking like he might throw up again.

"Do we just keep going?" Skiti asked, eyeing the tunnel the waadrech had come out of.

"The mission hasn't changed," Laanda said, squinting thoughtfully as she watched the dragon. "If it comes for us, we do what we must. In the meantime, we have some humans to hunt." Yglind's body tensed at her words, and Skiti wondered again if the two of them would fight each other for the chance to get the first crack at the humans.

"Let me take the rear," Aene said, staring down at a set of golden-lighted symbols hovering in the air just above her gauntlet. "I think I can slow it down if it tries to get too close." She flicked her fingers, and the glowing figures disappeared.

"Skiti?" Laanda whispered, tilting her head toward the entrance. Skiti nodded, though she wasn't sure why she had to go first. Or rather, she knew why, as she was the best climber and the most trained to look for traps, but if a dragon had come out of the tunnel, why were they in such a hurry to go in there?

She extended her Omni into trident form, pausing mid-shift as the waadrech lifted its head briefly to stare at her, then continued its meal. Skiti used a moment of noisy slurping to slide the Omni the rest of the way out, then took a tentative step toward the entrance. The creature's eyes stayed on her as it turned its head up and snapped its jaws a few times to swallow a chunk of innards, but it made no move toward her and soon dug its snout back into the carcass.

Skiti's skin crawled as she felt it watching from behind, but she forced one foot in front of the other and soon passed into the darkness of the tunnel. The Maer's amulets threw off her dark vision but gave off enough residual light that she could make her way through. The tunnel was so narrow at one point she wondered how the creature had squeezed through, and she had to wait a moment when Yglind got stuck and had to remove his shoulder plates again.

"Yes, let's go through the dragon-infested bat tunnels to sneak up on the fucking humans without proper armor or shield," he muttered, but there was something gleeful about his whining, an undercurrent of thinly disguised bloodlust.

When they had gotten a few hundred yards in and there was no sign that the waadrech was following them, they took a moment to have a bite and a sip, and Laanda squatted and started drawing with the tip of her dagger in the dust. Skiti crouched next to her, studying the drawing.

"If I remember correctly, this tunnel drops us in the old furnace room by the number five shaft, right?"

"It's been years, but that's what I remember," Skiti agreed.

"And there's a passage connecting the furnace to the copper gallery."

"Right. Should be a short walk from the furnace."

"And how long until we reach this furnace room?" Yglind crouched down next to them, shining his light down at the lines in the dust.

"Shouldn't be more than an hour," Skiti said, though there were a few spots where they'd have to climb. The Maer were pretty slow at that, and Ardo was looking drained, though he maintained a stoic face.

"I'm ready," Yglind said, standing up to a stoop, as the chamber was a little too short for his height.

Laanda stood, grasping her axe handle with both hands in a gesture that immediately drew everyone's attention.

"Once we emerge on the other side of these caves, we will need to be quiet and ready for anything. Skiti will go a little way ahead, beyond the range of your amulets, and get a peek at what we're walking into." Laanda flashed

Skiti a quick blink that landed like a feather in her heart. "Ardo, are you sure you're up to this?"

"I'm absolutely certain." Ardo still looked a little diminished, but he stood up tall and strong as he spoke. Aene uncrossed her arms and put her hands on her hips, her eyes fierce yet hollow. The stress and fatigue were taking their toll, but these Maer had heart.

Laanda put a hand on Skiti's shoulder and leaned her helmet in to touch her forehead.

"Go with the gods," she murmured.

The descent was slow but steady, and with the exception of a few rock crawlers and crevice spiders, which skittered away at her approach, Skiti saw nothing other than rock and dried guano. She hissed her "okay" signal back to Laanda every so often, pausing for long enough to hear the response, then continued to the next turning point. As she descended into a rounded chamber with water dripping somewhere inside, a putrid stench struck her, making it hard to focus on her holds. She hissed the "stop" signal, then turned and studied the chamber. Almost everything was the same temperature, so she only saw the cave's contours vaguely, but an oddly shaped pile shone in her dark vision with the faded light of something recently dead. She listened carefully but heard nothing other than the drip drip drip of water and her own low breathing. She found her way down to the cave floor and crept toward the heap of warmth, which she was now sure was the source of the rank odor that sent her stomach lurching up into her throat. She squeezed the Omni and focused for a moment, and the head of the trident lit up, casting a bluish-white light over the area. She covered her mouth with her hand, almost giggling when she saw that she was standing ten feet away from a pile of dragon shit the size of a small hulshag.

She considered running back to warn Laanda, but there wasn't much point, so she continued, marking the exit with a chalk streak so the others could follow. She wound her way down and, a few accidental detours aside, was pleasantly surprised at how well she remembered the route. She stopped when she smelled a change in the air, and she knew she was not far from the exit into the furnace room. She found an area where the passage widened a little and waited for the others.

"I remember this place," Laanda said, her eyes falling softly on Skiti. Her voice had taken on that distant, almost sentimental tone she used when speaking of the past, of their childhood. They used to explore the tunnels while their parents worked, and Laanda was always the one leading the expedition, princess though she was. Skiti had always taken such pride in following her, being strong for her, knowing the burden Laanda thought she hid from the world.

"How much farther?" Yglind whispered as he squeezed into the space, taking up more room than Skiti and Laanda combined.

"Shouldn't be more than five or ten minutes more now." Skiti searched her memory for the exact contours of the final leg. "I'll ping you a little more often now."

Laanda touched her on the shoulder and nodded her forward. Skiti took a deep breath, smiled at her, and crept down the tunnel into the growing darkness.

The flow of air hit her suddenly as she poked her head around the final bend. She studied the last bit of tunnel and saw the faint contours of the opening, the cast-iron grate firmly in place, with nothing but cold, dark stone beyond. She listened to the silence for a full minute before creeping down the tunnel on soft feet, ducking though the roof was tall enough she didn't need to. When she reached the grate, she stopped again to listen, and again she heard nothing. She eased on the light of her Omni just enough to study the edges of the grate, which showed no signs of being touched in recent memory. She manipulated the buttons on the Omni so the end released into a half-dozen tentacles. She directed them between the rusty bars and around to the lock, which fortunately was oiled enough it didn't take an inordinate amount of time to unlock. She left it closed, knowing the grate would make a racket when she opened it, and she wanted backup in case the humans came running. She returned to the bend and hissed for the others to join her.

Laanda moved in relative quiet, given the muted armor she wore, but Yglind's armor was jingly, and Skiti could almost feel his footfalls through the ground. They slowed down as they approached, and even Yglind managed not to create an excessive amount of racket.

"I unlocked the grate." Skiti close-whispered so her words would not carry around the corner. "I'm ready to open it and climb down, but I want backup."

"I'll cover you." Laanda slid her axe into its loop and swung her crossbow around. Her visor was down, but Skiti felt the concern in her voice.

"I'll be ready," Yglind hissed, and Skiti clenched her jaw at the sound. He probably thought he was whispering, but he might as well have been shouting, as far as anyone or anything living underground was concerned.

"You have no missile weapons?" Laanda looked Yglind up and down, disdain evident in her posture.

"By tradition, I carry none. I prefer to meet my opponents in—"

"Egg." Aene tapped him on the helmet. "Nobody cares." Skiti stifled a giggle as Yglind's head snapped to face Aene, his sigh audible through his visor. "I'll cover you too." Aene tapped her gauntlet, which glowed faintly. Skiti hoped Aene didn't have cause to use it any time soon, but she was curious to see it in action. She'd seen the evidence of what it had done to the hulmar, but she'd missed the fireworks.

Laanda nodded, and Skiti sent the Omni's tentacles through to turn the latch. It was not as well-oiled as the lock and resisted. She reconfigured the six tentacles into three and was able to get enough leverage to wrench it open a crack with a screech that echoed through the room beyond. Skiti winced at the sound, and everyone seemed to hunch their shoulders at the same time, but only silence followed the noise. Skiti braced both hands against the grate, grasping the bars with her gloves and pulling with all her might until it groaned all the way open. She uncoiled her livesteel cord, bonded one end to the grate frame, and let it dangle to the floor twenty feet below. More silence ensued, and she looped the cable and slapped a tension pulley on, then lowered herself down. She landed without a sound and turned about, taking in the hulking shape of the old furnace, the two wide entrances, the channels carrying a trickle of dripwater out through the drain below. She sensed no sign of any life or recent activity.

She gestured for them to descend, which they did, one by one, until they stood in a tight circle around the rope, facing outward. Laanda lit the tip of her axe, and the contours of the room came clear, the high ceiling, the half-dismantled furnace, the great chimney. Yglind crouched, his fingers running through the dust on the floor, tracing lines in the air in the direction of three sets of footsteps that circled and crisscrossed the room, leading in and out of the corridor on the east wall in the direction of the old copper gallery.

23

Ardo's stomach groused at him as he busied himself by check-ing Yglind's bandages and his armor, making sure everything was strapped on tight.

"Everything is fine," Yglind said, pulling his leg away and taking Ardo's cheek in his gauntleted hand, guiding him to standing as he lifted his visor. "You've done all you can do now. The rest is up to me."

Ardo clapped Yglind's shoulder and turned as he saw Laanda pull her axe back out and gesture Skiti toward the tunnel entrance where the footsteps in the dust led. Yglind lowered his visor, held up his sword in front of his amulet for a long moment, then stalked over next to Laanda. Ardo blinked hard a few times, gripping his staff and trying to steady his breath by inhaling long and slow, but every part of him felt shaky, wobbly. Aene's grim smile did little to lift his spirits, but he moved over behind Yglind with Aene at his side. Laanda faced them for a moment, her eyes hard and serious, then closed her visor and nodded to Skiti, who disappeared into the tunnel entrance.

Laanda nodded her head one, two, three, as if keeping time, four, five, six, then strode forward, leading with her axe. Yglind followed, his sword gleaming in the low light of his amulet. Ardo's stomach roiled once again at the bloodlust he felt coming off Yglind in waves. He glanced at Aene, who flicked her wrist, and her body shimmered with the now-familiar force armor. She nodded, and they followed Yglind and Laanda into the dark passage.

They had gone no more than fifty feet when Ardo heard a loud hiss, then a series of horrid coughs and gasps coming from the darkness of the tunnel. Laanda tapped her axe tip to life, sending a flood of bright white light down the hallway. Skiti lay gasping on the floor, surrounded by a cloud of greenish mist. Laanda started running, and Aene called, "Wait!" but it was too late. Laanda reached the cloud, and as she crouched over Skiti, she too began coughing and gasping and fell onto her back. Yglind started forward, but Aene latched onto his arm and physically spun him toward her.

"Idiot!" she hissed. "Just give me a second." She tapped her amulet, closed her eyes, and the shimmering grew brighter around her head, encasing it in a bubble of glowing light. "Stay here," she whispered, pointing at Yglind, who nodded with a huffing sigh. Ardo's heart lurched as Aene hurried down the hall and lifted Skiti to a half-standing position, slumped over Aene's shoulder. They stumbled their way out of the cloud, and Aene dumped Skiti into Ardo's arms. His eyes and throat burned with the fumes that lingered around her, and he lay her surprisingly heavy body onto the floor as gently as he could, coughing all the while. Aene soon returned with Laanda, who collapsed against a wall, her head lolling to the side. Aene struggled with Laanda's chin strap, which Ardo helped her undo and removed the helmet. Laanda's face was pale and rubbery, her eyes red and watery.

"The fucking humans will pay for this!" Yglind bellowed, staring down the dark hallway.

"Egg, shut the fuck up!" Aene hissed. "If they didn't know exactly where we were before, they do now."

"Let them come!" Yglind roared, raising his sword so it clanged against the low ceiling, his voice reverberating through the hallway and into Ardo's bones.

"I swear to gods I don't know why they let an idiot like you lead a Delve," Aene mumbled, tapping her gauntlet and scrolling through an array of golden symbols, then stopping and tapping the gauntlet again. A shimmering wall appeared, blocking the tunnel in front of them. "That should hold them off for a bit while I figure out how to help our friends here."

Skiti let out a faint hiss, and her face grew red. Her fingers clawed at her throat as her back arched and her feet kicked wildly against the floor. Ardo dropped down over her, panicked, and could only think to hold onto her hands so she wouldn't scratch herself.

"Come on, Aene, do something!" He'd seen her use her gauntlet to heal wounds and stop infections, but he wasn't sure what she could do about this, whatever it was.

"Calm down, I'm working on it," she muttered, scrolling through the lighted symbols and wincing. "Is it magic, or just poison? Fuck, this chip is running low too. Fuck!"

"She's not breathing, Aene. She's not breathing!" Ardo's voice trembled as he grasped Skiti's cheeks, staring into her vacant eyes.

"Then fucking move aside." Aene bumped him out of the way and knelt over Skiti, whose body was convulsing, foam leaking out of her nose and the corners of her mouth. Aene's fingertips glowed, and she inserted them inside Skiti's mouth and closed her eyes. Her face drew tight as she mumbled a few words, and Skiti bucked, sucking in a huge gasp of air, then vomited bloody foam. Ardo helped Aene roll her onto her side, but Skiti flopped over onto her back again.

"Keep her sideways!" Aene said, backing away and popping the chip out of her gauntlet. It clattered on the floor as Ardo rolled Skiti back onto her side, and another stream of foam spilled out, thinner this time. Skiti's breath came in ragged bursts, but she was breathing.

"Laanda too," Yglind said. Ardo glanced over to see him crouched over Laanda, who was spasming and foaming at the mouth.

"I fucking know, Egg," Aene said, fumbling with a chip, which finally popped into the gauntlet with a click. Skiti coughed, and Ardo patted her gently on the back. He heard Aene's mumbled words and turned to see her glowing fingers in Laanda's mouth, with the same result. Laanda sat up suddenly, coughing bloody foam, which coated her beard and armor, then she turned to the side and retched noisily while Yglind held her. Aene sat back hard against the corridor wall, her eyes red with burst blood vessels before she closed them and covered her face with her bloody hands.

Skiti gave one more feeble cough and rolled onto her back, looking up at Ardo with watery, kind eyes.

"Thanks," she croaked, raising a trembling hand to wipe the mess from her beard.

"Shhh." Ardo gently removed her hand, pulled a handkerchief from his vest, and cleaned her face and beard as best he could. "We've got you."

Skiti blinked, then her eyes rolled toward the force wall Aene had put up, which glowed golden in the darkness.

"Neat," she said, then her eyes narrowed, and she raised a finger to point toward it. "Not so neat."

Ardo followed the direction of her finger and saw a small globe floating in the air just on the other side of the barrier, glinting with the reflected glow.

"Aene?" Ardo called, but she was already at his side, staring at the glowing orb.

"How many of those fucking things does he have?" she muttered, defeat in her voice.

"I don't care how many floating glass balls he has," Yglind snarled, moving to stand in front of the orb and holding up his sword. "When I get finished with him, he's not going to have balls left of any kind."

"Your word to the gods' ears, Egg." Aene stepped forward, standing beside Yglind, and stared at the orb. Ardo stood up and joined them, feeling Yglind's rage bleed into him. He hoped Yglind would cut the mage's balls right off, but if need be, Ardo would crush them one by one with the tip of his staff.

Ardo and Yglind kept an eye out while Aene, Skiti, and Laanda slept. The glass orb had vanished after a few minutes; presumably, the humans had seen everything they needed to see, but if they were doing anything about it, it wasn't immediately apparent. No lights reached them, and other than the sound of the Timon's snoring, the mine was utterly silent. Yglind paced to the furnace room and back, over and over, hovering for a moment each time he returned to where they rested. Ardo wished he could do something to help Yglind relieve his tension, but that would have to wait until they got back to a more civilized location.

Aene's sparkly wall remained in place for a while, then suddenly dissipated like golden embers thrown from a fire. Ardo considered waking Aene, but it was clear they were going to need her at her best, and neutralizing the poison had obviously taken a lot out of her. Or had it been the number of spells she'd channeled in such a short time? She'd used four in the space of several minutes, and he knew each spell took something from her. He wondered, if he'd been born in different circumstances, whether he might have had the chance to study. He still planned to, once he completed his service with Yglind, though it was painful to think of a future in which they didn't spend their days together.

Once they returned to civilization, Yglind would no doubt have earned his stars and be put into a leadership role. He might be sent off to command forces in distant lands or stay close to Kuppham as an advisor. Ardo would still have a chance to remain at his side, but if the Delve was successful, Yglind was destined for hibernation sooner or later. The thought Ardo kept locked in the back of his mind seeped out, and he saw the dark, hazy vision of Yglind lying strapped to a stone table as a chanting mage poured tarry black liquid into his mouth. He'd heard one of the squires describe the ritual, and he'd worked hard to suppress the grisly images. He stared into the tunnel's darkness, half wishing the humans would kill him so he didn't have to live to see his lover sent off to the doom of immortality.

Aene woke first, looking disoriented and surly, but by the time she came back from squatting in a corner of the furnace room, she looked close to normal except for her bloodshot eyes. They ate a piece of sporecake and drank a bit of water while they waited for Skiti and Laanda to wake up. The Timon were both a little groggy and slow at first. Laanda seemed to recover quickly and was soon chewing on sporecake and sipping water like one who had not eaten or drunk for a week. Skiti looked rather the worse for her experience, wan and wobbly behind the brave face she maintained when anyone looked at or spoke to her. In other moments, Ardo saw her deep fatigue, a look of hopeless exhaustion, and he wondered if she would be a liability when things finally heated up. She was tough, he thought, tougher than he was, and something told him she would pull her weight when all was said and done.

They began moving again, with Skiti out in front as before, looking only half-alive, with a forced smile on her face. She moved slowly, and Ardo noticed Laanda counting to ten this time before following. The corridor was long and straight, wide enough for them to walk two abreast without having to crowd. Laanda held up her hand, and everyone stopped.

"She told us to wait," Laanda whispered, though Ardo hadn't heard a thing. The Timon seemed to have some special whisper skills Ardo had never heard of before. "If memory serves, the copper gallery is very close. Dim your lights."

They lowered their amulets to glow, standing in tense silence for a few moments, then Skiti appeared from the shadows, worry etched into her features.

"They have a barrier up over the entrance, like the one you use," she whispered, glancing at Aene's gauntlet, "except it's greenish and more like hard glass than sparkles. There's a low light off to the side somewhere in the gallery, but I can't see what's causing it because of the barrier."

"Can you bring it down?" Yglind hissed to Aene.

"Probably," she whispered. "It might take a minute, as I don't know what his power base is, but I can find a way."

"We should assume they know we are coming and will be ready," Laanda said in a hushed voice, shaking her head. "I don't like this setup at all."

"We could climb up the overflow channel and surprise them," Skiti whispered. "If we went back to the furnace room, we could squeeze through the channel there and down into the drainage system, then come up into the copper gallery from below. They won't be expecting that."

Laanda shook her head, pointing at Yglind with her chin. "He would never fit. Nor Ardo, I expect. Aene would, though. Easier than you or me."

"I'm sticking with Yglind and Ardo. No offense," Aene said.

Laanda blinked understandingly. "Skiti and I will go. We'll climb up and be ready as soon as you disable the barrier. With any luck, I can hit the mage with a surprise shot from my crossbow."

"Are you seriously suggesting we split up?" Yglind asked, flipping his visor up to show his furrowed brow. "That's the number one rule of a Delve. Never split up the party."

"Well, you might be on a Delve, but we're not." Laanda spoke with sharp-edged politeness. "We're here to put an end to these *skinfuckers*, as you put it."

"So are we!" Ylglind's voice started to rise, then he lowered it back to a whisper. "I just don't think it's such a good idea to—"

"To contradict the queen of the Timon in her own territory? Most people would agree."

Yglind's brow softened; it was hard to tell in the shadows of the corridor, but Ardo thought he might have cracked a smile.

Ardo and Yglind stood watching as Aene studied the barrier. It resembled thick glass with a slightly greenish tint, and it seemed solid, as opposed to the one from Aene's gauntlet, which looked airy and insubstantial. The room stretched off into the darkness, empty save assorted piles of rubble and old mining equipment.

"He used the same barrier before, when we found them near the exhaust vent." Yglind leaned in close, his breath hot and warm as he whispered in Ardo's ear. "It was hard like steel, and it blocked sound as well."

"I think I've got it figured out." Aene turned to face them, a self-satisfied smirk on her face. "You might want to get your helmet back on because this won't take but a couple of seconds if it works, and gods know what will happen once we move into that room."

Yglind's eyes hardened at her words, then softened again for the briefest moment as they fell on Ardo's. He blinked and pulled on his helmet, tightening the straps and adjusting it so it sat neatly in the grooves of his neck guard. Ardo did a quick spot-check of Yglind's armor, but he'd already checked several times. Everything was in place, and Yglind looked like a right god of war with his Forever Blade and golden bronze armor.

"You two distract the mage, and I'll engage with their knight," Yglind said. "The Timon should be in place by now. Hopefully, they will be able to help."

Ardo nodded, though he wasn't sure what he could do against a mage of such power. But if he could take a spell intended for Yglind, that would be better than nothing. Aene blinked at them, then turned back toward the barrier, tapping her gauntlet into life and flicking through the lighted symbols for a moment until one symbol grew larger, then disappeared. She touched her fingertips to the barrier, closed her eyes, and mumbled a few words. Her body tensed in concentration as if she were pushing against the wall, then all at once, it vanished, and she tumbled through the doorway into the dark room.

Aene froze in place, her head turned toward the light, then waved her gauntlet in a swift arc, creating a bubble of golden light several feet around her. Her barrier glowed blinding blue as two lightning bolts hit it, but it seemed to hold. Yglind charged through the entrance, passing behind the bubble, and at another gesture of Aene's, a section of the force wall flowed off to surround Yglind. Ardo ducked through the doorway, taking cover behind Aene's bubble as Yglind took off running toward the light.

Through the faint haze of the bubble, Ardo could make out two figures, the tall, armored knight and the rail-thin mage, who hurled another pair of lightning bolts at Yglind as he ran. Yglind's bubble burst in a shower of blue and golden sparks, but he kept running toward the knight, who stepped forward, swinging their sword in a theatrically wide arc and bracing for impact. Ardo took advantage of the multiple distractions to move around the other side of the bubble and run in a low crouch toward the mage, who was heaving for breath even as he raised his arms for another spell. A ball of blue light surrounded his hands, and he swiveled toward Ardo with darkening eyes and a wicked smile.

24

━ ● ━

Aene flipped through the symbols above her gauntlet in a panic, still jittery from the lightning. *Too slow, too slow,* she thought, then the mage staggered, the glow in his hands dimming as he slumped to one knee, a crossbow bolt jutting out of his back. He glared toward a dark corner, where Laanda and Skiti must have emerged, then his hands whipped around toward Ardo, who was now running at full speed toward him, and the blue glow built up again until it was so bright, Aene had to look away.

Aene's head shook as she clenched her teeth and reached deep into the chip, draining it until the brightstone cracked, and directed its power with all her strength toward the mage. A loud *pop* sounded, followed by an explosion of sparks and smoke, and two more blue bolts shot out of the commotion and slammed harmlessly into the ceiling above. Aene collapsed with the effort, holding herself up on hands and knees to see Ardo sprint into the sparking cloud, whipping his staff sideways. The hollow crunch of metal on bone rang out, followed by a pained scream that did not sound like Ardo.

The clang of crashing blades drew her attention, and she turned to see Yglind and the knight standing with swords crossed, Yglind leaning forward as the knight braced themself, then pushed off and leapt back, swinging their sword around in a flourish. Yglind held his sword at a strange angle, circling his opponent, then they fell on each other in a blur of flashing metal, rough grunts, and ear-splitting clangs.

A *boom* sounded from the cloud of sparks surrounding the mage, and Ardo's body catapulted through the air and bounced on the stone floor, his staff clattering away from his motionless body and rolling to a stop. The cloud dissipated, revealing the mage heaving for breath, clutching his arm, his face wrenched with pain and fury. He yelled something in his language, then turned just as Laanda barreled toward him, axe held high and swinging down for his head. He spread his fingers wide, and a glowing force like thick green glass appeared just in time for Laanda to crash into it and roll to the side, her axe clanging on the floor. The mage swept his hands slowly sideways, and the pane stretched around him, continuing as he turned in a circle until he was surrounded by a cylinder of glassy force ten feet in diameter, reaching up to the ceiling twenty feet above.

Aene sat back on her heels, looking over to Ardo, who had pushed up onto his forearms and was shaking his head. Her fingers felt thick and clumsy, and she fumbled to remove the spent chip and insert a new one as she heard Yglind roar in pain. She turned to see him stagger back, blood dripping from a cut on his forearm where his armor had been sliced open like a quince rind. The knight pressed their advantage, darting forward with a flurry of quick strokes, which Yglind parried as he moved backward. Aene didn't know much about swordplay, but she knew enough to tell he was getting his ass kicked.

She took a few steady breaths and turned to watch the mage as he pulled a taper from his robe and lit it by touching it with his finger. Aene's eyes flitted to Laanda, who was being helped to her feet by Skiti. The mage waved the flaming taper in a large circle, once, twice, three times, until the air in the patterns he had traced seemed to flame of its own accord, growing larger as he held his taper high. He chanted, his arms raised wide, and the space in the center of the circle of fire turned pure black, darker than the shadows of the room. She couldn't hear what he was chanting through the force wall, and the din of clashing blades was like a mashtorul hurling pots and pans around a kitchen. A quick glance at Yglind and the knight showed Yglind had regained his footing, and the knight stumbled as Yglind landed a glancing blow to their helmet.

Aene took another deep breath, then flicked through the spells stored in her gauntlet. To try and take down the force wall, she'd need to be touching it, which was risky, so she pulled up the Web Net and turned toward the knight in case things took a turn for the worse. She knew Yglind would never forgive her if she interfered with his sacred combat, but she would never forgive herself if something happened to him on her watch, nor would the High Council. Ardo had gotten to his hands and knees and recovered his staff. He used it to push himself to standing, then limped over toward Aene. They watched as Yglind and the knight swung, blocked, and parried more and more slowly, both heaving for breath. Laanda stood watching as well, gripping her axe in obvious frustration. Skiti fiddled with her Omni, then pressed it against the barrier. It glowed bright blue at the point of contact, and the mage turned away from the circle of fire, which was now taller than he was, and stalked over to face her, his fingers spreading into wide claws.

The mage touched the barrier, and a chunk of it shattered into dust. Before Laanda or Skiti could react, he shoved his hands forward, and the two of them hurtled backward as if they had been knocked over by a powerful ocean wave. He shouted some words, and Aene turned to see a hooded figure emerge from the shadows behind Yglind, a bandana covering their mouth and nose, and hurl a tiny red ball against Yglind's helmet. The ball burst in an explosion of powder, and Yglind staggered back, coughing. He stood still for a moment, swaying slightly, then crumpled to the ground as if boneless. The clang of his helmet on the floor made Aene's stomach lurch. She stood up, studied the distance for a moment, and launched the glowing ball of the Web Net. The masked figure was backing away from Yglind, staring down as if in horror at his motionless body. They turned at the last second, and Aene saw a flash of green eyes beneath the hood.

Feddar ducked, but the Web Net had already spread too far for him to avoid, and it snapped tight around him, the bright golden strands pressing his limbs to his body. He fell awkwardly onto the hard stone floor, but Aene did not hear the telltale *clunk* she was wincing and waiting for. His hood had fallen back as he fell, and Aene could see the collar was still attached. The knight stared down at Yglind, then at Feddar, whom they picked up and slung over their shoulder, Web Net and all. Their gaze fell on Aene for a moment, and she felt exposed, as if the knight sensed how pathetic she was and almost felt pity. They turned and ran toward an opening that had appeared in the barrier, which then closed behind them. Feddar's weight hardly seemed to slow the knight as they followed the mage and disappeared into the blackness at the center of the circle of fire. The fire went out in a puff of smoke, and the silence left in the absence of their footfalls was eerily complete.

Aene spun as Ardo sped over to Yglind, moving quickly despite his hobble, stripped off Yglind's helmet, and laid his ear on Yglind's chest. His eyes closed for a moment, then a smile emerged, disappearing as his eyes opened and blinked reassuringly. Aene hurried over to where Skiti and Laanda lay, both moving their limbs a little but making no move to get up. Aene crouched by Skiti and took her hand.

"Not again," Skiti mumbled, grasping Aene's hand and letting herself be pulled up to sitting. She stared at the darkness where the barrier and the flaming circle had been, but nothing remained other than a few wisps of fading smoke and the smell of scorched eggs. Laanda sat up, shaking her head as if to clear it and looking up at Aene with bleary eyes.

"They got away," she half-whispered, still staring at the place the humans had disappeared into.

"Most importantly, no one died." Aene shuffled over near Laanda, who pulled her helmet off and showed a face wracked with pain. Laanda looked down at her foot, moved it a little, and let out a sharp cry.

"It's not broken," she hissed through clenched teeth. "I don't think. But no way I'll be able to put weight on it."

"Let me help you get that boot off, and I'll see if there's anything I can do," Aene said. Laanda nodded, and Aene began unlacing and unbuckling the boot, which seemed made to fit snugly, but with Laanda's ankle already swelling, it was almost impossibly tight. She managed to undo the laces and shimmy the boot off, though Laanda's pained breath and whining groans had Aene sick to her stomach. When she finally got it all the way off, Laanda let out a huge sigh.

"Soma, my queen?" Skiti offered a lozenge, which Laanda took and tucked into her mouth without hesitation, smiling and chucking Skiti on the cheek with her gauntlet.

"How'd you make out?" Laanda asked Skiti, seeming to forget Aene was even there, which made her job easier. She pulled up the Healing spell and channeled it into her fingertips, which she moved lightly over the skin until she could feel the contours of the torn and twisted tendons. She could almost see them with her fingers, as if they glowed brightly in a spectrum of light only accessible to touch. The spell flowed through her into every muscle and ligament. Tears began to smooth, knots untangled, overstretched bands retracted and recovered their elasticity. The power flickered for an instant, indicating the chip was at half power, and she pulled back, letting the spell flow back up through her and pool in the gauntlet.

"Wow, it feels...almost like it never happened!" Laanda rotated her ankle, then pressed it into the floor, tentatively at first, then firmly, pushing herself up to standing, still favoring the leg, but not by much. She put her hands on Aene's shoulders and looked up at her, eyes deep and warm. "Thank you."

"The gauntlet did most of the work. I—"

"Nonsense." Skiti waved her off with an exaggerated gesture as she stood up with Laanda's help. "I know enough about magic to know the skill it takes to use even the most advanced magical tech. You are phenomenal."

Aene blinked and turned her eyes down for a moment, and they fell on Skiti's Omni.

"I must admit, I never imagined your metal magic—I mean, mastery—could yield such a wide array of results. And that Omni is truly a marvel to behold."

"Well, it took a team of artificers years to build it, so I can't really—"

"He's awake!" Ardo called, his voice high and excited. All eyes turned toward Yglind, who was rubbing his eyes and smacking his lips. "You're awake," Ardo said in a low voice, holding Yglind's face in his hands.

"What in the gods' shit happened?" Yglind croaked, taking Ardo's wrists and pulling himself halfway up to sitting, then falling back hard on the ground. "I feel like I took a pouch of soma and washed it down with a bottle of mushroom wine."

"Knockout powder," Aene said, crouching by Yglind. She did not mention that it was Feddar who'd thrown it. She still hadn't wrapped her mind around that. Was he truly on the side of the humans, or had he known the knight wouldn't attack Yglind if he was incapacitated and done it to end the combat without any death? "I can try to clear your mind a bit if you want."

"That would not be unwelcome." Yglind shielded his eyes, and Aene pulled up the Alertness spell, which she had left on the gauntlet from her last exam period and could never bring herself to remove, despite its taking up a precious slot. She drew a little of the power into her own mind, which grew sharp and focused, then poured most of it through her fingertips into Yglind's temples. He let out a groan of relief and removed his hand from his eyes, which looked clearer now. He sat up with Ardo's help, then took the waterskin Ardo offered him and drained half of it in a set of long gulps.

"Let me guess: the fucking humans escaped," he said wearily, looking around the room.

"I think I broke the mage's arm, if that helps," Ardo said.

Yglind grinned and whacked Ardo on the shoulder. Ardo winced in pain; he'd taken quite the tumble, and Aene hadn't had a chance to look after his wounds.

"It really fucking does," Yglind said as he pulled himself to standing, using Ardo for leverage. "Now we just have to figure out where the fuck they went, track them down, and finish the job."

25

Yglind gnawed on one of the sporecakes, which had not gotten any tastier or easier to chew since the last time he'd tried one, but it did the job well enough. Laanda was standing with her face in one of the whisper cones while Skiti stood nearby, fiddling with her Omni. Aene had closed the wound on Yglind's arm and touched up some nasty bruises on Ardo's back and shoulders, and everyone seemed in shape to move. Yglind's palm itched whenever it wasn't touching the pommel of his sword, especially when they were standing around. Laanda turned back toward Skiti and exchanged a few words in their language, then they both rejoined the group with long faces.

"They're not answering my whispers," Laanda said in a grave voice. "They're short-handed, so it could just mean they're taking care of business, but the whisper room is on the critical list, so things would have to be pretty bad for them to leave it unattended."

"Unless the humans have found a way to disrupt the system," Skiti said, drumming the tips of her fingers together. "If they figured out where the main tube is, they could destroy it, just like they did half the whisper cones, and the keep would be cut off."

"Do you really think they're clever enough to do that?" Laanda shook her head.

"The fucking humans are wily as weasels," Yglind growled, almost feeling a grudging respect for them. "They figured out how to get in through your exhaust vent."

"If they wrecked the whisper tube, it's going to be absolute hell to fix," Skiti grumbled. "Between that and the Magni, the chimney, and the giant fucking holes they've blown everywhere, not to mention the exhaust vent, it's almost like they're doing everything in their power to make sure this mine won't be operational for a long time." Her voice fell as she finished.

Yglind's stomach churned as he thought about the havoc this would wreak with the war effort. The automatons, great and small, relied on brightstone, as did the gauntlets and the circlets, and the Maer were already desperately short on supply. They'd been digging test mines all over the Silver Hills, hoping to find additional pockets, but only the Timon seemed to have the knack for finding it. He felt Laanda's probing eyes on him, and he wished he were wearing his helmet to deflect her gaze.

"This is all because of *your* war," she said in a voice like an anvil.

Yglind's ears burned with the accusation, but he couldn't deny it.

"No one expected things to begin so soon, and certainly not like this, but you are right. There's no other explanation." He looked down as Laanda's eyes burned into his. "But there's one thing that still puzzles me. They break into the mine and cause all kinds of damage, then they kind of disappear for a while, only to reappear, cause more havoc, and vanish again." He found his voice rising, and he lowered it. "We haven't been able to stop them, so if they were after the brightstone, wouldn't they have just gotten it by now?"

Laanda shook her head, her jaw tense, but her voice was even. "The brightstone pits are the most secure location in the mine. More secure than the keep, even. The only way in is a pair of hardsteel doors with enough enchantments on them to stymy a Grand Wizard. This human mage may be powerful, but I don't see them getting through those doors."

"Feddar said they were here to disrupt operations, but he didn't mention the brightstone," Aene said quietly, twisting the braids in her beard. "Humans don't seem to use it."

"But they know we need it," Yglind growled. "They're trying to choke our supply here and at the other mines as much as possible for as long as they can."

"Other mines?" Laanda said, her voice taking on a melancholy tone.

Yglind closed his eyes for a moment as he realized what that meant to the Timon.

"The last reports we got from the Stream before we lost connection said at least four other mines had gone dark on the same day."

"Timon mines?"

Yglind nodded. "I'm sorry."

"War with the humans is closer than we thought," Ardo said in a low voice.

"War with the humans has already begun. Can't you see that?" Laanda's voice rose to a shout, and she turned away, clenching her axe with shaking arms. When she turned around, her face was hard and dark. Yglind's palm itched, and he rubbed it over his pommel, then drew the sword, feeling its power surge through him.

"If it's war they want, then war they'll get!" he shouted.

"The patient general is the victorious one, Egg." Aene stepped to him, touching him on the arm and fixing him with hard, bright eyes. "Now more than ever, we need to keep one of them alive, to take back to the High Council and find out exactly what the humans are planning."

Yglind bared his teeth at Aene, who did not flinch. Whatever twisted obsession she had with the human thief, she also had a point.

"When we catch up to them, find a way to take out the fucking mage. And you," he said, pointing at Skiti, "trap the thief with your Omni if you can. If you approve, of course." He inclined his head toward Laanda, who nodded, her face stony and cold.

"Agreed. The thief lives if we can manage it. The others die."

They made their way slowly back toward the keep, keeping to the same routine, with Skiti scouting in front and the rest of them following with just enough light from the amulets to see. It was slow, tedious movement, and Yglind's teeth ached with fatigue as he struggled to maintain his focus, scanning the darkness, listening for anything amiss. Skiti stopped at a storeroom by one of the smaller shafts, and they took a moment to refill their waterskins and stash a few more sporecakes in their pockets and their mouths. Yglind had hoped perhaps ones straight out of the tin would be somehow fresher, but they had exactly the same pasty texture and bitter aftertaste. It was starting to get to him.

Laanda cleared her throat. "I'm going to try the whisper cone, so be quiet for a minute." Everyone froze all at once, and Yglind stopped mid-chew. Laanda put her face to the cone and started whispering, then turned her ear, smiling and nodding as a faint hissing emerged from the cone. She went back and forth a few times with whoever was on the other end, then straightened up, eyeing Skiti for a moment before turning to Yglind and his companions.

"The humans' signal appeared in the lower tunnel, and they're now at the gate to the brightstone pits." Her voice was grave but with confidence beneath it. "I seriously doubt they'll find a way through it. But if they do…" She clenched her fist. "We must hurry down right away."

"That's going to be quite a climb in our condition," Skiti said quietly. "Not that we can't, it's just—"

"Find the strength," Laanda said, hefting her axe and moving toward the door. Skiti took a long drink from her waterskin, then secured it on her belt.

"Let's do this." She nodded to Laanda, who followed her out the door without a backward look.

Yglind took a deep breath and joined them, and soon Skiti began climbing down the nearest shaft and Laanda a minute later. He started a mental count, trying to relax his breathing. The stress of recent events, plus the lack of proper sleep, had his breath edgy and shallow. Ardo stood staring at the shaft opening, a distant look in his eyes, probably doing one of his little meditations. Aene squatted down, whipped out her dice, and moved them in three quick circles before dropping them unceremoniously on the stone.

"Do you really think now's the time?" Yglind snarled, struggling to retain his count, which was nearing its end.

"This is for me, not us," she said, moving her hand in a circle over the dice, then snatching them up and dropping them back in her pouch.

Yglind's time was up.

"What did they say?"

Aene cocked her head and looked down, then back up, her eyes glistening in the low light of the amulet.

"I think it's going to be okay in the end."

"Your lips to the gods' ears," Yglind said as he lowered himself down into the shaft, winking at Ardo, whose eyes looked suddenly sad.

Yglind climbed down as quickly as he could, but he sensed the distance between himself and Laanda growing. It was infuriating how fast they could climb, being so much shorter than he. He looked up to see Ardo lowering himself into the shaft, his glowing amulet casting swinging shadows as it dangled. Yglind didn't love the idea of Aene being up there alone, but it was what they had decided, and she could take care of herself as long as—

The dragon's roar was so loud that Yglind felt the vibration in the ladder's rails. He looked up, sure it was coming from above, and saw Ardo's form dark against a blinding light.

"Not this fucking time!" he heard Aene scream, and the light burst even brighter, forcing Yglind's eyes shut. Even closed, he saw glowing yellow blobs, felt his eyes burning, and when he opened them again, the edges of his vision were filled with it. Only in the center of his vision, where Ardo's body had blocked the light, could he see anything. The dragon screeched, and Yglind heard a crackling sound, followed by a higher-pitched screech of pain and rage.

"Get a move on," Aene shouted, and Yglind heard her clamber into the shaft. He moved down as quickly as he could, though it was difficult with his blurred vision.

"I can't see," Ardo cried.

"Feel your fucking way down, godsdammit!" Aene screamed. "It's—" The end of her sentence was swallowed by a roar that echoed inside Yglind's helmet, which he banged against the ladder involuntarily. He almost lost his grip on the rung as one hand moved instinctively to cover his ears. A cacophony of ringing, shouting, and scrabbling erupted, and he gritted his teeth against the pain and moved down one rung, then another. Another roar sounded, erasing all other sounds and pitching him into a world of pain and confusion. He stopped, holding tight onto the ladder, hoping the ringing would clear, that the growing yellow blobs in his vision would dissipate, but all was noise and light and darkness, then a great weight came crashing down on him. His hands lost their grip, and he fell back against the opposite wall of the shaft, crushing the air out of his lungs. He nearly blacked out with the shock of supporting another Maer's weight with only one foot braced on the ladder and his back smashed against the wall.

He smelled Ardo's breath, heard his muffled voice, and the weight slowly lifted, but Yglind was wedged in the shaft, and his back sang with pain when he tried to reach out for the rungs again. He groaned, though he could barely hear even his own voice, and a hand grasped his, pulling him up as his back exploded in agony. He screamed but held on, and his other hand soon found a grip on the ladder. The pain in his back steadied a little once he was upright again.

"...keep moving," came Ardo's voice, as if through a closed door. Yglind straightened up, his back still on fire, and slid his foot down to find the next rung. The dragon's roar sounded again, but it too was muffled, and he steadied himself enough to move down a few more rungs. He looked up past Ardo, and in the sliver of his vision that remained, he saw Aene's slight shadow against the light of a golden grid above. A distant clattering sound filtered through, and the grid bent but did not break. After another burst of clattering, which might have been rock bouncing off steel or stone, the dragon's roar sounded one more time, then stopped, leaving only the ringing of a thousand distant bells to fill the silence.

Yglind's vision slowly returned, and the sound of feet on ladders began filtering in.

"I think it's gone." Aene's voice mixed fear and optimism. "That's the last time I get stuck on solo watch."

"It's a good thing it was you instead of me," Ardo said. "He'd have eaten me for breakfast. Hey! I can see a little!" He waved his hand in front of his face, smiling down at Yglind.

"Sorry about that," Aene said, stopping a few rungs above. "I had been keeping that flash on the tip of my mind just in case. I'm glad it worked."

"You don't have to shout," Laanda hissed from just below Yglind. "Are you trying to broadcast our exact location to the humans?"

"I would think the dragon's roar might have tipped them off," Yglind whispered. "Sorry, that roar kind of deafened me."

"I can imagine," Laanda said softly. "It was bad enough farther down. Is everyone okay?"

"I held him off," Aene said in between deep breaths like she often used to cool down after a big magic expenditure. "Gonna need to put a new chip in once we get down, though."

"Skiti's at the lower exit. Says the coast is clear. If you're ready, we should get moving."

Yglind's breath grew shallow as the pain in his back sent icy shivers through his head, but once he'd descended a few rungs, the pain subsided to a burning ache. By the time he reached the bottom, the ringing in his ears had grown faint, and his vision was normal, though he knew from experience his back was going to be stiff as hell for the next couple of days. Skiti gave him a quick nod, then exchanged a few words with Laanda, who nodded and replied, turning to Yglind as Ardo descended.

"We go about an hour down this passage, then take another shaft down, which lets out near the brightstone gate. If the humans are there, it's not going to be the best place for a fight. The tunnel is narrow, only wide enough for one, so we'll want to think hard about how to approach this."

"How far from the bottom of the shaft is the gate?"

"Maybe two hundred yards. Whoever's in front is going to get a faceful of whatever the mage wants to throw at them."

"I got you covered," Aene said, slumping against the ladder and heaving for breath. "Let me swap out this chip, and I'll ready a shield that should be able to take a shot or two." She popped out the old chip, dropped it in a pocket, then fished around for another, frowning as she looked down.

"One more left after this one." She slid it into the slot and closed the cover, and the gauntlet lit up, golden lines running the length of her fingers. "And to think I had to beg them to send me with this many."

"I'll go behind you, with Skiti at my back," Laanda said, her eyes darting to Yglind as he opened his mouth to complain. "This is our mine. No discussion. You can back me up, and Ardo will bring up the rear."

Yglind clenched his teeth and blinked. He hoped Laanda wouldn't take away one of his kills, but she was the queen, and they were her guests. "As you wish, my...Laanda."

"Ardo, be on the lookout. They'll know we're coming and may have some tricks up their sleeve."

26

━ • ━

Skiti ran her fingers over the Omni's controls as she walked behind Laanda and Aene down the narrow tunnel. The light from Aene's amulet was making it impossible to see more than twenty feet ahead, but memory told her they were getting close.

"Are you sure you don't want me to scout ahead?" she whispered.

Laanda shook her head once. "Not until we get closer. You won't evade their notice, not in this environment, and that mage will light you up before you have a chance to raise your Omni." Skiti's heart warmed at Laanda's protective instinct, but she wasn't sure if Aene had the stealth needed.

"Well, I can't see a damned thing with that amulet in my way."

"The Maer can't see a damned thing without it. Nor the humans either, it would seem. Maybe we can use that to our advantage somehow."

They continued in silence, Skiti mulling over the possibilities, but she couldn't think of anything they could do. Even if they destroyed the humans' light source, the mage could produce light from his fingertips as long as he was upright. When they approached the final turn, Laanda whispered to Aene to stop and extinguish her amulet, which she did, along with the other Maer. It took a few moments before Skiti's dark vision kicked in, but it showed her nothing except the contours of the tunnel ahead and no tinge of light or heat from the corner.

"Go ahead just to the turn and have a quick look," Laanda hissed, scouring the darkness ahead.

"I don't see any light from here," Skiti whispered, and Laanda shook her head. Skiti pictured the shield shape she'd prepared back in the castle, though she had no idea if it would stop the mage's lightning. It might even conduct it, channeling it all through her hands to fry her from the inside. She focused instead on the dome, which was a bit trickier to pull off, but she'd managed against the hulmar. If she could get it up in time, it might disperse the charge without her being in contact with it. Assuming she was faster than the mage.

She approached the corner on soft feet, listening intently for any noise, but the mine's silence was absolute. She eased her head around the corner, and though she couldn't make out a lot of detail, she could see the gate, which appeared intact. There were no heat signatures nearby, not even residual ones. She whispered the safe signal, and moments later, Aene's amulet glowed back up, and the group approached, not as silently as Skiti might have liked.

"It looks like they're gone," she said once they reached her.

"I can't decide if I'm glad or mad about that." Laanda lifted her faceplate for a moment to scratch her beard. "Let's proceed cautiously at any rate."

As they approached the gate, the smell of charred metal reached them. Skiti held up her hand for them to stop, then turned on her Omni's light and moved toward the great steel doors. The area around the lock was blackened in a rough circle, but the gate and lock appeared intact. Whatever magic the humans had used hadn't been nearly hot enough to damage the glamored steel, and there was no evidence of openings in the rock nearby, which had multiple layers of hardsteel webbing laced throughout.

She studied the area with her light, making sure there were no unwanted surprises, then moved to touch the gate, which was cool, as she'd known it would be. She waved the others forward.

"The brightstone is safe at least," Laanda sighed. "They must have gone east to the number two shaft. I wonder where they'd go from there."

"If they can't reach the brightstone, they'll try to get back into the keep, see what other damage they could cause," Yglind said. Laanda scowled at him, and he raised his hands. "That's what I would do."

"You're probably right. I should warn them." She flashed Skiti a concerned look as she moved to the whisper cone beside the gate and hissed her message. The only response was silence. She hissed again and again. Nothing.

Laanda closed her eyes, and Skiti could see her fatigue in the way her eyelids twitched. When she opened them again, they were red and watery but shone with a fierceness that stirred Skiti's heart. Laanda was so often occupied with the minutia of running the mine and the keep that she seldom showed such pure emotion. Her deadly determination was contagious, and Skiti's mind hardened at the thought of the task ahead.

Laanda flipped down her visor and started marching without a word. Skiti scrambled to catch up, and the Maer hurried behind them.

"It's a good hour at least back to the castle, including a long climb," Laanda called over her shoulder, apparently no longer concerned with stealth or secrecy. Yglind kept so close that Skiti was worried he would stumble over her. She could hear his eagerness in the sound of his breath inside the helmet and his long, awkward strides, as he had to crouch slightly in the low tunnel.

When they reached the shaft, Laanda immediately clambered up without speaking or waiting for anyone. Skiti followed her more closely than usual, given Laanda's evident hurry and the dragon's unknown whereabouts. If the creature was waiting for them at the top of the shaft, Skiti wanted to be nearby to give Laanda some cover with her Omni.

When she reached the top, Laanda finally stopped to catch her breath and suck down most of her waterskin. Skiti did the same. They would be at the keep gate in half an hour, and they would need every ounce of endurance they could muster if the humans were about. Once the Maer had emerged and breathed for a minute, Laanda picked herself up from the wall where she had been leaning and hefted her axe.

"At this point, anything goes," she said, turning toward the Maer. "I know you want the thief for your High Council, but after what happened in the copper gallery, one false move and I'm taking him down. I expect you to do the same."

"Hopefully that won't be necessary," Aene said firmly. "I can subdue him with a simple spell from my gauntlet."

"If you can see him, and if the mage isn't busy frying your eggs." Laanda pointed with the head of her axe, which Aene stared at thoughtfully for a moment. Skiti hoped this thief situation didn't drive them apart. "Remember what happened last time."

"How could I forget," Aene said with a sigh.

When they finally approached the keep gate, Laanda sent Skiti ahead to scout it out. There were no heat signatures outside, but the area around the gate was a little warmer than the surrounding stone. And there was something strange about the gate itself, which Skiti couldn't make out until she was a little nearer. As she got close enough to see it more clearly, she saw that the gate was wide open, and several lifeless forms were sprawled across the gatehouse floor. Skiti tapped her Omni for light and saw the corpses belonging to three Guard, two of whose armor didn't fit quite right, as if it had been made for someone else. Skiti stuck her head out the door and hissed Laanda over.

"Good gods," Laanda gasped in Timon, kneeling by one of the bodies and removing her helmet. "It's Feyer. She only completed her training last month."

"How the fuck did they get in?" Skiti muttered in Maer.

"It doesn't look like they forced their way in," Aene said, studying the door. "Either they opened the door with magical means, or someone opened it for them."

"If the thief had a device that could freeze us in time, it's no stretch to imagine them being able to open a door," Yglind grunted.

Skiti felt the blood rush to her face, and she stepped right into Yglind's space, almost touching him, though her head only came up to his breastplate.

"This is not just a door!" Skiti felt her voice rising in anger, then lowered it to a hiss. "The keep gate cannot be opened except from the inside. It is physically impossible, no matter how much magic—" Her throat hitched, and she spun away, covering her face in her hands as a sob surged out of nowhere. Seeing Laanda close the Guards' eyes with her fingers triggered the waterworks, and Skiti cried like she hadn't done since she'd lost her mother. Laanda looked up with burning red eyes, then stood and pulled Skiti in for a hug against her armor.

The Maer remained silent, giving them space as they clung to each other until the spikes on Laanda's breastplate started digging into Skiti's shoulder, and she pulled back.

"We need to figure out if they're still inside the keep, and if so, what the hell they're doing," Skiti said.

"We need to look for…" Laanda paused, closing her eyes for a moment. "We need to protect whoever's still here."

Skiti glanced at the whisper cone, then at Laanda, who shook her head.

"If they're still inside, they could be monitoring the whisper network."

"They could be watching us any time," Aene said, squinting toward the raised portcullis leading out of the gatehouse. "Keep an eye out for those little glass balls."

"I don't know where they are, but I can tell you where they went," Yglind said, crouching by the open portcullis. He pointed at three sets of large bloody footprints leading out of the gatehouse and into the keep.

27

Ardo followed the group through the arched doorway into a series of hallways, but the footprints petered out after the second turn. Skiti quietly opened a door and stood staring into the darkness without moving for a long moment, then closed the door again with gentle finality. She eyed Laanda, shaking her head, and continued soft-stepping down the passage. She checked two more doors and gave similar reactions, though after the third one, she looked like she was going to be ill. Laanda moved to the door, heedless of Skiti's pleading look, and flipped up her visor. Ardo couldn't see her expression, but the way she stood in the doorway made him want to cry. She flipped her visor back down before closing the door and turning back to the group.

"Not all are accounted for. I think some of the Guard might have gone to protect the civilians."

"They'd be in the safe rooms if they followed protocol," Skiti said.

"They would. They did." Laanda said in a voice like she was trying to convince herself. "It's two levels down," she added, turning toward Ardo's group. "We'll take the ventilator shaft." She eyed Yglind, and a faint clucking sound echoed out of her helmet. "I hope you'll fit."

The entrance to the shaft was behind a hidden door, indistinguishable from the gray stone of the walls. Skiti opened it by forming the tip of her Omni into a key. She peered up and down the shaft, then nodded to Laanda and lowered herself in. The shaft was half the width of those in the mine, and it was a snug fit, even for her. Laanda gestured Yglind forward.

"If you're going to have trouble fitting, we best know about it right away."

Ardo heard Yglind's huffy breath as he turned around and backed into the tube, his armor scraping against the metal edges. After some maneuvering, he managed to lower himself down onto the ladder, and his helmet soon disappeared into the darkness.

"You two follow close now." Laanda slipped into the tube with practiced ease and was soon out of sight. Ardo and Aene stood looking at each other, then Aene threw up her hands, crouched, and turned around to slip into the narrow shaft.

"I almost got eaten by that dragon last time. It's your turn to be fucking bait." She winked at him, then moved down and out of sight.

Ardo waited a moment since he figured Yglind was probably moving slowly, but then he heard a strange noise coming from somewhere down the hallway. He squeezed himself into the shaft and gently pulled the door closed behind him. It sealed tight with a metallic click.

Down, down they went into the darkness, the glow from their amulets providing a dim yellow light. Yglind's armor scraped against the metal walls the whole way, so there was little chance of stealth if the humans were paying any attention whatsoever. Ardo wasn't wearing metal armor, and he was nowhere near as wide as Yglind, but even he found it a tight fit and was relieved when he saw light appear from below and realized they had arrived at the next level down and not been immediately attacked. He clambered down as quietly as he could and exited another door like the one above, contoured to resemble the passage walls. Laanda gestured everyone close in and only spoke when their heads were almost touching.

"Skiti is going to check on the safe rooms," she whispered, and Skiti nodded. "We think the remaining Guard will have helped everyone hole up in there. They're big enough to hold the entire population of the keep in an emergency for up to a week, though I imagine it's none too comfortable."

"Maybe they'll be able to tell us something about where the fucking humans are," Yglind hissed.

"That's my hope. We'll go to the next intersection, so if they come from one way or another, we'll see them." She fingered her axe blade, looking up at them through her open visor. "Something tells me they're going to hunker down somewhere and wait for us. I just don't know where."

"My money's on the temple," Skiti said, eyeing Yglind. "I've noticed how you Maer hate the low ceilings, and they're about your height. The temple has the highest ceilings in the whole keep."

"Plus, it's got a wide-open space around the altar," Laanda added, "so there's no way to sneak up on them. Go check in with the safe rooms, and I'll think on how we want to approach this."

Skiti touched Laanda's arm with a gesture Ardo was pretty sure was more than friendship. It was like the way he touched Yglind before a dangerous situation or when they would be separated for a time.

Skiti blinked at the rest of them and padded down the hall, making no noise as she disappeared into the shadows. Laanda gestured them forward, and they walked a couple of hundred feet until they came to an intersection. They walked just past it, and then Laanda stopped, turning to look in both directions.

"We stay here and keep quiet," she said. "Skiti will be back soon, so if you want to catch a breather, now's the time."

Ardo felt Yglind's hand on his shoulder and leaned back into him. Yglind's arms wrapped around him, and Ardo felt Yglind's breath on his ear. Though the helmet and armor prevented them from truly touching,

Ardo felt safe in Yglind's embrace, and he closed his eyes for a moment as they breathed together.

He knew once they got close again, Yglind's sword would take over, and he would become entirely focused on killing the humans. He dreaded seeing Yglind like that again. He enjoyed watching Yglind fight when it was just for sport, but things had gotten personal with the humans, and they would not leave this mine without blood being spilled. He put his hands around Yglind's arm, though he could not feel the warmth beneath the mail and padding, and Yglind squeezed him tighter in response.

Skiti appeared out of nowhere and moved to Laanda, grasping forearms with her.

"A dozen Guard and just over half of the civilians are in the safe rooms."

"So few?" Laanda's voice was weak.

"There may be more. They didn't know. It seems one of the humans...just appeared out of thin air and let the others in."

"The fucking thief," Yglind snarled. Ardo glanced at Aene, who tensed but remained silent.

"I think it may have been like that portal they went through," Skiti said. "Some kind of teleportation spell. I don't know how the thief got past the Guard in the gatehouse to open the gate, but they think that's what happened. Once the humans got in, it seems the remaining Guard held them off for a time while the rest herded as many civilians as they could find into the safe rooms. The others may be hiding in the shroomery, but they didn't know."

"We should go there first to find out," Laanda said, and Skiti nodded. "If they're there, maybe they can tell us where the humans went. If not, we'll head for the temple."

They walked down a series of corridors to a spiral staircase cut into the rock. A pair of metal doors with a wheeled lever was set in the wall next to the stairs.

"Normally, we'd use the elevator, but..." Skiti shrugged, then turned and disappeared down the stairs. They waited for a little while, then she must have summoned them with a whisper Ardo couldn't hear. Laanda nodded, then crept down the stairs, with Yglind and Aene close on her heels and Ardo bringing up the rear as he had before. The staircase was narrow enough that Yglind had to move sideways, and Aene flashed Ardo a wicked little grin when Yglind got stuck for a moment.

His heart pinged at the almost childish glee in her eyes. Had something changed between them? He touched his chest, wondering if what he felt was just the tension of the moment or if it could be something more. He still loved Yglind—more than ever—but did that mean he couldn't develop feelings for someone else too? Laanda's loud hiss signaled a stop and Ardo stood, rolling his staff back and forth across his fingers. He heard whispers, too distant to comprehend, then Aene spoke in a low voice:

"Be ready to move in five."

When the signal came, Ardo and Aene exchanged a glance, then he followed her down into the ever-retreating shadows cast by their amulets. After a dizzying number of turns, they emerged into a cavernous space, much wider than it was high, filled with scores if not hundreds of low stone platforms. Tiny brightstone lights streamed from devices suspended above each bed, laying a ghostly glow over some of the most luscious fungal displays Ardo had ever seen. There were numerous beds crowded with the fuzzy white globes of silver spores so prized by the Maer and, apparently, by the Timon as well. There were rockear and honeycomb fungus, too, along with some other varieties he'd never seen before.

Aene's hiss pulled him forward, and he hurried to catch up. The whole group was jogging now, crouched down. They ran a zigzag path through the maze of fungus beds along the edge of an area filled with heaps of dirt, mulch, and logs. Aene disappeared around the edge of a particularly large pile of wood, and Ardo followed, pulling up short as he saw the others face to face with two armed Guard standing with shoulders squared and axes in hand.

Laanda hissed something in Timon, and the Guard relaxed, but only a little. One gestured them to follow, and they turned and walked between two more piles to a hefty-looking steel door.

"We must input the code," one of the Guard said, flipping up a panel and struggling to remove their gauntlet.

Laanda gestured Skiti forward, and Skiti inserted her Omni into the lock. The door popped open, revealing two rather surprised-looking Guard and several dozen civilians armed with what looked like farming tools. They knelt at the sight of her.

"Enough of that," Laanda said, removing her helmet. "This is war. Tell me what you know."

28

Aene sat cross-legged on the floor, half listening to Laanda talk strategy with Yglind and the Guard. Ardo hovered behind Yglind, then turned around as Aene pulled out her scrying dice and started shaking them gently so they clicked rather than clacked together. She raised her eyebrows at him, and he glanced back at Yglind, then walked over and squatted across from her.

"Gonna give it one more try, are you?" Ardo murmured, his eyes soft with fatigue. They hadn't slept in...she couldn't remember how long, and that didn't look to change any time soon. Aene's eyeballs ached, and she considered giving herself a boost with the gauntlet until she remembered she only had a chip and a half left.

"I figure it's now or never," she replied, and Ardo's eyes crinkled with his smile. He settled down all the way and crossed his arms over his knees in what might have been an imitation of the meditation poses of Cloti's acolytes. She had tried a few of Cloti's cycles after seeing them on the Stream, and she'd found them helpful in centering herself, but she'd been too nervous about her views being tracked, so she hadn't kept up with it. As she warmed up the dice by moving them in slow circles, she could have sworn she felt Ardo's positive energy in the way the dice moved in her cupped hands.

When she dropped them, her vision went black as images flashed in her mind. Lightning arcing across open space. Blood flying. Laanda's axe slipping out of her hand as she fell, light as a feather. Skiti falling to her knees, crouched over Laanda's motionless body. Aene's hand on Feddar's hairless cheek. His green eyes, darkened by shadow, gazing up at her as she moved atop him. Energy pulsed through her, coiling in her loins, her fingertips, and her head until the darkness faded, leaving her gasping and clutching Ardo's fingers.

Ardo's eyes met hers, and she gripped his hands tightly as her breath steadied. Ardo did not speak, but his eyes had a somber depth to them as if he had sensed something of what she had felt.

"Are we going to make it?" he whispered.

"I think so." Aene glanced over at Laanda and at Skiti, who looked away from Laanda and Yglind to blink softly at her.

"And what about the thief with the pretty eyes?" Ardo's grip shifted, softening, and she felt his fingertips warm on her palms. As she looked back at him, something in his eyes brought back the memory of their frantic coming together, his confusion mixed with his desire to please her, his complete submission to her will. She longed to see that look in Feddar's beguiling green eyes.

"We may yet have our moment when all is said and done." She squeezed his hands, then let go, scooping up the dice and dropping them into her pocket.

"We're going to hole up here and sleep for a couple hours while they stand watch," Laanda said, gesturing to a set of bedrolls against the wall. "It seems the humans are in the temple, as we suspected. Their mage appears to be resting from his injuries, and I think we'll do better with a bit of a rest ourselves."

"We should strike while their defenses are down," Yglind growled, but Laanda stopped him with a glare.

"Look at yourself!" she hissed. "You're dead on your feet, and Aene looks like she could barely stand up."

Aene pushed herself shakily to standing, blinking in acquiescence. "She's not wrong, Egg. I need a little rest if I'm going to do my part to stop the mage."

"There'll be plenty of time to sleep once the fucking humans are dead!"

"Yglind," Ardo said, touching him on the shoulder. Yglind shook him off, throwing up his hands.

"Fine. I'll just lay down in my armor and pass out from unspent rage."

Aene wasn't sure if she'd slept, exactly, but something touched her toe, and she sat bolt upright, her gauntlet firing up without her being aware she was doing it.

"Looks like you're ready," Yglind said, squatting to offer her a hand and lift her to standing. "Toilet's over there." He pointed to a corner covered with a curtain. "Just follow your nose."

It was pretty ripe in the room, Aene realized, which was not surprising, given that there were forty people crammed into it. The Timon's faces were drawn with tension, fatigue, and sorrow. Aene could hardly imagine what it would be like if half of her city were slaughtered by humans. It was said their reach did not extend beyond the edges of the Silver Hills, but if they could do this kind of damage here, with only three, she shuddered to think of what would happen if war truly broke out. Some said it was inevitable, and a few even claimed it had already begun, but she'd never imagined the humans being able to reach all the way to Kuppham. Until now.

Once she'd used the bathroom and splashed a bit of water on her face, she tapped her gauntlet to check the charge on her chip. It read just over half full, so enough for two or three spells before she would have to swap it out, hopefully not in the middle of a fight. She shuddered as she pictured the mage's angry eyes, his hands in claw shape pouring forth bolts of jagged lightning. With the charge she had, she could absorb two, maybe three of his blasts, though he might change it up and hit them with something else. She popped out the chip and swapped it with the last fresh one, hoping that would last her for whatever was to come.

Her heart was full of dread as she watched Ardo checking Yglind's armor, trying to adjust it where the knight's sword had torn an opening in the forearm. Yglind stood erect, impassive, his eyes fixed on the wall, no doubt imagining the blood he would spill. Ardo touched up his neck guard, then tiptoed up to give him a peck on the lips, which Yglind seemed to accept without encouraging it.

Aene turned away, and her eyes fell on Skiti, who was tightening the straps on Laanda's greaves. She was not Laanda's squire, Aene was pretty sure about that, but her exact role was something of a mystery. At times it seemed like they might be in a relationship, but when Laanda got all queenly, Skiti reacted as any subject would, though perhaps with more fervent dedication than most.

Ardo approached, and they shared a quiet smile as he took her hands in his.

"We're counting on you," he said, his eyes tender and serious.

"Well, then you're fucked, aren't you?"

Ardo snorted and let her hands go, half-turning toward Yglind as if to see if Yglind had noticed them touching. Yglind was no fool. Or rather, he wasn't that kind of fool. He knew what had happened, and he had no reason to get chippy about it, but she couldn't rule out a little bit of jealousy. He and Ardo had been partners for some time, and though Yglind definitely fucked around, Ardo had always seemed completely devoted to him. It was part of what had made it fun, feeling Ardo's conflicting desires swirling together with her own. She smiled to herself, hiding it with her hand when Yglind's head swiveled toward her, a scowl growing on his face as if he had read her mind.

"I've got crossbows for everyone and anything else you might need." Laanda gestured toward a table where an array of weapons was laid out. "I want everyone to take a shot at the mage as soon as he's within sight." She picked up one of the crossbows, moving a lever to pull the string back over the latch, and inserted a bolt. "Standard trigger action, and this lever should be easy enough for any of you to use." She handed it to Aene, who took it with a frown.

"I'm not much good with one of these. I haven't shot since I was in school."

"I hope you had a good teacher. At any rate, your chance to hit is not zero, and you might distract him, which is almost as good. Take a shot, drop it, and use your gauntlet after."

Aene nodded, looking down at the crossbow, which felt solid but was lighter than expected. It was made of polished wood, burnished dark with much handling, and smelled faintly of oil.

"The rest of you take your pick, and we'll—" Laanda stopped as a series of quick, rhythmic clicks sounded on the door. She nodded to one of the Guard, who turned a crank in the wall, and the door popped open. Another Guard stood outside, huffing and pointing and saying something in Timon. Laanda listened, then pushed past him through the door and stood, staring at something Aene could not see. She only half-turned her head as she gestured for them all to join her. Aene hefted her crossbow and followed the others out the door and into the cavern.

A glass ball floated in the air, like the ones they'd seen before, but this one glowed brightly, casting icy shadows on the ceiling above. Its glow expanded, forming a large oval, which grew thinner and more defined until it took on the shape of the knight in a ghostly glowing outline, standing with arms crossed, faceplate up, a sneer just visible inside their helmet.

Yglind surged forward, standing face to face with the figure, who pulled out their sword, longer than their arm, and held it with both hands, the tip inches from Yglind's face. Yglind dropped his crossbow and pulled out his own sword, and they stood, blades nearly touching, eyes locked on each other. The knight shifted their sword to one hand and pointed to Yglind, then began to fade, dissolving into the glowing oval, shrinking until there was nothing left but a glowing ball floating in the air. The ball began moving, and Yglind stalked after it.

"Wait, we need to—" Laanda called, but Yglind did not react. He kept walking, sword erect, staying a few feet behind the ball, headed along the outer wall toward another spiral staircase opposite the one through which they had entered. Laanda glared at Aene and Ardo, then gestured at Skiti with her chin, picked up the crossbow Yglind had dropped, and took off after Yglind at a fast trot. Skiti fiddled with something on her Omni and flashed Aene and Ardo a grim smile before running after Laanda. Ardo patted Aene on the shoulder as he followed them, and Aene took a deep breath and hurried after.

29

Yglind followed the glowing ball, which he could see was glass like the others. It moved at an awkward speed between walking and running, so he loped along after it, his muscles waking up, his mind coming clear as his Forever Blade hummed in his hand.

"Yglind," huffed Laanda, who was jogging right on his heels. "Move aside and let me go first. This is our mine, and you are our guest."

"No one is getting between me and that knight," Yglind growled. "You can pass judgment on me later. They and I have unfinished business." His forearm throbbed where their sword had cut him, though Aene had mostly healed it. He still couldn't believe the sword had cut through his armor. It was supposed to be triple magic-hardened, but the human's blade had wormed its way underneath the scales and exploited a hidden gap in coverage.

"Take your godsblasted crossbow at least." She shoved it into his arm, and he slowed down enough to sheath his sword and take the crossbow from her.

"I'll only use it against the mage or the thief," he grumbled. They didn't abide by the warrior's code, so they did not get the same courtesy as the knight. Despite their cruelty, the knight had shown themselves to follow a combat code not very different from Yglind's, though clearly twisted in its view on civilian casualties.

"How quaint," Laanda said. Yglind shook off his aggravation and maintained his focus on the glowing ball, which took them down several long corridors and a spiral staircase into another corridor, this one wider than the others. A waft of fresh cedar smoke hit Yglind as they followed the ball.

"We're getting close to the temple," Laanda said. "We should stop and regroup."

"I'm not stopping until we find the fucking humans and smite them to the ground."

"Skiti and Aene can absorb the mage's first spells, give us a chance to take a shot at him, then you and I can go after the knight while they work on him."

"The knight is mine!" Yglind shouted, his blood thrumming hot in his ears. He stopped, facing Laanda, who squared her shoulders in response, not flinching in the slightest. She might have even been leaning toward him. He took in a deep breath and relaxed his stance, though his muscles were twitching and his heart jittery. "If it pleases your Highness to allow me to claim this combat."

Laanda's posture somehow relaxed even as she stood up straighter.

"How can I deny you the pleasure? I will make sure the mage is brought down and keep an eye out on the thief as well."

She glanced toward the globe, which had continued moving. Yglind inclined his head slightly, then spun toward the globe and started jogging again. It led them down a long passage, which widened as it ended in a pair of large, ornate steel doors encrusted with hundreds of glowing brightstones in the shape of an infinity symbol. The globe stopped in front of the door, and everyone caught up, standing in a semicircle around the wide area just outside the entrance. The globe floated motionless in the air, hovering at eye level. Aene stepped forward, the lines on her gauntlet firing up, and sent out a bubble of golden light, which flowed around the globe, then shrank until the globe appeared to be gold instead of icy blue. At a gesture from Aene, it floated toward her, and she pulled out a heavy black velvet bag and held it open. The golden globe descended into the bag, and she tied it off and tucked it in one of her many pockets.

"How do you know it's not a weapon?" Yglind asked. The humans were known to use such devices in their spying operations, and some of them were said to explode.

"I can read its energy. It is a scrying device, not a weapon, though how it can project images, I'm not quite sure." She pursed her lips and shook her head gently. "Human magic is mysterious and frankly quite impressive. If he didn't need killing so very, very badly, I'd love to take their mage back and see what he could teach us."

Yglind nodded, studying the door. He had never seen so much brightstone in one place, and to use it for mere decoration seemed almost sacrilegious, but it was the most beautiful thing he'd ever seen. It almost distracted him from thinking of what was on the other side, but the image of the knight taunting him through the glassy barrier flashed in his mind's eye, and he felt his sword calling to him. He looked down at his crossbow, hoping it wasn't a mistake to start the battle without his sword in hand, but Laanda's point was well taken. The knight was a formidable opponent, but the mage had power enough to take them all out in an instant.

"I assume they must be inside," Laanda said, sidling next to Yglind and flipping her visor up, then turning to face them all. "The temple is a large, circular room around a hundred feet wide with a domed ceiling reaching over fifty feet high." She paused, making eye contact with each of them. "In the center is a pool whose vapors can bring about a strong sense of euphoria, so steer clear of that. There are rows of benches around the pool, enough to seat all of…" She trailed off, and her eyes seemed to soften, then harden suddenly like ice over a lake. The Timon had suffered horrific casualties; Yglind wondered if they would ever be able to recover. "There is only one other exit, a passage leading to the cremation chamber, which has a chimney, but it's impossible to climb. There is no other way out besides these doors."

"I expect they'll be waiting for us." Aene adjusted her gauntlet, her face tight and grim.

"I'll join you heading in first," Skiti said, stepping forward and fiddling with her Omni. "We've made a modification I think might help deflect a blast or two. Between you and me, maybe we can buy them some time."

"Crossbows first," Laanda said. "If you see the mage, take a shot."

Skiti slid the Omni into her belt loop and swung her crossbow around on its strap. "Ready when you are, my Queen."

Laanda's eyes crinkled, and she lowered her visor. Yglind followed suit, his fingers twitching for his sword even as he held the crossbow up and cocked it. He moved to stand behind Skiti, who was short enough he could shoot over her head, and Laanda moved behind Aene. Yglind felt Ardo's hand touch his back, and he leaned into it for a moment, then reached for one door handle while Laanda wrapped her gauntleted hand around the other.

"On my mark," Laanda said. No one moved for a moment as the silence seemed to swallow them.

"Now," she whispered, and she and Yglind pulled at the heavy doors, which opened without a sound.

The domed room was lit with hundreds of brightstones running in a spiral pattern up toward the center of the dome. Yglind scanned the darkness, and a faint movement in the shadows caught his eye. He swiveled his crossbow and fired at the dark figure, who moved his arms in a swirling motion, and the bolt veered off course and clattered to the floor. Four more bolts shot off in rapid succession, all of them deviating at the last second.

The figure swirled his arms again, and flames burst out of his fingertips, tracing a figure eight in the air. Yglind sensed movement to his left and pulled out his sword as he spun to see the silvery blur of the knight rushing toward him, sword drawn and held low. Yglind took a few steps toward the knight, who was suddenly lit up with hot orange-yellow as the whole temple seemed to blaze with flame and echo with its dull roar. Yglind felt its heat, but Aene must have done something to slow it, and he quickly forgot about the flame, his companions, and everything else except the fearsome vortex of steel hurtling toward him.

The knight had momentum, and they swung their sword in a high arc that came crashing down on Yglind's upheld sword, wrenching his shoulder a little as he parried it sideways, back-stepping to avoid some of the impact of the charge. The knight stopped and swiveled with unbelievable control and swung two more times before Yglind could fully recover, and he found himself stumbling backward as he barely kept the heavy blade at bay.

The sizzle of lightning flared to his left, and he heard shouting and running, but he was too busy keeping the knight's hammering blows from slicing him in two to spare a glance at the others. He found a little rhythm in the knight's attacks, which he was able to briefly disrupt by closing the distance between them and forcing the knight's sword to the outside with a deft twist of his blade. He pressed his momentary advantage, running his shoulder into the knight's chest, then slamming his pommel into their helmet, which sent them reeling.

Yglind stepped forward and swung overhead with all his might, but the knight recovered in time to raise their sword and deflect the blow, which Yglind felt in his bones would have been the end of the fight had it landed. Instead, he found himself parrying a frenzied attack as the knight's huge sword seemed to come at him from all directions at once, moving with impossible speed. Yglind missed his shield terribly, but he was able to adjust quickly enough to protect himself, though one of the blows landed on his hip, slicing through his mail but not making it past the padding. It was the second time the knight had broken through his armor, which was the finest in all of Maerdom. He managed to give himself a little space when the knight's attacks subsided for a moment, and they circled each other, breathing heavily, eyeing each other through the slits in their visors.

A scream to his left drew his attention for a moment, and he saw Laanda lit up with blue energy, her back arching as her axe dropped from her fingers. His blade raised instinctively just as the knight bore down on him again, and he scrambled backward, barely managing to parry the punishing blows. His breath was running short, and his hip ached from where he had taken the hit, but the knight kept coming, and Yglind kept inching backward.

Despair rose in him as he realized for the first time since he was a kid that he was facing a superior opponent. His wrists ached from blocking strike after strike, and he felt each clash of their blades in his bones. One particularly vicious blow made him lose his grip, and before he could find it again, the knight's sword flashed silver in the light from the thousands of brightstones overhead, and Yglind's left shoulder blazed hot as the blade sliced through his armor and cut deep into his flesh. He dropped to one knee in pain, fumbling to re-grip his sword, and the knight paused, lowering their sword a hair and taking a step back.

"So, you do have a sense of honor after all," Yglind snarled through his pain. His left arm hung limp at his side, and warm blood soaked his padding and spattered onto the floor. The knight stood immobile, silent, impassive, and though Yglind could not see their face through the visor, he knew the expression he would see if the helmet were off. The self-satisfied smirk of a warrior having gotten the better of another in battle, daring them to stand up again and face their inevitable end. Yglind had no doubt worn this expression more than once. His blood pounded in his ears as rage surged through him, and he pushed himself up to standing, swinging his sword around and getting back into his fighting stance as blood flowed hot down his chest. Shouts and shuffling feet and a groan of agony sounded to his left, but he did not turn his head to look.

The noises grew distant as he focused on the knight, who had raised their sword and lowered their stance once again. He imagined himself in the arena back in Kuppham, with every Maer in the city cheering or jeering at him. Though none could doubt his skill, many would relish the tale of him being bested by a skinfucker in single combat.

Yglind felt a roar rise up within him, fueled by his embarrassment and the pain in his shoulder, like boiling copper searing his flesh. He lumbered forward, making a point to move more awkwardly than he felt, and swung half-heartedly. The knight sidestepped his clumsy attack and swatted his sword down, and Yglind planted his front foot, wheeling about and using the momentum of his spin to land a quick blow to the knight's ribs. It didn't penetrate the plate armor, but it knocked them off kilter just enough, and as they held their sword out for balance, he took the opening and swung his sword in a high arc and brought it crashing down on their wrists.

They howled in pain, and their sword clattered to the floor. Yglind kicked it away, brought his pommel up, and smashed it into the knight's chin. Their head popped back, and Yglind swirled the sword around and put all his strength into a sideways swing to the neck, which was partially exposed. He felt his blade bite through the mail, and blood sprayed in a jagged arc, a few droplets finding their way through the slit in his visor and landing hot on his face. The knight's hands clutched at their throat, and they sank down onto their knees, blood pumping from the wound and coating their gauntlets with an oily red slick. Yglind watched, fascinated, as they fumbled at their chin strap, finally loosening it enough to pop their helmet up. It clanged to the floor, rolling a few feet away. The knight's eyes were wide and panicked, and they pressed their gauntleted hands uselessly against the wound as their posture slumped and they crumpled to the floor.

"Yglind!" Aene shouted, and as he swiveled toward her voice, he grew suddenly dizzy and had to fall to one knee to avoid passing out entirely. His left arm was now completely numb, and he was still bleeding. If he didn't get some medic's balm or Aene's healing touch soon, he was done for. He flipped up his visor to get a better view of what was happening and saw Aene and Skiti crouched behind a shield of golden light. Laanda and Ardo lay sprawled on the floor, and the mage stood, covered in a thick layer of what looked like green glass. Yglind's heart leapt into his throat at the sight of his lover's motionless body.

30

ene braced as the mage stomped over, now more than twice his usual size with the strange wizard glass he was encased in. He raised a fist, and the layer of glass around his hand thickened and swelled to the size of an anvil. He brought his fist down on the shield, which burst, sending Aene and Skiti tumbling backward. She tried to bring it back up again, but her chip was dead.

"Yglind!" she shouted again, turning to see Yglind on his knees, covered in blood, his left arm hanging limp, his sword sagging to the ground. The mage raised his now impossibly wide foot to stomp on her, but before he could bring it down, Skiti's Omni flared out into a half-sphere, covering them both.

The sphere bowed beneath the blow, then sprung back, and the mage teetered backward and fell to the ground with the smack of a great rock falling. Aene popped out the chip, which skittered across the floor, and she pawed around in her pocket until she found the last half-used chip and wrestled it into her gauntlet. The glass encasing the mage dissipated, and he stood up slowly, sweat and blood streaking his face. His sleeve was torn, and the wound from Laanda's throwing axe still wept blood, but his mouth pulled wide into a wicked grin as he pressed his hands together and a cloud of black smoke formed around them, sparking and crackling.

Skiti swung her Omni, and the half-globe spread out like a net and flew through the air toward the mage, but he ducked underneath it, and it fell on the ground behind him. He opened his hands, and the black smoke filled the space, obscuring Aene's vision and sending her coughing to the floor as dozens of shocks wracked her body.

Each shock made her suck in more of the smoke, and her vision swam with little sparks punctuating the swirling darkness. The shocks continued, and she lost control of her limbs, which spasmed on the floor as her mind grew more and more distant. She heard coughing and a strange gurgling sound like someone choking on their own blood, which she hoped was the knight and not Yglind.

The smoke gradually cleared, and she gained just enough control of her body to lift her head to see the mage stalking toward her, hands sparkling as they'd done right before the forked lightning that had felled Laanda and Ardo. She raised her gauntlet, trying to clear the fog in her brain enough to summon the magic, but it was no use. She glanced over at Skiti, who had rolled onto her side and was struggling to get up, but she looked to be in the same shape as Aene.

The mage stood above them, both hands glowing with blue-white energy, his wicked grin accentuated by the ridiculous mustache that ran along his jawline and connected to his sideburns. What an inglorious end, she thought, to be killed by someone with such atrocious facial hair.

She clenched her jaw and tried to concentrate again, but her brain felt mushy, and she couldn't conjure enough focus to even light up her gauntlet. A shadowy form sped out of nowhere and stopped behind the mage, whose grin twisted into a snarl as he spun around and was immediately enwrapped by a thin gray rope that wound itself around and around him with little whipping sounds, binding his arms to his sides. Feddar's eyes sparkled like emeralds from beneath his hood as he stood holding one end of the rope.

Aene's heart flooded with relief, which lasted only a second before a huge shape surged out of the shadows, rising up behind Feddar, black scales and jagged teeth glinting in the light from the brightstones. Feddar's brow quirked in worry, and when he turned and saw the dragon, his mouth fell open, and he dropped the end of the rope.

The creature moved forward in two ponderous steps and rose on its hind legs, throwing the bound and seething mage into shadow. He uttered a series of low syllables, and the rope unwound itself with remarkable speed, pooling on the floor in haphazard coils. His hands still crackled with energy, but before he could raise them, the dragon's mouth opened wide and slammed down on him with an audible crunch, squirting gruesome crimson streaks across the floor. Feddar stood gaping at the beast, which chomped several times in rapid succession, sending a torrent of blood gushing to the ground, along with one of the mage's booted feet, sliced cleanly off at the ankle.

Feddar fell to his knees, retching voluminously, and Aene slammed her eyes shut but could not erase the sight of the mage's boot with jagged bone and shredded, bloody flesh spilling out. She opened her eyes, staring down at her gauntlet as the sound of crunching and slurping sent a wave of nausea crashing over her. She steeled her mind, picturing the waterfall she had summoned before, the point of stillness between gravity and time, and the gauntlet flared into life. Power surged through her, and she looked up to see the dragon's head raised, mouth half-open to the ceiling, snapping several times as it swallowed its oversized meal.

It shook its head, flinging blood and fleshy bits, some of which landed on Feddar, who scurried back out of the way, stopping to dry-heave before continuing his desperate scrabble. The dragon lowered down onto all fours facing Aene, who had drawn up to a crouch, though the shaking in her limbs at the sheer size of the beast would not allow her to stand up all the way. Its massive jaws dripped gore, and the oblong pupils set in eyes like golden dinnerplates narrowed as it seemed to study her. She held her gauntlet up, letting a bright light flare from it, and the dragon blinked several times, drawing its head back. A low, rattling noise emanated from it, then its mouth opened, and the rattle erupted into a gurgly sound like an enormous belch, which staggered Aene with the stench of bile and blood. Its nostrils flared as it sniffed noisily, and it turned toward Feddar, who had pulled back to sit on his knees, his face pale and slick. It eyed Laanda and Ardo, sniffing in their direction for a moment, then turned back to Aene, cocking its head sideways and fixing her squarely with one enormous eye.

Aene pushed herself to standing and extended the light into a shape like a long golden whip, a personal modification of the Power Sword spell she had been fiddling with. The creature blinked, and she gave the whip a twirl, careful not to swing it in its direction. The dragon's lips curled up to show all of its teeth, then it turned and lumbered away, whipping its tail against the puddle of blood on the floor, sending a shower of tiny droplets raining down on Aene. She closed her eyes and pursed her lips until the mist subsided, then opened her eyes again to see the creature disappear into an impossibly narrow crack high in the opposite wall.

"Aene," Yglind moaned. She turned and saw him on his knees, leaning on his sword and covered in his own blood, which pooled on the floor beneath him. She rushed over, almost slipping on the blood in her hurry, and gently removed his helmet. His eyes were half-closed, but he smiled weakly as she peeled aside the sliced remains of his shoulder plate and padding, covering her mouth when she saw the wound. His thick trapezoid muscle had been sliced through to the bone, and blood still wept from the opening, though with the amount covering him and the floor beneath him, it was hard to imagine he had much left.

"Did you kill the mage?" he whispered.

"The dragon took care of that. Hold still."

"I'm not—" Yglind coughed, a wet, painful sound, then swallowed hard. "—going anywhere."

Aene pulled up the Major Wounds spell, gritting her teeth against her sudden headache to summon the necessary concentration to connect with his flesh. Once the spell had begun, she only had to maintain focus and the gauntlet did the rest. The gauntlet stuttered for an instant as it hit the low power threshold, and she noticed the wound had stopped bleeding and part of the muscle had sewn itself back together. She stopped the spell, found her jar of medic's balm, and smeared a dollop on all sides of the divot, holding Yglind's shoulder as he writhed in pain.

"That stings like a bastard," he groaned, but his smile returned, and his breathing seemed steadier.

"Hold tight. I'm just going to go check on Ardo and Laanda." She turned to see Skiti crouched over Ardo, holding her fingers to his neck, and Skiti blinked and nodded. He was alive. Laanda sat slumped over her folded knees, and she glanced up at Aene as she knelt by Ardo.

"How's Yglind?" Laanda asked.

"He'll live. You?"

"It feels like I've got hotiron burns on every bone in my body." She winced as she braced her hands on the ground and tried to stand, but she collapsed with a grunt. "Look after Ardo. I'm just going to sit here and hurt for a while."

Aene flashed her a smile and knelt by Ardo. Skiti pointed to a black mark on his neck.

"I think those are just surface burns," she said, moving her hand in a circle above the mark. "Laanda's armor caught that, but it didn't stop the damage on the inside. Hopefully, he's just passed out."

"Well, I've got just enough charge left to try to bring him to. If that doesn't work, we're going to have to do it the old-fashioned way, like in the Time Before."

"Meaning?"

"Say a prayer and wait."

"I'll say one anyway." Skiti ran a hand down from her forehead to cover her face and held perfectly still.

Aene pulled up the Alertness spell, which was usually used to relieve fatigue, but she hoped it would work. She pressed her fingers into Ardo's temples and fired up the gauntlet. Her heart raced as the spell ran through her, then into Ardo, who took a deep breath as his eyes flew wide open.

"Yglind," he croaked, his eyes darting around wildly.

"He's fine," Aene cooed, cradling Ardo's head in her hand. "It's all going to work out, just like the dice said."

"And the humans?"

"The fucking humans are dead," Yglind said, kneeling unsteadily beside Ardo and taking his hand. "Except the thief." He gestured with his chin, and Aene looked over and saw Feddar wiping his face with a cloth, still wearing the cruel collar the Timon had installed.

"Skiti, would you please remove Feddar's collar?" Aene asked in as steady a voice as she could muster.

Skiti raised her eyebrows and glanced at Laanda, who shook her head, her eyes dark and hard. "I'll need a full Council vote on that, after what he's done."

Aene stared into Feddar's eyes, which had a soft, defeated look to them, then turned to Laanda. "He saved my life. Our lives. If he hadn't bound the mage, we'd all be dead."

"If he hadn't helped them in the first place, more than a hundred of my people wouldn't be dead!" Laanda's voice rose to a shout, echoing through the great room. "The mine is in ruins. It will take us months to get it back to normal operating capacity, if we even can with the numbers we have remaining." Her face was red, and her voice trembled. "Do you have any idea what that will do to our economy? And who's to say the humans won't send another expedition? This whole thing was because of your fucking war with them! I'm sure your leaders will just consider us collateral damage." Laanda's fists were clenched around her axe, whose head rested on the floor.

"The High Council will send help. They sent us, didn't they?" Aene tried to keep her voice low and reassuring, but she could see by Laanda's reaction that it was no use.

"Yes, and a fat lot of good it did us. There's no *help* that can undo what they did. What *he* did. I should just kill him myself." She picked up her axe and turned toward Feddar, who had risen from his knees and stood with his palms facing Laanda.

"I didn't kill anyone," he said in Southish. "I tried—"

"Shut your whoreson human mouth before I split your head like a fucking log." Laanda pointed at him with her axe, then turned her head to Aene, her eyes red and blazing.

"You gave your word," Aene said in as level a voice as she could muster, flexing her fingers slightly to gauge how much power was left in the gauntlet. It wasn't much. She glanced over at Yglind, who blinked and eased his hand to the pommel of his sword. "You tested his blade. He's innocent of any deaths."

"Innocent?" Laanda shrieked, spinning toward Aene. "He knows what he did, what he's responsible for. And my promise was based only on incidents that happened before. What he's done since then does not fall under that agreement. *He* is the one who let them back into the keep, where they slaughtered another fifty of my people. He bears responsibility for those deaths, under *our* law, in *our* mine. And I declare his life forfeit. Skiti, bind him!"

Skiti flicked the Omni she held at the ready, and a silvery-gray ball of tightly coiled strands flew through the air toward Feddar. His arms went wide as he spun away and planted his foot to run, but he slipped in the puddle of his own vomit and stumbled. The ball spread out into a net, which fell upon him and tightened with a thousand tiny clicking noises. His flailing limbs were bound tight to his body, and he froze in place, then fell face-first onto the floor.

Aene flared her gauntlet into life, casting a bright glow, and Laanda shrank back, covering her eyes with her hands.

"Laanda! We are allies, and we could be friends. But if you lay a finger on our prisoner, it is *your* life that will be forfeit." She focused on the light, shaping it into a dozen glowing golden daggers, which floated in the air, pointed at Laanda. She was pretty sure the chip didn't have enough energy to launch the spell, but Laanda didn't have to know that.

Laanda turned to Feddar, then swiveled her head back to Skiti, who stepped toward her, tightening the cord connecting Feddar to the Omni as she went. Skiti's eyes were soft, and she reached out a tentative hand toward Laanda.

Laanda whipped her head toward Aene, then back to Skiti, who took a half-step closer and laid her hand on Laanda's steel-encased arm. Skiti's eyes were wet, and a fat tear rolled down her cheek, followed by another. Laanda's face broke in an instant, twisting like a wailing toddler, and she let her axe slump as she leaned into Skiti's body. Skiti wrapped her arms around her, and they clung to each other, sobbing and saying a few words in their language. The net around Feddar released, and Aene let her spell dissipate.

She looked to Yglind, who stepped closer and held out an arm as if for a hug, but he paused, his eyes questioning, hesitant. It was the first time in all the time she'd known him that she'd ever felt comfortable touching him. She wrapped a gentle hand around his waist, leaning away from the sticky, bloody mess of his torso, and gave him a squeeze. Ardo approached and leaned awkwardly into them both, one hand over Aene's shoulder and the other on Yglind's face.

"We fucking did it," Yglind said. "We killed the godsdamned skinfuckers."

Aene peeked through the space under Ardo's armpit to look over at Feddar, who stood as if in shock, but his eyes glimmered when he caught her glance, and his lips curved into the faintest smile.

31

Skiti slid into the bath across from Laanda, the heat of the water melting her weary muscles and loosening the strings of tension in her mind. Laanda's eyes were closed, and she slowly sank beneath the water, bubbles rising as her mouth and nose went under. Her arms floated out to the side, ribbons of red rising from spots of crusted blood the water dissolved from her skin. They would need another bath after this one, but Skiti luxuriated in the perfumed warmth, the quiet, the lack of anyone trying to kill them.

Laanda's head emerged from the water as slowly as she had gone under, and she ran her fingers through her hair, leaning over sideways to let it fall into the water so she could untangle it. She angled her head halfway upright.

"Would you pass me the pick?"

"Let me help you with that." Skiti grabbed the pick and scooted around the bath's built-in bench to sit next to Laanda, who blinked a soft smile as she turned away so Skiti could have full access to her hair.

Neither of them spoke as Skiti worked out the crusted dirt, sweat, and blood from Laanda's hair, easing the pick through one tangle at a time. It was quiet and calm in the bathroom, with a shaded brightstone lamp casting a warm glow over the rounded walls. The only sound was the trickle of water running in from the dragon's head faucet and the irregular slooshing of wastewater through the overflow. When Skiti had finished with the worst of the knots, she scooped out a palmful of shampoo and worked it through Laanda's hair until it was white with lather from her scalp down to where it draped into the water. She touched Laanda gently on the shoulders, and Laanda slowly leaned back. Aene's hands guided her, moving to frame her face so the soap wouldn't get in her eyes when she went all the way under except for her face. Laanda opened her eyes, fixing them on Skiti.

The hurt in her gaze was raw, flagrant, crushing, and it twisted Skiti's heart to know there was nothing she could do to help. No tonic she could offer, no words of comfort, no restraint could free Laanda from the blame she heaped upon herself for every life lost. Laanda stared at the ceiling, as if she were replaying the awful memories of the past two weeks in her head. Skiti could almost see those moments flashing in the glint of Laanda's eyes. She moved her hands down through Laanda's hair, cradling the back of her head, and Laanda rose to sitting. She reached her arms behind her head and clasped Skiti's wrists, leaning her head back against Skiti, and they sat like that for a long, long time.

Skiti rapped on Laanda's door, which swung open. Laanda stood in her full regalia, her necklace and crown glittering in the lamplight.

"I love seeing you like this," Skiti said as she closed the door behind her.

"Like what?"

"Like a queen." She looked down sheepishly. Laanda had a tumultuous relationship with the word, but in this moment, there was no other word to describe her.

"I'm too ugly to be a queen." Laanda leaned over her mirror and scrunched up her face.

"Saying things like that, maybe you're too stupid to be a queen. Laanda, you're Magnificent." Skiti gestured from Laanda's face to her broad shoulders and down to her powerful waist and legs.

"Thank you." Laanda touched her on the arm, then turned and picked up the engraved scroll case they'd made for their letter to the Maer High Council.

"Are you sure about this?" Skiti gazed down at the case, which looked elegant, almost fragile, in Laanda's strong hands. Were they really going to leave the mine behind and make for the Jagged Mountains deep in the South? What welcome would they find there among the clans of Timon who had mined those hills for thousands of years?

"I'm sure." Laanda's eyes were distant, melancholy, but less sad than Skiti had expected. "Our partnership with the Maer has brought us great wealth, but nothing is worth this." She closed her eyes for a moment, her fingers tightening around the scroll case. "Could you imagine living here with the ghosts of the dead haunting your every step? The blood has been washed from the floors, but the stain of our loss is indelible."

Skiti wanted to hug her, to offer what comfort her feeble arms could muster. Her heart felt hollow, and she did not know where she would find the strength to keep it from imploding. She took a tentative step toward Laanda, who seemed to sense her need, and pulled her into a tight embrace.

"We're burying the dead in this mine, not the living." Laanda's voice was deep and soft in Skiti's ear. "We honor them by forging a new life for ourselves and our people."

Skiti closed her eyes as Laanda's arms wrapped around her more securely than the tightest restraint. It didn't stop the pain, but it kept the void inside her from drawing her all the way in for a moment.

Laanda released her, holding her at arm's length, her eyes crinkling with her faint smile.

"Go see to the thief. I'll meet you and the Maer in the great hall shortly."

Aene was sitting just outside the prison cell, talking in low tones in Southish to the thief. Aene pulled back as she entered, and Skiti saw her fingers slip from the thief's as she turned around, flashing Skiti a guilty look. Skiti blinked at her, hoping to convey her understanding, though as she thought about the scores of lives lost, she had half a mind to activate the collar and end the human's life right here and now. She summoned Aene with her eyes, and Aene joined her in the hallway outside. Skiti closed the door and held up the pair of livesteel cuffs in one hand and the control ring in the other.

"I've keyed this ring to you and you alone. Push this button while touching the ring to the cuffs, and they will release."

Aene nodded somberly and reached for the cuffs, but Skiti pulled them back.

"If you release him and he gets back to the humans, I will personally hold you responsible for the consequences of whatever may come."

Aene blinked her assent. "You needn't worry about that. My duty is first and foremost to the Maer High Council, and I would not betray that trust." She reached out for the cuffs, her eyes softening. "Or yours."

Skiti handed her the ring, which Aene examined for a moment, then tucked it into a pouch.

"It wouldn't do to let him know I have the key," she said.

"Let's go in there, and I'll show you how they work."

Skiti led Aene into the room and approached the bars, shooing the thief back with her hands. Two Guard flanked her, wrist axes at the ready, and the thief slunk back against the wall. Skiti opened the lock with her Omni, letting the Guard in first. They moved to both sides of Feddar, who shrank between them, his green eyes wide and wet with worry.

"Hold out your hands," she commanded in Southish, and he obliged. She eyed Aene and draped the fat coil of the cuffs over his wrists. The thief let out a sigh through clenched teeth as the cuffs tightened. "They're designed to keep the same tension, so long as you don't struggle against them. They can't be removed except by the Maer High Council. Do you understand?"

Feddar nodded. "Are you going to remove this collar now?"

Skiti blinked, gesturing for him to turn around. "This may prick for a moment as the hooks release." She brought the Omni up next to the mechanism, adjusting the fine controls, and she saw the muscles in the thief's neck tense at the Omni's clicks. "Just relax," she said and inserted the needlelike tip of the Omni into the tiny hole in the collar, which released with a loud click. The thief jerked, then his shoulders sagged as Skiti gently lifted the hooks out of his skin. She dabbed the pinprick wounds with a piece of cloth, then laid the collar on the table.

"Thank you," the thief said in a low voice. "But don't think I forgive you for putting it on me in the first place."

"I'll keep that in mind each time I pray to honor the hundred and twenty-four of my clanmates your friends slaughtered in this mine with your help." She gripped her Omni, realizing how easy it would be to lift it under his chin and shoot a spike directly into his brain, but she had seen enough blood for many lifetimes.

"Are you prepared to officially take him into custody?" Skiti asked Aene, gesturing to the paper on the table.

"I am." Aene picked up the gilded pen and signed in careful letters. Skiti added her signature, blew and blotted the paper, then rolled it up and tucked it into its leather case, which she handed to Aene.

"He will be delivered to you as you exit the mine. We will say our good-byes in the great hall shortly," she said. "We may have different perspectives on what happened and what is to come, but for what you did for me and for my people, I thank you from the depths of my heart."

Aene placed a hand on her chest and closed her eyes.

32

Ardo stood between Aene and Yglind in the great hall facing the assembled Timon, who stood in long rows against either wall. Feddar sat sullenly in a corner watched by two stone-faced Guard with wrist axes in hand. Yglind's armor had been cleaned and repaired, and it shone golden in the light from the brightstone chandelier. Ardo had helped trim his facial hair, and Yglind had never looked so handsome, but there was something troubled in his eyes. Ever since the battle with the knight, he'd lost a bit of his confidence, replaced by a strange bitterness. It might have been the fact that he didn't get his five kills unless the hulmar counted. Though by bringing back Feddar, he had surely cemented his place in the Time to Come.

"I was beaten," Yglind had murmured in bed the night before.

"But you killed the knight, my lord," Ardo had reassured him. Yglind had turned away, or tried to, but his shoulder was still healing, so he'd turned his head away instead. Ardo hadn't seen what had happened, but the result surely spoke for itself, didn't it?

Laanda approached, decked out in fine black velvet adorned with intricate patterns of silver thread. An elaborate necklace hung around her neck, glittering with countless tiny brightstones, and a crown of woven gold and silver filaments sat atop her head like an ethereal flame. She carried a scepter in one hand and a metallic tube in the other. Yglind stepped forward as she neared, moving a little stiffly because of his shoulder, and dropped to one knee.

"Queen Laanda," Yglind said in a voice so restrained, Ardo almost didn't recognize it. "I am sorry we failed to protect your people. I will carry this burden to the end of my days." Ardo couldn't see Yglind's face, but his voice quavered at the end as though he were on the verge of tears. Ardo's heart swelled at the sound, and his own tears burst forth, running hot through his facial hair until they cooled in his mustache.

"It is a burden we both share, Yglind Torl." Laanda gestured for him to rise, which he did unsteadily. "We all did what we could, but with the powers arrayed against us, it was not enough. Many sleepless nights await us all as we ponder what we could have done, what might have been, but we are here today to discuss the future, not the past."

The tone of her voice chilled Ardo's heart. The Delve was over, and the future Ardo had to look forward to was watching Yglind be put into hibernation and losing him forever. He steeled his jaw against the tears that surged, but there was no stopping them. Laanda turned slowly, making eye contact with each and every Timon in the hall, then returning her gaze to Ardo's group. She held out the cylinder, which Yglind took, holding it up to study it.

"What you hold in your hand is a declaration that our contract with the Maer for brightstone is officially ended. Inside the tube, you will find our final delivery, for which we will not accept payment since we must end this long-standing agreement so abruptly. We have decided, after long and arduous discussion, to leave this mine and seal it up so that no one, Timon or Maer or human, may ever access its riches again. This mine will heretofore and forevermore be a monument to the community that once thrived here and the many souls that will never again walk its halls." She bit her lip, tears slipping from her steely eyes. "I ask that the Maer High Council respect our wishes and leave the site undisturbed, but I should warn you that we will be leaving in place mechanisms that will wreak great destruction on anyone who chooses to ignore our designation."

"It shall be as you say." Yglind bowed, holding up the case, then stepped back in line with Ardo and Aene.

Laanda barked a few curt words in her language, and the Timon lining both walls straightened up. Laanda raised her scepter, then lowered it, and the hall swelled with the low hum of a hundred voices finding their pitch, then rising into a haunting note that they held for a very long time.

Ardo's heart thumped in his chest, and he found Yglind's hand and gave it a squeeze, which was gently returned. One voice, high and clear, pierced the air, and a half-dozen others joined in, harmonizing in a lower octave, followed by still more, their melodies moving past each other in an overlapping set of rounds, climbing ever higher. Laanda alone did not sing, and as the song reached its peak, she began to walk. The voices rejoined in a middle range, moving together, then in harmonizing groups. Yglind pulled Ardo forward as he followed Laanda, and Aene joined them, inexplicably holding Yglind's other hand.

The Timon Guard filed in behind them, holding Feddar firmly by both biceps, and the rest of the Timon followed, still singing. Their song echoed through the halls, creating reverberations that vibrated Ardo's very bones. In their song, he felt their sadness, their loss, their despair, but a softer note crept in, that single high voice rising above the haunting drone of the chorus. Though Ardo understood not a word of what they sang, that voice gave him a sliver of hope that the Timon might find a new home now that they were leaving this one behind. He puzzled over their decision; though the humans had wrought great destruction in the mine, their skill with stonework was unmatched, and they could surely repair any damage and rebuild, given time. Perhaps they had seen the writing on the wall, that any association with the Maer meant war with the humans, whose appetite for cruelty was now on full display.

The Timon stopped following them once they passed through the keep gate, with only Laanda, Skiti, and the two Guard holding Feddar joining them. They took a large elevator up, which moved more quietly and smoothly than any Ardo had ever used, as if it were floating on air instead of pulled by cables and counterweights. No one spoke, and when they exited the elevator, the air seemed a little fresher. They walked down a series of hallways until a crack of light appeared before them, widening from above to become a square of warm yellow sunlight. Ardo glanced up at the ceiling and saw the cables ripped from their moorings and realized they had made it back to the gate through which they'd entered. Laanda stopped just inside the gate and growled a few words to the Guard, who let go of Feddar and stood aside.

"May we meet again in kinder times," Yglind said, bowing to Laanda.

"If we meet again, it will be in the Time to Come," Laanda said. "Farewell."

The morning sun hit Ardo on the face, warming him to his core. He inhaled a deep breath of pine-scented air, and for a moment, he believed that everything was going to be all right.

Yglind was unusually pensive for the first few days of their trip. The news they received through their circlets was depressing—the humans had hit all the major brightstone mines all at once and taken down some of the big signal towers as well. The High Council had declared a state of emergency throughout the Maer lands. War was upon them. Ardo's friends and family were glad to hear from him, as there had been some losses in the groups sent to the other mines. He'd mostly kept his circlet in his pocket, as he had enough grief to process without the added woes of the world at large.

Ardo had made little overtures each night, hoping a good orgasm would snap Yglind out of his funk. Yglind had played the injured shoulder card, though Ardo could tell from the way he carried himself that his shoulder wasn't causing him too much pain. Yglind had let Ardo dress and wash the wound, which was looking better each day, and by the time they passed Mount Galantz, the wound was healed enough that it no longer needed treatment.

Aene spent much of the trip speaking with Feddar, teaching him Maer, against Yglind's wishes, but Yglind didn't seem to have the energy to fight her on it. As far as Ardo could tell, Aene hadn't slept with Feddar yet, but by the way they looked at each other, how Aene touched Feddar as she laughed at his pronunciation, he could tell it was only a matter of time. A tingle of jealousy welled up inside him, then faded as quickly as it had arisen. His moment with Aene had been just that. Her heart was locked on Feddar, just as Ardo's was tethered to Yglind. He wondered if they would ever even see each other again once they returned.

They had traveled for five days and would reach Kuppham in a week more, and Ardo ached for Yglind. He'd even had to take care of himself a couple of times while Yglind slept to assuage his frustration. So when at last Yglind had asked Ardo if he'd help him wash his wound in a little spring they'd found, Ardo's heart leapt at the subtle invitation in Yglind's voice. Aene had waved them off with a smirk, then returned to practicing verbs with Feddar, who proved a quick study, perhaps due to the extra attentions of his tutor.

The spring sat in a copse in the middle of a great plain, with packed dirt around a small pool of water that bubbled slightly in the center. The trees and underbrush would provide excellent privacy, Ardo thought, and as they shucked their boots and the rest of their clothes, his cock stiffened in anticipation. Yglind glanced down at Ardo's half-mast, and a smile spread across his face as his own cock bobbed a bit, swaying awkwardly from side to side.

He stepped into the pool, which had flat stones laid across the bottom, as was common in springs along well-traveled paths. He eased into the water, his eyes growing wide and his mouth forming an O at the icy water, which came up to their stomachs. They washed their privates, underarms, and faces quickly, then stood up and took turns with the old blanket they used as a towel. Yglind took the blanket outside the copse, his thick, rounded ass flexing with each step, and laid it out in the sun.

When he returned to the copse, Yglind's eyes showed a different spark than usual, something needier, almost vulnerable. Ardo's balls twinged at the sight, and he put his hands on Yglind's chest, massaging the slabs of his pectorals and gently tweaking his rough nipples. Yglind nosed Ardo's face up and kissed him more softly than he ever had before as his hands trailed down Ardo's back, cupping his ass and pulling him close. Their cocks pressed into each other's bellies, and Ardo moved his hands to Yglind's broad back to remove what little space remained between them.

They kissed, slow and soft, for a very long time. Yglind pulled back from the kiss, wrapping his big hands around Ardo's hips, and leaned in to flick his tongue across Ardo's nipple. Ardo gave a little squeak of surprise, which turned into a moan as Yglind licked and sucked each nipple, moving one hand to cup Ardo's balls while the fingers of his other hand traced lines up and down his cock, circling the head with a touch so light Ardo grew faint.

Yglind lowered down to his knees, kissing the hair along Ardo's stomach as his hands continued their torturous ministrations, squeezing and releasing his balls as he slowly pumped Ardo's cock. He held it tight at the base, and Ardo looked down in amazement as Yglind's tongue began licking and circling his head. Ardo clutched the hair on the back of Yglind's neck, closing his eyes and steeling his jaw as he felt himself creeping toward an early climax. It had been a very long time since Yglind had—

Ardo groaned as Yglind opened wide and took him all the way in, then pulled out slowly, closing his lips tight at the last second, so it made a soft little noise as Ardo's head popped out. Ardo felt himself right on the edge, and he pushed Yglind's forehead back, stooping halfway to a crouch so he wouldn't spill so soon.

"Yglind, gods, I—" Ardo stood up, still throbbing, painfully close.

Yglind rose with him, the steel in his eyes stopping Ardo's words, then kissed him, softly again, with none of his usual mad fervor. The slow burn had Ardo's body singing with desire and he pressed into the kiss, gripping the hair on the back of Yglind's head as his flickering tongue desperately sought entrance. Yglind finally relented, letting Ardo explore his mouth, their tongues intertwining. Yglind pulled back again, his eyes full and probing, and he turned around, leaning his ass against Ardo's cock and pulling Ardo's wrists around his chest.

"You are always so good to me," Yglind murmured, raising Ardo's fingers to his lips and kissing them one by one as he pressed his ass into Ardo, moving up and down until Ardo feared he would pop.

"I live to serve you, my lord," Ardo managed, though the words felt different coming out this time. They had evolved this love language between them, this play upon their lord and squire roles, but the rules of the game seemed to be shifting beneath Ardo's feet, and it was as bewildering as it was intoxicating.

"I know you do...and I need to ask you to serve me in a different way now." He reached behind him, grasping Ardo's cock and sliding it between his legs so it nestled in the space between his balls and his hole.

"Anything you need," Ardo whispered.

"Did you bring the oil?" Yglind asked, lowering himself so Ardo's cock strained against his weight, threatening once again to erupt.

"Of course, my lord." Ardo pulled away, crouching again for a moment, and hurried over to pull the bottle of herbal oil he had laid next to the towel. He turned to see Yglind crouched over a large round stone on the edge of the little clearing in the center, his arms braced against the stone and his legs spread wide apart. Ardo's stomach dropped, and his balls ached to see Yglind in this position. He uncorked the bottle as he approached.

Yglind glanced over his shoulder as Ardo splashed the oil onto his hand and slicked him up, gently massaging and probing. Yglind closed his eyes and let out a stuttering groan as Ardo slowly pushed two fingers in, reaching around to run his other hand up and down Yglind's hot shaft. Ardo smiled as he rubbed his fingers against Yglind's pressure point, and Yglind gasped, eyes wide, wild, hungry.

"Fuck me, Ardo," Yglind pleaded. Ardo slid his fingers out slowly, then gripped his own cock until it was tight and shiny, holding it stiff as he gave it a quick coating with the oil. He circled with the head of his cock, pressing in for a moment, then circled again. He felt Yglind getting closer to letting him in with each pass until, at last, the tension was just right, and he pushed in slowly, breathing hard through his nose to keep from losing it just from the heat and the pressure.

"Don't move," Ardo hissed through gritted teeth, and Yglind held perfectly still for him, though the throbbing warmth was almost more than Ardo could bear. He raked his fingernails gently across the hair on Yglind's back, closing his eyes and picturing the dark tunnels of the mine, the water dripping from the rock, the smell of the place, anything to distract him and bring him back from the edge. He felt himself settle, and he opened his eyes again to see Yglind craning his neck around to stare at him with those big, vulnerable eyes. A sudden fire built in Ardo's chest, and he gripped

Yglind's hips and pressed deeper into him. Yglind grunted and turned to face the stone.

Ardo pulled halfway out and thrust in again, their bodies crashing together, and again, harder this time. Yglind changed the angle of his hips, and Ardo felt that ineffable tingling in his balls as he thrust in over and over. He knew he was living on borrowed time. He seized Yglind's cock and shucked it all the way, then began pumping it as fast as he could, hoping the oil left on his hand was enough to reduce the friction, but none of that mattered now as they moved together in a frenzy. Ardo felt the rush growing inside him, too powerful to stop, and he held Yglind's cock as tight as he could and thrust upward once, twice, three times. Yglind's moans raised to a desperate whine as Ardo poured himself inside Yglind, finishing him off with a flurry of frenetic strokes until his hand was slick and sticky. Ardo held in place, feeling another wave building inside him, and he let out an animalistic groan as he spilled again, then collapsed onto Yglind's broad back, breathing into his neck, covering it with tender little bites, until at last, the throbbing subsided. Yglind began to twist sideways, and they separated as Ardo pulled back, then fell into Yglind's arms.

"I hope I served you well, my lord," Ardo whispered into Yglind's sweaty ear.

33

— • —

"Where are you from?" Aene asked Feddar as they made their way up the jagged path that zigzagged toward the first low ridge of Yaeger's Hump. Feddar moved a little awkwardly because of the livesteel cuffs, but his cheerful demeanor hid any discomfort he might have been feeling.

"I was born in Gheil, the second-biggest city after Wells. It's in the west, along the Low River. It's known for its honey—and mead, of course."

"It sounds lovely." Aene pictured a city in the middle of a great field of clover, bees buzzing in golden afternoon sunlight. "What about your parents?"

"My father was a singer, and my mother was a professor."

"At university?" It had never occurred to Aene to think about human universities. "Professor of what?"

"Folk history," Feddar said. "She wrote a book comparing different versions of stories about the Time Before, trying to trace their origins to specific times and places. She theorized each one had a common historical event at the core, which she could get to if she collected enough variations on each one. She even compared them to Maer versions of some of the stories when she could get hold of them."

"It sounds fascinating," Aene said, though she couldn't imagine there was a whole lot of demand for folk history on the eve of war. Maer cultural institutions had taken a serious hit in the past decade, and universities had been particularly affected. Aene had been lucky enough to study something deemed practical for the war effort, so her program was well funded, but she'd still had to fight to get enough brightstone chips for the Delve.

"She's retired now. They bought her out when they closed her program. She still writes, though I'm not sure who's reading her treatises nowadays."

It felt unreal having this conversation with a man who was surely marching to his death, or at least a life of imprisonment and torture. Perhaps if he cooperated fully with the judiciars, he would be spared the worst treatment, but once this trip was over, he would never again breathe free air. Aene thought about the carnage the humans had caused the Timon and, by extension, the Maer, but it was hard to hold the lively, charming man before her accountable. After all, his group's mission was not much different than her own, though on different sides of the conflict.

Each night she bound his feet and tied the cuffs to a tree in case he took a notion to flee in the middle of the night or worse. But if he had any intention of doing so, he hid it well, and he readily offered his hands and feet to her rope, watching her with sharp eyes as she bound him with careful loops and secure knots. She had noticed him sneaking glances at her body as she worked. He seemed to have a particular obsession with her breasts, peeking at them whenever the angle permitted. She pretended not to notice and even loosened her robe so they showed a bit more, smiling to herself and biting her lip when her head was turned away.

For her part, she relished the shocking smoothness of his wrists and ankles, the way his veins showed through the pale skin on the inside of his forearms. He wasn't hairless, not exactly; scattered rough hairs lined the backs of his arms and all over his legs, as well as what she could see of his neck and chest. The only part of him that was as hairy as a Maer was the top of his head and his beard, which appeared to have been shaved in the not-too-distant past and was now growing out. She couldn't help trying to scry what lay beneath his robes, whether the hair around his privates was thick like a Maer's or sparse like that on his arms and legs. Once when he was bathing, he'd caught her looking, and she'd turned away, pretending to check her gauntlet, heat flowing from her ears to her face and down to her loins.

Ardo and Yglind had finally started having sex again, thank the gods. She'd half considered taking her frustrations out on Ardo, but seeing the way he looked at Yglind told her that was no longer an option. Deep down, she was glad for both of them. She'd worried that Yglind's preoccupation with recent events had flattened his spirit, which she'd come to see as mildly endearing when it wasn't maddening. After their lovemaking, Yglind would begin snoring noisily, and Aene would watch until she saw Ardo's breathing become regular. Then she'd scooch her bedroll closer to Feddar, and they'd whisper together like little kids whose parents were sleeping.

Feddar's eyes always stayed with hers, and his smile never left his lips, even when he was sleeping. He never complained about the ropes, though it must have been horribly uncomfortable sleeping like that. Each night, she considered untying him, ripping his clothes off, and putting her fantasies to the test, but wisdom always prevailed, though at a greater cost with each passing day. As they got closer to civilization, Aene realized if she was ever going to scratch this itch, the time was now.

She secured him extra carefully that night, taking her time to wrap the rope neatly, touching his calves and wrists with her fingers as she smoothed down the rope. While Ardo and Yglind were doing their business, she knelt by Fedar and reached out for his face, and he did not flinch as her fingers ran over his stubbly cheeks, hairless forehead, and shiny nose. He just watched her, his eyes shining greenish-black in the starlight. He made the tiniest little sound, the very beginning of a groan, as her fingers traced through his mustache, and she ran her thumb across his lips. He puckered slightly, kissing her thumb, and she pushed his lower lip down, then pulled her hand back.

"Don't stop," he whispered in Maer, and she ran her knuckles along his cheek to his hairless ears. She folded his ears down, then gently rubbed his earlobes, and he made the sound again, a little more desperate this time. She responded with her own *mmm* as she slid her fingers down to wrap around his throat, holding gently but firmly. She glanced over at Ardo and Yglind, who were in the second half of their lovemaking, and she leaned in close and pressed her lips to his. Her heart stuttered, and her head grew light as she slipped her tongue in to taste him, just for a moment. His tongue responded, and his lips gripped hers, but she pulled up, pressing her hands into his chest.

"Don't stop. *Please,*" he said in a quiet moan. Aene just smiled as she let one hand slide down his stomach, lightening the pressure as her fingers reached his pants and the unmistakable heft of his cock straining against the fabric. He was as hard as a tree root, and his breath grew shallow as she wrapped her fingers around his length and held them in place, feeling him throbbing beneath her touch. Yglind's grunts sounded louder and louder from behind the rock where he and Ardo had gone for privacy, and she knew they would finish soon. She released the pressure slowly and moved her hand up to cup his cheek once again.

"Patience," she whispered. "We'll wait until they're well and truly asleep, and then I'm going to have my way with you. If that's what you want."

Feddar blinked his wide, shiny eyes, and nodded his head slightly.

Aene lay next to Feddar, whose arms were stretched behind his head, the livesteel cuffs tied to a sturdy scrub tree. His sleeves had slid down past the elbow, showing part of his biceps. He had lean muscles, not the slabs and chunks of a warrior, and the sight of his bare skin, especially the inside of his elbows, made her want to lick and bite his tender flesh. They whispered in the dark, talking about their favorite foods, places they'd been, things they'd seen...anything but the dark future looming before them.

When Yglind's snore sounded and Ardo lay snuggled facing away from them, Aene scooched in closer so they were barely touching, only her breasts pushing against his chest and the points of her hips touching his. She kept her lips just out of his reach and his mouth quirked to one side as their noses touched. Heat poured off him, and she pressed in closer until she felt him throbbing against her, his lips pouting toward hers. She gave in and turned her nose sideways and fell upon his mouth as she ground herself against his hip bone, reaching between his legs to softly caress him through his pants.

"You're going to kill me before we even make it back to the High Council," he murmured when they came up for air.

"Well, I definitely am now," she said, rising to her knees and yanking his shirt up to expose his chest, though she couldn't take the shirt all the way off because of the cuffs. She ran her fingernails up his stomach, letting them tangle in the hair that curled up around his belly button, then spread her hands out and ran them up the shocking expanse of bare skin that ended in little clouds of hair around each nipple. She stuck two fingers of each hand in his mouth, rubbing them against his tongue as he sucked on them, then made wet circles around his nipples, stopping to pinch and flick every time his breathing pattern changed. She moved her hands around his neck and lowered her mouth to kiss and suck all over his chest, relishing the smooth feel of his skin, like the palm of a hand that had never done hard labor. She slid one hand down to grip his cock while the other joined her mouth, teasing his nipples, and the throaty little whine he made sent a shiver straight to her core.

She stood up and tore off her robe, looking down at him, her body warming with the burning intensity of his gaze. She planted her knee on one side of his head and swung her other leg over, feeling the rough stubble of his face through the hair on her thighs. She ran her fingers through his hair as she lowered herself down onto him. His silky tongue and tender lips rose to meet her, eager, agile, languorous.

His groans vibrated into her, and she pressed down and began to move, circling and grinding as his tongue worked her with deft strokes. She gripped his hair tightly and bore down harder, shifting back and forth so fast she briefly worried she might break his nose, but pleasure flooded her as his lips clamped down on her clit and held on, freezing her in place. She hovered low over him, her legs trembling as his tongue swirled around like a deranged machine, and she pulled his head up by the roots of his hair, smashing his lips beneath her as pressure coiled inside her tighter and tighter until she could no longer hold back.

Something inside her snapped, and she let out a hoarse cry as pleasure raged through her like water gushing through a broken dam. Her eyes locked on his, half-buried in her hair, as he held steady, maintaining just enough pressure and suction. He flicked his tongue across her clit one more time and she collapsed with that final stroke, falling forward onto his bound arms. She lay a hundred soft kisses on the tender skin of his wrists with her back arched and her cunt pressing against his face as the last few waves of pleasure lapped over her. His mouth relaxed, and he sucked in a deep gasp, which she quieted by pressing against him again.

"Don't think you're done yet, my dear." She lifted herself up and turned around, sliding her hands down his chest and over his stomach as she wiggled around to find the right position. His tongue met her again, flicking at an entirely different angle this time, sparking a new fire inside her. She pressed back into his face as she undid his belt and slid his pants down, gripping his cock with both hands. She gasped and held in place as Feddar's tongue found a delicate little sensitive spot and worked it over with gentle laps that sent a hundred little sparks shooting through her. She took in a deep, steadying breath and moved against his chin in slow circles until she found a rhythm, which she matched with steady pumps of his cock. He was shiny-hard by now, and she held him tight and lowered her mouth down.

She lay wet kisses all around his head, swiped her tongue around a few times, then took him in as fast and as far as she could. His mouth froze against her, and he let out a pained whimper as she worked him over, but his tongue soon continued lapping and licking, and they wound each other up higher and higher. Whenever Aene had to pause because Feddar's ministrations were pushing her close to the edge, she powered through and returned the favor, her mouth twitching toward a grin around his cock as his lips stopped moving.

The cycle repeated itself until Feddar's whines grew more and more insistent, and his legs began to tremble a little. She pulled her mouth away abruptly and pressed her cunt against his chin, rubbing back and forth faster and harder as his whine morphed into a long, pained groan. She held his cock tight as she ground against him, her mind floating farther and farther away from her body, which exploded with bliss just as Feddar's cock twitched, then spilled wildly into the air, once, twice, three times. She held him firm as the last of his seed dribbled down, as the last wave of pleasure receded, and their bodies relaxed into each other, hot, wet, and satisfied.

Aene ignored Yglind's sideways glances in the morning when he woke her with a gentle nudge of his foot. She and Feddar did not make love again in the final days of their journey. They lay side by side each night, barely talking, Aene's head resting on her stacked hands, but she did not dare to let herself get too close again. The moment they had shared was a mistake, she knew. If Feddar had somehow escaped, the damage to the Maer would be incalculable, and she already felt guilty enough for taking her pleasure with this helpless, hairless creature, though he clearly hadn't minded. She made sure to press her breasts into Feddar's face when she untied him each morning from whatever she'd found to secure his cuffs to, and she always let her hand stray across his morning wood as she moved to release his feet.

"You are a cruel woman," he said on the last morning as her hand lingered, cupping his hardness. His lips twitched into a crooked grin as he stretched his limbs this way and that, straining into her hand and revealing the lean muscles beneath his bare skin.

"I'm trying to give you something to remember me by, something to think about as you sit alone in your cell in the long, cold mountain nights." She turned away as tears suddenly welled up, and she wiped her face on her shoulder and shook her head to clear it. Her heart felt like it was being crushed in a giant fist, and she stood up as her tears trickled down through the hair on her face.

"You never know," he said as he maneuvered himself to standing, his pants tented with his erection, and accepted the waterskin she offered him. "I survived your Delve, and getting out of sticky situations is something of a specialty of mine." His green eyes sparkled in the morning sun, his lips so soft and plump she almost gave in to her desire to kiss him again, but she swallowed the heat rising behind her face and flashed him the brightest smile she could muster.

"Your lips to the gods' ears, Feddar."

Word of their arrival had spread quickly by the time they reached the outskirts of Kuppham, and the phalanx of armored warriors moved aside and bowed to them as they passed through the great bronze gate, which opened from within and closed behind them with a great clank. Feddar's face grew pale and slick, and he looked like he was about to throw up. She wanted to go to him, take his head in her hands and pull it to rest against hers, to whisper a thousand reassuring words, but there were too many Maer watching. She flashed him a small smile through her tear-filled vision and angrily wiped her eyes on her filthy handkerchief, then fell into step behind him so she wouldn't have to see his face again.

The Captain of the City Guard curled his lips into a snarl as he saw Feddar, and four warriors grabbed him roughly by the arms and dragged him away. Aene let her tears flow as Feddar turned his head toward her one last time, flashed a crooked smile, and disappeared into the crowd down the main road leading toward the Tower.

Those who entered its stony confines were seldom seen again, but her heart nursed a faint spark of hope. He had survived Yglind and Laanda's wrath. If anyone could make it out of the Tower alive, it would be Feddar.

34

Y glind stood next to Aene before the assembled Council in his full armor, now repaired and shiny. He recognized more than half of the faces from his family's social events, but he didn't really know any of them. He had once visited the Council chamber on a school trip, and he had marveled at the great bronze chairs, the elaborate frescoes covering the walls and rounded ceiling, and the huge shining bronze Soulshape, which towered behind him. He had dreamt of this moment ever since he was a child scrapping with wooden swords in the training yards, but his heavy heart felt no joy at this occasion. He wished Ardo were here, but squires were not allowed at formal ceremonies. He had never questioned it before, but as he stared out at the jowly faces, the bejeweled beards with their fashionable white streaks, the family crests embroidered in gold thread on velvet robes, a sour fire burned in his stomach. He suddenly understood why the Maer empire was destined to fall.

"You think the High Councillor is taking a shit, or what?" Aene whispered.

Yglind cleared his throat, stifling a giggle. As if on cue, the shining double doors opened, and Haadris entered, walking with the unassuming gait of a Maer accustomed to commanding attention. The low murmurs of the Council stopped suddenly as he rounded the U-shaped arrangement of the chairs, then turned toward Yglind. He inclined his head slightly, then sat in the Great Chair, his huge hands wrapping around the frasti heads on the armrests. He fixed Yglind with a heavy gaze, then blinked and spoke.

"Your Delve has been declared a success." His deep voice echoed hollowly off the walls. "You slew two human saboteurs and captured the third, who has already given us much valuable information on the movements and intent of our enemy. You faced creatures of the deep not heard of for some time, and you emerged victorious." He paused, a slight frown creeping over his face. "I regret the losses suffered by the Timon, for which you bear no responsibility and which surely would have been greater had you not been there to stop the humans. We should have sent you sooner."

He tucked his mouth to his hand for a moment and gave his head a little shake. Yglind felt unaccustomed tears rising up as Haadris tried to absolve him from blame, but Yglind knew better. The bulk of the Timon losses had occurred while he was in the mine. He was the one who'd failed to stop the humans several times when he'd had the chance. He had been bested in single combat against the knight, who'd had him on his knees and could have ended him, but they'd respected their code. Yglind could have done the same when he'd disarmed them, but his bloodlust had taken over, and he'd killed an unarmed opponent in direct opposition to all his training. That part hurt more than anything else.

When Haadris finished his speech and stepped forward with the Forever medallion, Yglind's throat twisted with unspent tears. Aene stepped aside, and Yglind lowered his head so Haadris could place the medallion around his neck. It bore the shape of his family's crest, the mashtorul, set in a thick bronze disk whose weight he felt from the pressure of the chain on his mail. He wasn't so sure his actions had honored his ancestors or that they merited this ticket to the Time to Come. It was some consolation that his newfound status would get him his pick of postings, so he could be there on the front lines when the humans inevitably betrayed the truce. His hand found the pommel of his Forever Blade, and he felt his lips curl into a grin as he pictured the looks on their skinfucker faces when they saw it bearing down on them in the bloody heat of battle.

"Your election has been duly witnessed by the High Council, and preparations for your hibernation chamber will begin at once." He leaned in close, touching Yglind on the shoulder, and whispered, "Here's hoping you won't need it for a very long time."

Yglind had chosen a spot in a valley at the edge of the Maer-human border, where he hoped to be the vanguard of the Maer forces in the Time to Come if he wasn't sent straight to his ancestors in the coming war.

The polite applause of the Council rang hollow in Yglind's ears. He bowed to them as he had been instructed, then turned to Aene, who stood off to the side examining a large purple gem that hung from a slender silver chain around her neck. He held out his elbow, and she stepped forward to link arms with him. The applause grew a little louder, and the Councillors stood up as Yglind and Aene walked past them and out the big brass doors, which were opened by two liveried guards. They walked down the long hallway, their footsteps and the clinking of Yglind's armor ringing off the empty walls.

"That's a pretty prize you've got," Yglind said, gesturing toward Aene's gem, which he could now see was cut in an abstract, geometrical replica of the Soulshape. "What's it do?"

"It doesn't *do* anything, Egg. It's just a pretty bauble." She stared at it for a moment, then raised her eyes to his, her steps slowing as they approached the door to the courtyard. "Are you ready for this party?"

"I should be, but..." He fingered his medallion and shook his head. "I've wanted this all my life, ever since I was a little furball. The Time to Come.

It's always been this golden dream, like sunshine after rain. But now? It feels like a death sentence."

"We're all going to die one day, Egg. At least you get to choose."

The crowd assembled in the airy courtyard broke into choreographed applause when they emerged, but their claps and whistles fell thin on Yglind's ears. Of the seven teams sent out to the sites of the human attacks, only four had returned, and one of the knights had since died of his wounds. Drumbeats rose, drowning out the applause, and the crowd parted to reveal the path leading to the pavilion sprinkled with copper dust, which glittered in the afternoon sun. Yglind's heart lifted when he saw Ardo standing at the head of the path. He strode over, squeezed Ardo in a tight embrace, then pulled back enough to kiss him full on the lips.

The applause grew, mixed with laughter and cheers, and Yglind raised Ardo's arm, spinning him so the crowd could get a better look at him, though they would never appreciate Ardo's role in the Delve nor in Yglind's heart. Ardo raised his other hand in an awkward greeting, bowing slightly to the crowd, his eyes shiny and bewildered.

"Come on, love," Yglind said into Ardo's ear, pulling him to his side and squeezing Ardo's waist tightly against his. "Let's eat and drink until we can't anymore, then fuck until dawn. We've earned it."

The war went badly from the start. Half of Yglind's soldiers were sick with Ulver's cough, and a few of them had died coughing up brownish globs of their diseased lungs. Yglind had been lucky enough to catch only a mild case, but he'd caught a horse's hoof to the head during a skirmish. Though they'd repelled the first wave, he'd suffered from blinding headaches and poor balance and had been sent back to Kuppham for treatment.

He followed the news through his circlet as much as he could bear, but his head throbbed when he wore it for more than a few minutes. There was nothing but bad news and propaganda in the Stream anyway, so he kept it on his bedside table most of the time. Ardo was at his side as often as Yglind would let him, but the worried look on his lover's face was sometimes too much to bear, so he'd pretend to be tired, accept Ardo's gentle forehead kiss, and close his eyes until Ardo left. He occasionally tried to do the little meditation exercises Ardo had gotten so obsessed with, but they only made him angry that he was stuck in a bed instead of out spilling skinfucker blood with his battalion.

Even when he'd mostly recovered, Yglind's balance was never quite right again, and he did not return to the battlefield. The few times he'd accepted Ardo's amorous overtures were bittersweet affairs, brief moments of passion amidst a sea of despair. Lying in each other's arms afterward, he found a fleeting peace, but visions of his hibernation haunted him even then. The somber chants of the mages, the guttering candles, the tarry liquid they would pour into his mouth. The utter loneliness of the forever darkness.

He joined the War Council, playing their strategy games with pieces on the big table, half-following their heated arguments on where to deploy the great automatons, where to mass troops, and where to pull back. Though no one said it out loud, they all knew the end game was in sight. The bronze pieces representing the Maer forces became fewer and fewer, clustered closer to Kuppham as the northern strongholds fell one by one. When half the War Council fell ill with Ulver's cough and they suspended their strategy sessions, Yglind was summoned to Haadris' chamber.

Haadris sat facing the open window, a goblet hanging slightly off-kilter in his hand. He gestured for Yglind to approach without turning around, and Yglind quietly set down his heavy bag and sat in a cushioned deerskin chair opposite the High Councillor. Haadris' face was long and somber, and the faint smile he summoned when Yglind met his eyes was brief and unconvincing.

"It won't be long now," Haadris said in a gravelly voice.

"No, it won't," Yglind agreed, taking the goblet of mushroom wine Haadris poured for him.

"It's going to be hell getting you to your hibernation site, but we have a team assembled and a distraction planned to get you past the human forces near Valleys Road."

"High Councillor, are we sure this is the best use of our resources?" Yglind stared down into his wine, then eyed Haadris over his goblet as he drank. He thought of the soldiers who would die in this distraction, the families they would leave behind, just so he could be bound in dark magics for some illusory future gain.

Haadris blinked slowly. "The war is over, Yglind. It may drag on for several years yet, but there is no path to victory for the Maer. Not in this time." He drained his goblet and poured another, sloshing a little puddle of wine on his desk. "The only way we make it through is in the Time to Come. We will need leaders then, clear thinkers, strategists. We will need *you*, Yglind."

Yglind swallowed the wine that pooled in his mouth, then took another large gulp, spilling some into his beard. Haadris spoke like a true believer, but Yglind was not convinced. Even if the magics did work, if they kept him alive for a thousand years or more, what effect would that have on his mind? What kind of world would he wake up to? What good would it be to travel across time to wake up without Ardo at his side, surrounded by strangers who spoke a language he did not understand?

"I will do what I must, High Councillor," was all he said, choked as he was on the bitter tears that burned their way through his sinuses.

"Dammit, Yglind!" Haadris shouted, pounding his fist on the table, sending little ripples through the puddle of wine he had spilled. "You speak of your sacred duty as if it were a burden! Our time here is almost over. The Time to Come is the only future we have left." He picked up his goblet, waved it near his mouth, and set it back down. "I know we've made a mess of things, and I weep at night when I think of how the great Maer leaders of the Time Before would see us, our excesses, our hubris, our folly. But the pain in my heart when I imagine a future in which there are *no* Maer, when the glory of our civilization is no more than dusty ruins sinking beneath the indifferent earth—" His mouth found his goblet, tears slipping from the corners of his eyes as he drank. "You *must* do this, Yglind. There is no future in the present."

Yglind stood, picked up his bag, and set it on his chair. His face burned with shame, but his mind hardened against any hesitation. He had made his decision.

Haadris' face contorted in disbelief as Yglind opened the bag and lifted his armor onto the table, piece by heavy piece, then dropped his shield on top, where it landed with a thud.

"What is the meaning of this?" Haadris stammered, standing and slamming his goblet down.

Yglind untied his medallion and tossed it across the table, and it skidded to a stop in the puddle of wine around Haadris' goblet. Tears flowed as he reached for his Forever Blade one last time. The pommel was hot in his hand, and the blade screeched as he yanked it from its ornate scabbard.

"Yglind, you cannot do this! Your family's legacy—"

The clang of the blade on the table sent shockwaves up his spine, and he held onto his chair for support as the sound reverberated through his skull.

The sword glowed angrily in the candlelight, and Yglind gripped the chair harder to stop his hand from creeping over to grasp the pommel.

"You are right, High Councillor." Yglind rose to standing, though his head was light and his legs wobbly. "The Maer of the Time Before would be ashamed of what we've done with their legacy." He unbuckled his belt and scabbard and laid them on the table. "But I will not hide from the present by seeking refuge in some imagined Time to Come. There is one who needs me now, and there is no future for me without him by my side."

Haadris picked up the medallion and dried it on his sleeve, his angry face softening into a thoughtful frown. He set it atop the shield and drummed his fingers on the table, then sat back, fixing Yglind with an inscrutable expression.

"You'll have to leave Kuppham, you know." A hint of softness crept into Haadris' voice.

"We will." As often as he'd imagined this moment, Yglind hadn't managed to think past it. Where they would go? What would they do? How would they survive?

"What if I told you there's a way you can still serve the cause from outside the city?"

Yglind pushed the bag off the chair and sat back down. Haadris held out the pitcher, and Yglind pushed his goblet forward to be filled. Yglind's heart stirred at the mischievous sparkle in Haadris' eyes as they clinked and drank.

"No one can know of this conversation except for your squire."

"Ardo's no longer my squire, High Councillor. He's just my partner now."

Haadris' smile was warm and genuine. "You'll need him by your side for what I'm going to ask you to do."

"As long as I have Ardo, there's no trial I can't endure."

Haadris tapped the table, then swiveled in his chair to rummage around in a drawer of his desk. When he turned back around, he held two shiny silver shields in his meaty palm.

"Yglind Torl, welcome to the Shoza."

The journey to the edge of Maer territory was long and harrowing, and Yglind regretted picking the most distant corner of Maerdom for his hibernation. It was strange seeing Gerd, the knight who'd been selected to take his place, wearing Yglind's medallion and carrying his Forever Blade, but the sword's grip on Yglind weakened with each night he spent in Ardo's arms. They did not make love during the journey, though it was not out of modesty. Yglind couldn't quite shake the feeling that it was all a ruse to trick him into hibernation against his will. The Shoza were known for their mental discipline, stealth, and spycraft, but Yglind possessed none of those things. Gerd spoke little during the trip, carrying himself in stoic silence as if he were already staring into the darkness of the Forever Kingdom. If it had hurt his pride to be selected by default, he never showed it, and the brief glances he shared with Yglind from time to time were filled with mutual respect and understanding.

They were nearly caught by the humans, only escaping due to the quick thinking of their mage, who'd used a pyrotechnics spell to draw the humans away from their position while they slipped through the narrow pass onto Valleys Road. They traveled only by night from there on, camping far away from the road during the day as seemingly endless columns of human soldiers tramped down the narrow path. The Stream had gone dark, meaning the humans had destroyed the northern signal towers. It was probably a blessing since the news was never good, and Yglind didn't know if he could stand to hear the name of one more stronghold that had fallen into human hands. The last report had suggested the human forces were massing near the Archive Valley, and preparations to bury the Archive were underway.

They took an arduous path around the last bit of Valleys Road, skirting the base of a tall hill with a chimney-like outcropping of rock above what was believed to be a deep, untapped vein of copper. All the Forever Shelters were built near potential mines in the hopes they could be used to rebuild in the Time to Come.

The last few nights, as they huddled together without fires beneath the wide, starry sky, Ardo told stories of the Thousand Worlds he'd heard at Cloti's temple, where he'd spent his days while Yglind was off at the War Council. Ardo spoke of secret passages between realities, invisible threads connecting minds across time and space. As they stared up at the stars, snuggled tight against each other, Yglind started to wonder if there weren't something to this Thousand Worlds. He even joined Ardo in his strange cycles of slow movement and breathing, which helped chase away his doubts and fears about what was to come.

They camped the last night in the valley below the town of Bachland, which they'd had to give a wide berth. It had been spared during the humans' initial incursions, being a small town of little consequence, but was now occupied by humans. Yglind's shelter had only just been finished before the humans had taken the town, and the handlers were relieved to find the shelter undisturbed, the stone door firmly sealed in place. It had taken them half a day to move the door, and Yglind's heart chilled as he saw Gerd descend the stone stairs into the darkness. The mage and her assistants followed him, carrying all manner of arcane equipment, and Ardo pulled Yglind away as the guards took their posts outside the entrance.

Yglind leaned against a twisted tree in the narrow, rocky ravine leading up to the shelter and closed his eyes, but he could not shake the vision of Gerd being strapped to a block and fed dark poison by the mage. He felt Ardo's warm forehead on his, and he dropped his hand to Ardo's shoulder and pushed back a little, looking down into his eyes, which were bright and glossy.

"I would have been lost without you, my lord." Ardo's voice quavered, and his eyes began leaking into the hair on his cheek.

"I'll never leave you, my love," Yglind said, his voice cracking as tears burst forth. "Whatever happens, whatever travails await us, we will face them together."

Their beards tangled as Yglind angled in to capture Ardo's eager lips. He felt the stares of the guards, but the wet heat of Ardo's mouth drew him in, and he lingered in the moment as his heart swelled.

The faint sound of a boot scuffing on stone pulled him from the kiss, and Yglind turned to see a figure in a gray cloak standing at the base of the little ravine. This figure hadn't been among their party, but Yglind had no doubt who it was or why they were here.

"Is that—?" Ardo whispered. Yglind nodded, and the figure lifted a flap on their cloak to show a silver shield like the ones Yglind and Ardo carried. Ardo started to turn toward the figure, but Yglind took him by the shoulders and pulled him back in, staring into his deep brown eyes.

As their lips met, the warmth of Ardo's embrace filled him with a hope he hadn't felt since he was a child. For the ephemeral infinity of their kiss, the troubles they'd left behind and the unknown struggles ahead of them dissolved. The past was a fading dream, and the future could wait.

This moment belonged to them.

Thank you for reading!

If you liked this book, or even if you didn't, please consider leaving a review on Goodreads, Amazon, or wherever your reviews live!

If you want to know more about the Maer, check out The Maer Cycle trilogy (character-driven non-epic fantasy), and for another angle to the world, my sword-free romantic fantasy Weirdwater Confluence duology may be of interest. There are connections between all the books.

You can subscribe to my newsletter, read about current and upcoming books, and more at my website, www.danfitzwrites.com

Acknowledgments

The Delve is my first self-published novel, and it wouldn't have been possible without a team of rock stars to help me through, including, but by no means limited to:

My wife Sarah, who's powerful and patient and anchors me in the best of ways;

My lifetime critique partner Beth Blaufuss, who was instrumental in helping me see the forest for the trees;

My fabulous beta reader and supporter, Susan Hancock, who gave me critical insight that helped me rewrite the ending;

My editor and sensitivity reader Charlie Knight, whose insightful nudges and superheroic knowledge of grammar and punctuation rules helped make this a stronger book with better relationships. Wherever I may have erred in representation of identities outside my own, it is through my own fault, not theirs;

My cover artist and designer, Luke Tarzian, who absolutely SLAYED on this one, in my humble opinion;

Rtistic Writer for the adorable artwork of Yglind, Ardo, Aene, and Skiti;

My Siblings in Smut, including but by no means limited to Krystle Matar, Fiona West, Connor Caplan, Angela Boord, Thomas Howard Riley, Maxime Jazz, Em Strange, Erika McCorkle, and so many others;

And as always, the brilliant, glittering hordes of the bookish community on Twitter: The book bloggers who were kind and generous enough to give this odd little book a shot, and who make the bookish world run; the fantastic author community, especially my fantasy and romance peeps; and all the wonderful people I've met along the way who share my love of a good story.

About the Author

Dan Fitzgerald is a fantasy and romance author living in Washington, DC with his wife, twin boys, and two cats. When he's not writing, he might be gardening, doing yoga, cooking, or listening to French music.

I write fantasy in part because the state of the world demands an escape, but also because fantasy provides another lens through which to view what we are living now. Part mirror, part magnifying glass, part prism.

I write romance because we need more love in the world, and sometimes we need to know things will work out in the end.

What you will find in my books: Mystery. Darkness. Wonder. Action. Romance. Otherness examined and deconstructed. Queer and straight characters living and fighting side by side. Imaginary creatures and magic with a realistic touch.

What you won't find: Extreme violence. Sexual assault. Unquestioned sexism or discrimination. Evil races. Irredeemable villains. Predestined heroes. An ancient darkness that threatens to overspread the land.